Praise for *The Hatter's Daughter* and the *Tales from the Riven Isles* series

'*The Hatter's Daughter* is an action-packed adventure of a retelling, and fans of the original story will love seeing the appearances of many reimagined characters – even as their seemingly perfect world of Wonderland is taken over by new and very dangerous forces that threaten heroine Faith and her entire Underneath. This book takes you on a wild ride down the rabbit hole and all the way up again, and it won't let you off until everything you've ever thought was impossible in this world becomes compellingly curious.'
Kelly Ann Jacobson, author of *Tink and Wendy* and *Lies of a Toymaker*

'*The Hatter's Daughter* is a fun and fresh adventure through a land of magic and encroaching decay. This fast-paced, magical tale is filled with charm and surprises, and features a world at once familiar and unique.'
M.H. Ayinde, 2021 winner of the Future Worlds Prize and author of *A Song of Legends Lost*

'Simpson's newest installment from the Riven Isles is filled with whimsy and wonder. Based loosely on the tale of Alice in Wonderland, we are introduced to the realm of Brigantia. With protagonists you can root for and a supporting cast of characters both old and new, this book will charm fairy-tale readers of all ages!'
Elana A. Mugdan, author of *The Shadow War Saga*

'Simpson sticks the landing with an epic conclusion. Fans of Andrea Hairston's *Master of Poisons* and other secondary world fantasy will enjoy this expansive magical adventure.'
Publishers Weekly on *Tinderbox*

'This promising debut features strong world building and well-developed systems of magic. It will appeal to readers of Kacen Callender's *Queen of the Conquered* (2019), N.K. Jemisin's *The Hundred Thousand Kingdoms* (2010), and L. Penelope's *Song of Blood & Stone* (2018).'
Booklist on *Tinderbox*

'A grisly murder, a missing box, a dangerous task, and a cranky magical talisman. Expect betrayals, intrigue, peril, and romance in this smartly moving fantasy.'
Jacey Bedford, author of the *Psi-Tech* and *Rowankind* series, on *Tinderbox*

'W.A. Simpson begins with a simple tale of revenge and quickly weaves a grand adventure bound together with the threads of fairy tales and fey creations...where possessed staffs speak, wil-o-wisps roam, and Jack's giant vine protects the world both above and below.'
Troy Carrol Bucher, author of *Lies of Descent*, on *Tinderbox*

'*Tinderbox* is a riveting tale about personal strength and hidden magic.'
Foreword Reviews

W.A. SIMPSON

THE HATTER'S DAUGHTER

Tales from the Riven Isles

Book Three

Following *Tinderbox* and *Tarotmancer*

This is a **FLAME TREE PRESS** book

Text copyright © 2025 Wendy A. Simpson

FLAME TREE PRESS
6 Melbray Mews, London, SW6 3NS, UK
flametreepress.com

US sales, distribution and warehouse:
Simon & Schuster
simonandschuster.biz

UK distribution and warehouse:
Hachette UK Distribution
hukdcustomerservice@hachette.co.uk

Publisher's Note: This is a work of fiction. Names, characters, places, and
incidents are a product of the author's imagination. Locales and public names
are sometimes used for atmospheric purposes. Any resemblance to actual
people, living or dead, or to businesses, companies, events, institutions, or
locales is completely coincidental.

Thanks to the Flame Tree Press team.

The cover is created by Flame Tree Studio with elements courtesy of
Shutterstock.com and: annymax; Irina Bg; Sasha Black; Tatyana Mi; Pawel
Michalowski; Andrii Muzyka; Baza Production; and Atelier Sommerland.

The font families used are Avenir and Bembo.

Flame Tree Press is an imprint of Flame Tree Publishing Ltd
flametreepublishing.com

A copy of the CIP data for this book is available from the British Library
and the Library of Congress.

PB ISBN: 978-1-78758-911-7
HB ISBN: 978-1-78758-912-4
ebook ISBN: 978-1-78758-913-1

Printed and bound in Great Britain by Clays Ltd, Elcograf S.p.A.

W.A. SIMPSON

THE HATTER'S DAUGHTER

Tales from the Riven Isles

Book Three

Following *Tinderbox* and *Tarotmancer*

FLAME TREE PRESS
London & New York

CHAPTER ONE

The night Faith was born, there was fire.

Yet she wasn't afraid. Despite the smoke filling the air and the cries of panic, Faith knew she would survive. Her mother's arms were the safest place she could be. But her mother gave her over to someone else as she lay in her birth-bed. Faith knew the person and her scent and although she no longer felt safe, there was a measure of trust.

They hurriedly whispered words and whisked her away.

The night was cool and the farther they ran, the darker it became. Faith looked up and saw the moon a mere sliver against the velvet-blue sky. But somehow the person who fled with her seemed to know the way.

Faith also heard things. Crickets. The crunch of fallen leaves. And somewhere, a bird made a lonely sound. They arrived, although Faith wasn't certain where. She only knew that they had stopped. That her savior held Faith out before her. She whispered something Faith didn't understand, and then she dropped her.

Faith supposed she should be afraid, but she wasn't. She was floating, first in darkness that seemed absolute, then lights appeared. Objects of all sorts, table and chairs, a floating fireplace, shelves filled with books surrounded her. A thought came to her, *curiouser and curiouser.* Now what did that mean?

Her journey seemed like it would go on forever, but she stopped falling when she landed on a hard, smooth surface. She couldn't see what it was, but a sound drew her attention. It was like a long low creak, as though some being was stretching out its kinks.

Before she had more time to consider, a dark-skinned face appeared. Plump and bearded, with brown eyes that twinkled with knowledge, the man smiled down at her. However, it was his hat that caught her attention. It was shiny black, tall and smooth. At its base was a red ribbon held together by a jeweled butterfly brooch.

"So, there you are." He gathered Faith in his arms. "I am the Hatter, my dear. Most call me mad and you will come home with me."

Faith smiled up at him and giggled happily.

"Welcome to Brigantia." They came to a door a head shorter than the Hatter as he reached for the knob to open it. He had to duck down, almost not enough because the doorframe knocked his hat slightly askew. He lifted her above his head and turned in a circle, allowing Faith to see the surrounding wonders.

And there were many. Unlike the world above, here the sun shone brightly and bathed the strange realm in its golden light. In just a single turn, Faith saw thick forests, deserts of golden sand, fields of flowers that swayed in the breeze. Those nearby had faces in their centers, and they smiled and cooed at Faith, who did the same in return.

"The Caterpillar told me your name is Faith," the Hatter said.

Faith didn't have the words, so she clapped her hands.

"Look over there." He pointed to a castle of red and white, which stood with majesty on a hill in the distance. "That is the home of our sovereign queen and king. One of three royal couples who rule our world.

"And there, beyond the Forest of the Bandersnatch, is the Sea of Tears," he went on. "Where Alice wept tears of salt and joined in the Caucus Race."

Faith didn't understand, but she smiled again and spread her tiny arms wide.

"And over there –" he pointed toward two dusky mountains, "– is my home. Now it will be your home, and you will sit at the grand table with me and my friends and have tea."

Faith stayed with the Hatter forever.

"So live and grow in our Wonderland."

And Faith did.

★   ★   ★

It was a fine day. Faith grinned when she woke before she threw back the covers and swung her legs around, resting her feet on the wood floor and enjoying the coolness of the polished boards. She stood and hurried to the window, moved back the drapes, and opened the double panes wide, allowing the sweet-smelling breeze in. And on that breeze came the familiar voice – "Today, my beautiful daughter is celebrating her twenty and one."

It was special to her father, but to Faith, it was another day alive and living in this wonderful place she called home. To her, every day was a birthday – or an un-birthday, as her father and his companions liked to say. The White Rabbit, the March Hare, and the Dormouse were as much family to her as anyone.

Faith thought everything was perfect and saw no evidence to the contrary. She was aware of other worlds, connected by a vast Celestial Vine that wound its way through all the Riven Isles. She'd read from the White Rabbit's library about how people found perfection impossible in those places, that people were not perfect there. What a shame, Faith would say, that they had never lived in Brigantia.

On this day she would ride across the beach at the Sea of Tears. She wanted some time alone before the true festivities began. Faith was certain her father had invited all the citizens of Brigantia from each of the Three Kingdoms. Not that she minded. She left the window open and moved to her dressing table to wash up, and made a face at her reflection. Then she dressed, their maid having laid out her favorite suit last night. And to top it off, no pun intended, was the gift from her father. A decorative top hat that he'd made in secret, and it was the most beautiful one Faith had ever seen. She placed it upon her head, then tilted it at a jaunty angle.

Faith supposed she should walk slowly, but she'd never been one to take her time, so she rushed down the stairs. Her home was a nonsensical place, which suited her just fine, and in Brigantia, the nonsensical was the true nature of their world. She walked down the hall, past living portraits of centuries of Hatters.

"Good morning, Uncle Felix."

"Good morning, Faith."

"Aunt Philomena."

"Good morning, Faith."

"Cousin Randolph."

Then came the paper on the walls, changing color and appearance with the mood of the household. This time, pictures of bright sunflowers waving in an unseen breeze, and petals fell on the carpet. They didn't remain there for long as broom and dustpan swept them up by themselves. The clock on the mantel struck eight and a half when Faith walked into the kitchen.

Their housekeeper, Minerva, was busy at the stove making breakfast, as well as Faith's birthday lunch.

"Good morning, Minerva." Faith slid onto one stool at the cooking block. "Where is Father?"

"Outside." Minerva didn't turn away from her cooking. "The White Rabbit has delivered the invitations."

"Wonderful." Faith was eager to see, even though she was hungry. They had invited the Three Queens. It would be improper not to, even if they didn't come. Minerva placed a plate of biscuits and ham in front of her and a hot coffee with lots of cream and sugar. Faith wolfed it down, eager to go out.

"Thank you, Minerva." Once she finished, Faith walked out the back door and around the side of the house, searching for her father. He was there in the garden, looking tall, portly, his dark skin complemented by a full beard and curled mustache. He wore, of course, his signature silk top hat and his finest green waistcoat and trousers with a purple vest and crisp white shirt.

"Father, you didn't have to get so dressed up."

"Of course I did." He kissed her on the cheek. "I have spoken to the White Rabbit and nearly everyone will be here."

"*Nearly* everyone?" she asked.

Her father released his breath and removed his hat. He pulled a handkerchief from his pocket and dabbed at his balding hairline. "Well, the queens will not be coming."

Faith shrugged. "Expected." She stopped just short of asking about the one person she really wanted to be there. Rowan, Prince of Hearts, son of the Queen and King of Hearts. They'd once been companions, maybe even friends, but as the years passed, they'd lost touch. Faith didn't know why he was on her mind. She hadn't thought of him for ages. But she wasn't about to ask after him.

"However, the White Rabbit has brought many responses and says the gifts will begin arriving soon."

Faith gave him a hug. "Thank you, Father."

"For what?" Her father grinned.

"For all of this." Faith made an expansive motion with her hand. "I'm going to go for my morning ride."

"Make certain you're back in time."

"I will."

Leading from her home was a brick path that wound its way through a small stand of trees and into their private garden, where the living blossoms greeted Faith with birthday wishes and dipped their heads in a bow. All except for one, of course, the bleeding heart, who was never friendly to anyone.

Each bleeding heart blossom formed a sad face that dipped and rose even without the breeze, and each one that spoke voiced a different portent of doom. Most times Faith ignored them, but something made her stop that day and listen.

"Can the realm be like perfection? We challenge such a notion!"

This wasn't their normal whining. Usually, they asked 'what if' questions like, 'What if the Sea of Tears dried up?' or 'What if the Three Queens went to war?' The finest minds in Brigantia had taught Faith, so both scientifically and personally, she thought their questions were laughable.

"Can you see the darkness? Oh, woe to Brigantia!"

The words were disturbing. Faith sat down cross-legged in front of them. "What is this nonsense?" A question which she found ironic.

"They've been about this all day," said a nearby red rose with her high, lilting voice.

"What else have they said?" Faith asked, but the rose remained silent.

They all fell quiet for so long, Faith had to change her position. She stretched her legs out in front of her. "Bleeding hearts!"

"They find ways in," a single heart said.

"What does that mean?" But then the hearts were back to their usual questioning. Faith frowned at them, her brow furrowed as she ran their words over and over in her mind. "Does anyone know what they mean?"

The other flowers merely shrugged and returned to their swaying. Faith stood up and stretched before tugging her jacket down. A thought was building in the back of her mind. A thought she didn't want to entertain. It was her birthday and she would enjoy it.

Now that was odd, Faith thought as she continued until she came to their edible garden, where they'd planted fruits and vegetables indigenous to both Brigantia and the outer realms, courtesy of the White Rabbit.

Suddenly, Faith spied who she'd been searching for, before her delay with the hearts. His feathered head bobbed up and down between the tall rows of grapevines. "Argestes!"

The gryphon was startled and wore a panicked expression for a moment. Despite being a formidable-looking beast, Argestes was a scaredy-cat.

"Lady Faith!" Argestes got turned around trying to extract himself from the grapevines. He was a beautiful creature, with white feathers dotted with smokey gray, and his leonine hindquarters coal-black.

"You were at the grapes again," Faith scolded gently.

He dipped his head. "I'm sorry, milady." He was wearing a bridle, which must have made it difficult for him to filch the sweet fruit.

"I see you're ready for our ride?"

Argestes brightened. Despite his fear, he loved their rides. "Shall we go to the beach?"

"You know me too well." Faith always rode bareback as normal saddles didn't fit the gryphon. She was quite good at it. She chose not to fly, more for the gryphon than herself, for he feared doing so. It was silly that a beast meant to fly wouldn't.

"But you were late," Argestes said, as though there hadn't been a lull in the conversation. "What kept you?"

Argestes was not a beast who Faith normally confided in. "The bleeding hearts – they gave portents of doom, as always."

"But you've never paid them any attention before." He sounded confused.

"Something was different about what they said. Like trouble was just over the horizon."

"Well," Argestes said, "if there is, I know you will face the challenge. You have the Gift, after all!"

Faith nodded. She didn't know if she'd had the Gift since birth or if it had touched her once she'd entered Brigantia. She'd come from beyond Above Ground just like the Heroine of Legend, a young blonde-haired, blue-eyed girl who had visited many times but one day remained in her birth world. Yet, unlike her, Faith called Brigantia her home and had no desire to return.

Faith mounted and led Argestes through the trees until they were clear of the grounds. Once they were out on the path, Faith coaxed Argestes into a trot.

The path wound through the Bandersnatch Forest, on the outskirts of the village of Stoneacre. The path opened up and out, but she caught the scent of the salt air before coming to the stretch of golden sand. The Sea of Tears. Faith took a few moments to watch the surf coming in. Despite her not wanting to, she couldn't help but go back to what the bleeding hearts had said.

"Faith?" Argestes' voice broke into her thoughts. "Are you well?"

She stroked the gryphon's neck more to reassure herself. "Yes, I'm fine."

"Shall we run?"

"No, not yet, let's walk."

A gentle squeeze with her ankles and Argestes moved forward.

There was no trouble in Brigantia, at least not before Faith arrived.

And they taught her the history of their realm, so she knew there was nothing earlier. But how far back did their history go? For crying out loud, these things had never bothered her before, had they? And perhaps thoughts about troubles would bring them about. She had to be careful not to stew too much, she concluded. Just to be safe.

"Faith?" She hadn't noticed Argestes had slowed and come to a halt. Faith could feel his muscles trembling beneath her.

"Argestes, what is it?"

He danced nervously, his head moving back and forth frantically. "Something," he said, his voice a whine, "not good!"

"I see nothing." Everything was as before. The waves lapping gently, the breeze soft— Wait, there was a change. No longer did it have the scent of the salt sea but—

Argestes turned a quarter way and faced the Sea of Tears. There was a legend behind it; the Heroine had shed the tears of this sea when she'd eaten the cake and grew to a height rivaling the giants and wept at her stupidity, nearly drowning herself when the enchantment wore off and she'd fallen into the very sea she'd created.

But it was Faith who now faced the sea, the stench increasing as the waves continued to wash over the sand. The gryphon persisted in moving about nervously. Faith squinted and noticed something. There was a thin, dark line on the horizon that continued to expand and spread the length of the shore as far as she could see. When it was close enough and rose in a rolling wave, she saw it was ink-black.

Argestes stepped back as the wave hit the beach and froth bubbled until it was the color of soot. Behind it came a second wave, but this time as it crested, things took shape as they rose out of the water, floating above the wave itself. Barely human in appearance, these things continued their journey toward the shore, their features becoming more detailed. They resembled nothing from this world. Twisted faces with mouths agape showed glistening ivory teeth, sharp as daggers. They wailed like the lost souls of the dead, swaying to music only they could hear.

CHAPTER TWO

Argestes screamed, the sound breaking Faith from her shock, and before she could react the gryphon reared and bolted forward.

"Argestes, don't!"

The cry was lost in the sounds of thundering claws and paws. The wave rose, higher than any Faith had ever seen, and spilled over the shore into the gryphon's path. The nightmare beings crawled and reached with gnarled hands and turned the sand black in their wake. They took hold of Argestes and stopped his mad dash.

Argestes screeched again and reared as he struck out against an invisible foe, and Faith went flying, landing in the putrid froth. The air left her lungs. She turned to her side far enough to witness Argestes clawing at the demons and shredding them into what resembled oily strips of cloth. Then he was off, galloping down the beach and away from her.

The nightmares came for her next. When one touched her exposed flesh, it burned, and she screamed. This pain motivated her to act. She rolled onto her stomach and pushed herself up to her knees. More of them grabbed on to her, pulling themselves up, and seemed to melt into her skin. They made her flesh crawl, and for a few moments, a deep sorrow overwhelmed her. A longing for freedom, but from where?

Concentrate! Her Gift made her fingertips tingle. Faith focused on the pain, and she thought of the first thing that came to her mind – the feel, inside and out, the color and even scent, and she fed that into the ink.

The shadows filled the air with wailing again but this time from agony and perhaps fear, not from one but from dozens of them as their transformation became complete. Then what was once decaying hardened into precious metal. That was Faith's Gift. To make one thing into another. Transforming its makeup and form into something different. It went by many names: transmutation, or the more common Philosopher's Touch. The remaining beings withdrew, disappearing below the waves. Faith stayed where she was, taking deep breaths as rivulets of liquid gold flowed between her fingers. Had she imagined it all?

The blisters on her hands told her the experience was quite real. Faith shoved each hand under her arms and climbed unsteadily to her feet. Argestes had left no trace except for the displaced chunks of sand. Her head throbbed in time with the pain of her burned skin. Still, she concentrated on taking one step at a time. Continuing seemed nearly impossible as all she desired was to lie down and curl into a miserable ball. Nothing looked familiar anymore, and she wasn't certain she was going the right way, yet she continued. When her mind wandered, she kept it occupied by reciting poems from her childhood.

"How doth the little crocodile
Improve his shining tail,
And pour the waters of the Nile
On every golden scale!
How cheerfully he seems to grin,
How neatly spreads his claws,
And welcomes little fishes in
With gently smiling jaws!"

Were those beings the danger the hearts had spoken of? Well, they had to be, she reasoned. She had never seen them before, but what did they want in Brigantia, and why now? She would find out, if she could just make it home.

Faith was uncertain if she was hallucinating when she heard familiar and cheerful voices, but she recognized them and where she was.

"Do you realize we have no song for an actual birthday?"

"Why not just say a very merry birthday? It's a simple matter of removing the *un*."

"Now that's just nonsense!"

"Of course it's nonsense! Our world is—"

It took Faith a few moments to realize that they had seen her. Her father, the March Hare, and the Dormouse came awake and gaped.

"Faith!"

She managed to smile, not sure how, but it no longer mattered as her knees buckled. Her father got to her first, grabbing her up.

"Ye gods and monsters! What has befallen you?"

"Dear Faith, who has done this?"

Even the Dormouse said, "What? What?"

"My poor baby." The Hatter lifted her into his arms. It surprised Faith that he still could. "What happened?"

"It was – in the sea – Argestes threw me."

The March Hare pulled back one chair, but her father said, "No, no, we'll take her to the house! Bring the special tea!"

As he rushed with her toward their home, he muttered, "That blasted gryphon! Him and his cowardice!"

"Father…" Faith supposed she couldn't blame Argestes for running away. Maybe it was just a matter of common sense. "There was something tainting the Sea of Tears. There were horrible beings…"

Faith lost things in a haze after that and the next time she came out of it, she was in bed and her father was yelling for Minerva. Faith dozed, glad for those moments of being unaware, for when she was conscious the burning made her want to vomit. Next thing, Minerva was bustling around the room, rubbing a cooling salve on her hands and arms and wrapping them in clean cloth. Next, someone pressed a cup to her lips with a sweet liquid – tea, of course – and she swallowed.

It warmed her insides and next she drifted on the dark waves of the Sea of Tears with a cloudy sky above. These waves were gentle and deposited her on the shore. Faith pushed herself up on her elbows, frowning.

"How—?" Faith climbed to her feet. What was she doing back on the beach? She walked, with a faint awareness that she was going away from home. The beach gave way to rocky outcroppings, the sand replaced by groups of onyx stones with glittering silver specks on their surfaces.

It surprised Faith to find someone sitting atop one of the larger rocks. She didn't recognize him. Nor did she recognize her surroundings anymore. Brigantia, once green, was a barren wasteland of rock and scrub, as far as she could see. Not of her own accord, Faith continued to walk, and trepidation started in the pit of her stomach and rose to her chest. This was wrong.

She could hear the man on the rock weeping, and with the sound came that sorrow washing over her like the black wave from before. Tears welled in her eyes and trickled down her cheeks. Then she was right behind him, close enough that she could reach out and touch him. As with most dreams, she couldn't quite tell what he was wearing as he seemed shrouded in mist. She had the impression of long, dark hair done up in a braid down his back. Faith did not want to, but her movements were no longer hers. She laid her hand on his shoulder. He twisted around as though surprised, and Faith saw his face. His version of humanity was warped. Skin stretched over a skeletal face. His eyes were bulbous red gems that glinted with a ghost of light. Fleshy lips opened wide to show jagged teeth and the sound that came forth was one that Faith hoped never to experience again. He leapt for her, and Faith screamed as he took hold of her.

"You must help us!" His lips didn't move, but she gathered the words. "Only you can free us. It's been so long, too long – we crave the light."

Faith tried to struggle and move away from the thing, but she remained paralyzed.

"If we cannot come from above, we will come from below," he continued. "Do you understand me?"

He said the last words with such force that Faith pulled back. She stumbled and fell screaming again and expected to hit the hard rocks, but came awake in her bed.

Hurried footsteps sounded on the stairs, and her father rushed into the room. "Faith, what is it?" He crossed the space to her bed and grabbed her up, and Faith clutched the lapels of his jacket.

Guilt warred with embarrassment. Here she was a grown woman, and she was allowing a dream to frighten her and then clutching on to Papa like she was eight years old again. *Get hold of your senses, woman!*

"Father, something is happening," Faith said. "I can't say what, but I feel something is trying to invade Brigantia."

"My dear, why is that?"

Faith told him about the words of the bleeding hearts, the black wave, and her dream. "When I touched the black water and the man in the dream, I could feel sadness. A deep loneliness as though he was a prisoner far away from home." She wasn't sure how else to explain it.

For a moment, her father's gaze was unfocused. "There has never been sadness in Brigantia."

The way he spoke, and his blank expression, confused her. She'd never gotten that tone from him. "Father?"

He shook his head, seeming to return to himself. "Yes, we must see to this! I shall visit the palace at once."

"I'll come with you."

"No, no, my dear, you stay abed and rest. Those burns are nasty, according to Minerva."

"But—"

"Trust me, my love. I promise I shall return as soon as I'm able."

Faith was uncertain still, but she'd always trusted her father. "All right. Please take care."

He tipped his hat. "That I shall."

Not long after he left, Faith found she could not sit still or fall asleep again. Minerva brought her a tray with some soup and more tea, but Faith only took a few spoonsful before she gave a huff of frustration.

"I can't just sit here." She set the tray on her nightstand and pulled back the covers. She swung her legs over the bed and took a moment to sit up. Her headache was gone, but she could still feel pain from her burns. She knew her father feared the queen, which was understandable since the monarch had a penchant for ordering executions for the smallest infraction, although Faith had never witnessed any of these executions carried out. Of course, there was Rowan. Could she speak with him? Would he even believe her?

"Well, sitting here will accomplish nothing," Faith said aloud. Standing wasn't easy, but she managed. She dressed and approached her mirror. Her hair and face were a mess. She cringed. Minerva had left a fresh pitcher of water and a washbasin. The water was tepid, but Faith washed her face and brushed her hair. She realized she'd lost the precious top hat. So, she crept into her father's room and chose one of his, not a colorful one, but it would do. Her father said everyone should have a good hat.

She left her room and tiptoed down the stairs. Minerva moved around in the kitchen. Faith rushed out the front door and circled the house, spotting Argestes indulging in fallen peaches from the tree.

"Argestes!"

"Waa!" He reared up and planted his feet down. "Faith? Please don't be cross with me! The Hatter already—"

"Never mind that." Faith strode toward him. "You will take me to the palace."

He brightened, thinking she'd forgiven him. He knelt before her, and Faith climbed on. She patted Argestes on the neck, more to reassure herself that she was doing the right thing. Then they were off.

CHAPTER THREE

"Rowan!" Instructor Spindler brought the ruler down onto the desktop with a crack. "You're not paying attention!"

He hadn't been. It was undeniable. He'd been gazing out the window, observing the waves in motion on the Sea of Tears. He couldn't see the beach. Then his gaze traveled to the Blue Mountains. Rowan had to endure tedious lessons in Brigantia, despite its intentional nonsense. Well, of course he had to learn. "It is unwise to feel proud of being ignorant," his father had told him, on one of the rare occasions he spoke aloud.

His instructor had been droning on about his duty as high prince and as the firstborn. They expected him to keep his behavior as princely as possible. It seemed rather ironic that they required him to behave in the opposite manner they did.

Still, Rowan agreed with his instructors; he had little patience for nonsense, as he supposed he should. During his younger years, he exhibited the same level of silliness and illogical thinking as anyone in Brigantia. Over time, however, he became disconnected from everything. Although pleased with this, his mother, the Queen of Hearts, sometimes indulged in silliness too. As for his father, well, the king rarely spoke about these things, or about anything at all, for that matter. The queen held true authority, at least in their kingdom of Uthelan. To the east, beyond the Sea of Tears, Epaitopia lay, with the Red Queen as its ruler, and to the north at the base of the Frostfire Mountains stood Mazia, with the White Queen in control. Each person found contentment in remaining in their own kingdoms, except when they came together for Stixis Day. The discussion on that day was intended to be about kingdom matters, but they typically got sidetracked by the absence of urgent issues in Brigantia, which resulted in the women taking part in idle gossip and grooming, while the men dedicated themselves to hunting.

They killed nothing during these hunts, as most animals exhibited sentience as they were chased. Still, Rowan savored these moments, as he accompanied his father, free from his mother's presence, and the King of Hearts exhibited a different persona. He would laugh, drink, and raise a toast to whatever beast they had pursued, and their supposed prey displayed gratitude. But once they returned to the palace, his father closed himself off and anger would tighten Rowan's chest. He loved both his parents, but his mother…

As Rowan focused on listening to Spindler, he questioned if he possessed the power to transform their present lives if he ever took the throne, provided he even survived, or stuck around that long. Unlike the rest of his family, Rowan desired to explore what lay beyond the borders of Brigantia.

I can never leave. I have responsibilities.

Someone gently knocked on the door. Spindler growled like an angry dog and strode over, grabbed the door handle, and pulled it open. "Now see here—" He halted and stepped aside. "Your Highness, my apologies."

It was one of his younger sisters, who either paid no attention to Spindler or was unaware of his tone. Among his siblings, she was the youngest out of the ten royal children, yet they named her Seven. Rowan often wondered how that came about. Like all the younger ones, she was dressed in a white shirt and trousers, with crimson hearts all over her outfit. Rowan felt relieved not having to dress like that anymore.

"Big brother, come quick!" She ran to him and took his hand, pulling him from his chair with surprising strength. "People are gathering in the throne room! They are speaking of a horror that is taking over the land!"

His teacher rolled his eyes, but Rowan knew his sister was not prone to telling wild stories. Apart from himself, she was the most levelheaded of all of them.

Rowan stood and bowed low to his teacher. "May I go for now? I promise to finish my studies for the night." He didn't need to ask. As a high prince, mutual respect was of utmost importance. His teacher waved him on. Seven continued to pull him along.

"I know where we can go."

Rowan had the same understanding, but he let her take the lead. Above and overlooking the throne room there was a balcony that the queen sometimes used to address the citizens, without being among them, though it was still possible for her to bask in their adulation. Rowan and Seven stealthily entered the room behind the balcony and closed the door. Since no one was allowed to enter this room except for members of the royal family, they didn't worry over much about being discovered. Rowan and Seven lowered themselves onto their hands and knees and shifted the curtains aside. They continued to the balcony railing, which gave them a view of the throne room. Lying on their stomachs with their chins resting on their folded arms, they watched the scene below them.

The throne room had fewer people than he expected. Citizens visited the queen and king on Knikix Day, where they could air any grievance or make requests. It shocked Rowan that the Queen of Hearts allowed this impromptu gathering at all.

As Rowan and Seven watched, more people waited to enter the throne room. Their stories started out as rather tame but increased to near disasters. To Rowan, much of it seemed exaggerated. The situation might have descended into chaos if not for his mother's patience evaporating.

"*Silence!*"

Even Rowan jumped at her order. Everyone fell silent right away. His mother ruled as a no-nonsense monarch with a generous figure and an impressively strong temper. The other queens, despite being rulers of their respective kingdoms, always deferred to her. She took a moment to adjust the bodice and skirt of her gown before taking her seat. His father had not moved or spoken. The anger, familiar to him, rose in his chest at his father's ineffectualness. His mother was the true ruler, and his father was nothing more than a puppet. Rowan loved the king, but he wished the man would assert his power more. Not to disrespect his mother, but just to show that he ruled as well.

"White Rabbit."

"Yes, Your Majesty?" He appeared in their view and stood to the right of the queen's throne.

"You will note each tale."

"Yes, Your Majesty."

"Hatter, step forward."

The Mad Hatter had gone unnoticed by him. Master Carter took a few steps forward and got down on one knee. "Thank you, Your Majesty."

Rowan frowned. Where was Faith? He hadn't seen her in so long, he wondered how she fared. She was the most outspoken person in Brigantia and did not fear his mother, unlike others. He'd always admired that about her, although he'd never told her.

He wanted – needed to get closer. "Seven, return to the nursery."

She pouted. "But Rowan—"

"No arguments now." The stories had started to become a little too frightening, and he didn't want his sister to have nightmares.

"All right."

When they left the room, he sent his sister in the opposite direction, and Rowan took the stairs to the lower level and entered the throne room, hoping no one would notice him. He moved into the shadows next to the marble column that stood a few steps back from his father's throne.

The Hatter continued to talk, and Rowan once again remembered Faith. They'd played together as youngsters but drifted apart as they grew older. He regretted not staying in her life, but what choice did he have? He underwent extensive training to govern his kingdom and didn't have time for play anymore.

That's no excuse. She used to be your friend.

Rowan moved around to the other side of the column. He blew out his breath. "Show yourself and stay out of my mind."

Slit pupils and brilliant green eyes appeared, followed by a tiny nose and long gray whiskers, and became a disembodied, floating head.

"Now, my prince —" the Cheshire Cat grinned at him, "— I meant no offense."

Rowan, looking at the citizens, realized he had missed most of the Hatter's words. "I suppose you know of this?"

"Only what you do." The head bobbed up and down. "I'll learn more." The Cheshire Cat paused. "Something is amiss. The air in Brigantia has soured."

"You don't say," Rowan said. "It smells the same to me."

"Of course it does," the Cheshire Cat said. "But I am Cat."

After he vanished, Rowan wondered about the significance of his *cat* identity. *Never mind.* He returned to his previous position to continue to watch what went on in the throne room.

His mother spoke to the Hatter. "Faith, is she well?"

"Yes, she is, Your Majesty. She is being cared for."

Wait, what happened to Faith?

Rowan stepped forward. "Forgive me, but Master Hatter, I did not hear. What has happened to Faith?"

"You didn't pay attention, did you?" the queen demanded. "Come now, you have been standing there all this time."

He should have been aware that his mother knew of his presence. "My apologies."

His mother harrumphed in annoyance. "You will wait until we finish here. Hatter, if you will remain?"

"Yes, Your Majesty."

Rowan could sense the Hatter's impatience, likely his desire to return to Faith. He disliked delaying the man, but he needed to have information. As additional citizens stepped forward, the stories shared a common thread. Some individuals recounted a distinct narrative of vegetation and crops wilting, and wells and ponds brimming with the same dark substance discovered on the seashore. It would be disturbing if something had contaminated their water supply. No one had any idea of the how and why of it.

Once the last citizen spoke, the queen rose from her throne again. "Return to your homes, all of you. Stay away from the sea. We will investigate this and make our findings known."

"Your Majesty?" His mother looked at him in annoyance when Rowan spoke. "I would care to further investigate this. The stories themselves seem rather – well, they bear further research."

"Agreed." She motioned to the White Rabbit. "Give him the notes."

"Your Majesty," the Rabbit said meekly, "should I make a copy?"

"Yes, yes," the queen said dismissively.

The throne room had emptied of citizens; only his mother and father, the White Rabbit and the Hatter remained. Faith's father stood in one corner, gripping his hat firmly. "Come, Master Hatter." Rowan beckoned, exiting the room without pause. Just a few steps down the hall was a waiting room where the queen held audiences. Rowan assumed this location was as suitable as any.

The Hatter stepped forward and opened the door for him. "After you, Your Highness."

Rowan abruptly nodded and stepped into the room.

"Tea, Your Highness?" the Hatter said. "Yes, we must have tea!"

The man appeared nervous and eager to please. The servants always kept a tea service stocked and prepared, making it easy for the Hatter to remove the cap from the flame tin and place the pot on top. Painted wood boxes held a variety of tea leaves, as well as tools for straining and crushing them. "I understand you like lemon ginger?" the Hatter said.

"Yes." Rowan couldn't help but be pleased and waited patiently as the Hatter continued his preparations. He served Rowan first, then poured his own and sat across from the prince. His hands trembled on the cup, and some tea spilled over the edge.

"I'm sorry."

"Don't be." He felt sorry for the old man. "I assume you want to get back to Faith. But I would appreciate your patience with me."

The Hatter began his tale, although his gaze remained on his teacup. When he concluded, Rowan's finger began tapping on the tabletop, a habit he had learned from his mother. "I will investigate. Return to your home and attend to your daughter."

"Thank you, but," the Hatter began, "may I come with you on your investigation? I want to view this thing for myself."

Rowan understood the Hatter lacked fighting skills, yet his tone and expression hinted at a desire for retaliation, even without a definite strategy. Yes, he wanted to return to Faith, but his fatherly instinct also wanted to obtain any information he could about who had injured his daughter.

The White Rabbit returned and knocked on the doorframe. "I have the papers, Your Highness."

He hopped over and Rowan had to fight not to laugh. Despite the abundance of sentient animals in Brigantia, the White Rabbit never ceased to unsettle him. "Thank you."

Rowan scanned the reports while the Hatter sipped his tea. The stories ranged from plausible to highly exaggerated in his opinion, but all exhibited similarities. The Hatter's words to him and Faith's dream stood as the sole tale of its kind. It seemed like Faith had physically encountered this unknown entity. "Hatter?"

He started, almost dropping his cup. "Yes, Your Highness?"

"I would like to speak with Faith."

"If she is feeling well enough."

"We'll see what we find along the shore."

★   ★   ★

Honestly, Rowan was uncertain about what he would discover or do. He'd handpicked six guards to accompany him, along with the Hatter, and the White Rabbit, who was there to note anything unusual. They'd traveled on horseback and the group arrived at the shore of the Sea of Tears. "Spread out," Rowan ordered. "Whatever you find, no matter how small, report back to me."

The Hatter stayed at his side, still somewhat sheepish, but he held his head high as he followed Rowan to where the tide met the beach. Everything appeared ordinary. That was, until Rowan noticed something glistening in the sand. He dismounted and approached it. He found a flat, shapeless mass, with holes in its surface.

"Is that...?" the Hatter began.

"It's gold, all right." Rowan picked it up and examined it, feeling its weight. Faith's Gift had always impressed him. There was no other indication of a disturbance. He trusted Faith's words, but his mother might not be so accepting. Rowan loathed returning empty-handed. Although the gold was not proof that anything had occurred, he felt compelled to have something to show for this task. The sea and shore appeared as they should. Rowan wondered if it would be worth going outside Brigantia and finding an alchemist to do further research. Not that he had any idea where to locate an alchemist. Faith represented the nearest equivalent to one. In moments like this, Rowan regretted Brigantia's insular nature.

Rowan tried to sound as official as he could. "White Rabbit!"

"Yes, sir!" The Rabbit moved to his side.

"Are you aware of an alchemist beyond our world?"

"I am, Your Highness."

It didn't surprise Rowan. The Rabbit stood as the sole individual who always traveled beyond the borders of Brigantia. "Visit them and present them with this." He handed the gold to the Rabbit. "Have them examine it. Give them whatever fee they ask for."

"As you wish, Your Highness." The Rabbit bowed and hopped off.

One guard approached Rowan. "Your Highness, we've found nothing."

Rowan swore under his breath. "Bring three others and establish surveillance in this area. Give it three days. Get whatever supplies you need from the palace."

"Yes, sir!"

"If anything happens, report back. Do not engage, understand?"

"Yes, Your Highness!"

Rowan believed it served no purpose to use time in that way. "Let's get on then. I want to see the damaged crops."

As he turned, he caught sight of none other than Faith riding toward him on that gryphon of hers. What was she doing here?

The Hatter noticed his attention had shifted and followed his gaze. "Faith?" He dismounted and rushed toward her. Faith smiled in welcome, but to Rowan's surprise, she approached him instead.

"Your Highness."

"Miss Carter." Being overly formal was unnecessary. He'd never used that name to address her before. Few knew or called the Hatter by his true name. Faith's brow furrowed, first in confusion, then annoyance. The Hatter came up behind her and laid his hands on her shoulders.

Suddenly feeling bashful, Rowan continued, "I'm glad to see you're faring well."

He was rewarded with her smile. "Thank you. Did my father tell you what happened?"

Rowan nodded. "Yes. Is there anything else you can tell us? Something you may have remembered?"

She wrapped her arms around her chest. "No, I'm afraid."

"What about the Dokkalfar?" Rowan asked. No Dokkalfar had ever been in Brigantia. "Nothing specific you can recall about him?"

"Only the profound sense of sadness. His face was warped. I can barely remember what he looked like."

He'd been hoping to obtain more information. "I'm trying to determine what is going on here," Rowan said. "Many reports align with your father's account, but only you experienced a dream linked to it."

"What are you saying?" Faith bristled at his words and stepped forward.

"Just that—" Rowan quickly changed the subject. "Nothing. We found gold here on the beach and I had the White Rabbit take it to an alchemist."

Her face flushed, bringing out rosy freckles across her nose and cheeks. He'd always liked the look of those freckles against her light brown skin.

"Do not tell me it's nothing!" Her fists clenched and Rowan was quite certain she would pummel him no matter who he was. The Hatter tightened his grip on his daughter's shoulders.

She approached Rowan until they were nose-to-nose. "Don't think I won't—"

Something tickled Rowan's nose, and he turned his head aside just in time and sneezed.

"Why, of all the—"

"Tsk, tsk." The cause of Rowan's sneeze appeared. The Cheshire Cat floated in the narrow space between them. "Is this how friends behave toward one another?"

"He started it," Faith muttered, then winced at her own words.

Cheshire stretched his full length. "We must have civil words and cooler heads."

Now Rowan winced. Cheshire, as always, spoke truthfully. Still, he wasn't ready to give ground yet. "I am responsible for—"

"Yes, yes." The Cheshire Cat rolled over, his body now a translucent cloud, his face larger than Rowan's. "I heard you volunteer your services. I was there, you recall." His cloudlike body stayed still while his head turned to face Faith. "The prince is quite sorry for how he behaved."

Rowan sighed, defeated, and said, "Yes, of course, please forgive me. I...meant no disrespect."

Faith harrumphed but said nothing. Cheshire's face faded out, leaving only his grin. "Like the rat said, what fantastic creatures boys are."

Then the grin faded, leaving everyone, including Rowan, with no idea what to do next.

CHAPTER FOUR

Honestly, Rowan could be quite annoying sometimes. He'd changed since they last spent time together. Despite his added responsibilities, Faith found his inability to be honest with her irritating.

It was only because Cheshire had intervened that Faith hadn't pushed further.

Rowan finally said, "Those I've ordered to stay, if you find nothing, return to the palace. The rest follow us. I want to see the remaining damage. Lady Faith, would you accompany me?"

Her annoyance remained, but she was also curious about what else had occurred, so she nodded. She turned to her father and took his hands, squeezing them. "Father, why don't you go on home? I'll be all right. Make sure all is well."

"Well..."

She could see the uncertainty in his expression.

"Just take care, my little jewel," he said.

"I will."

Faith called Argestes over and mounted.

Rowan climbed on his own mount.

"Where to first?" she asked.

"The nearest farmland," Rowan said. "Farmers shared tales of crop taint."

Faith had no idea what to expect. The farm itself was of moderate size and had a variety of fruits and vegetables growing in neat little rows, from corn to peppers, lettuce, radishes, grapes, and squash. Like Faith's home garden.

They dismounted. "Stay here, Argestes."

"Fine by me." He was trembling. "This place has a foul odor."

They saw the damage as they moved closer. Corn that once stood tall and proud now was bent and shriveled, its flesh a slick green. Root vegetables showed signs of tiny paws digging, only to find a greenish-brown sludge. Many other foods were in the same sorry state. The worst part of it was the stench. Argestes had understated. It was beyond description. Both were unfamiliar with the awful odor. It burned down their throats and made them want to vomit. It was a fight to keep it down.

The farmer stayed on his porch, not moving closer. He looked like a hardworking person, aged, with a receding hairline and scruffy beard. The sun had wrinkled and burned his face. He dressed himself in the usual tan overalls. He seemed content to stay where he was and enjoy the pipe clenched between his lips. The scent of the smoke supplied some relief.

Faith couldn't blame him for staying far away. Grapes, tomatoes, and squash were the only unaffected crops. Rowan reached out and plucked a grape, sniffing it first before eating. Faith waited. "It tastes perfectly fine."

Faith picked one and ate it. "It does." She looked at where the farmer stood. "We should harvest them for him."

Faith expected his resistance, but he surprised her with a simple, "You're right." It pleased her.

Faith, Rowan, and the guards set to work until they harvested the good crops. When they approached the farmer's house with their baskets full of foodstuffs, the old man stood staring at them while he took a drag on his pipe. "Thanks, Yer Highness, Miss Faith, but I don't want it."

"They're safe," Faith said. "We tasted them ourselves. We'll discover what's happening."

He huffed. "It's evil magic, I tell ye, ain't no bones about it. Never seen its like in Brigantia, and I been here since before ya both were born." He tapped his pipe on the sole of his boot before feeling around his overalls until he felt the pocket he was looking for and pulled out a tobacco pouch. He went about filling and lighting his pipe again.

"Have you seen anything like this before?" Faith asked.

"Like this, no." He took a few puffs. "But ain't it obvious? It's dark magic come from the dark fey."

"Dark fey?" Rowan said in disbelief. "There's never been dark fey here."

"Seen none, eh?" The farmer cackled. "You sure? They were here. Long time ago. Even before the Heroine."

Rowan didn't respond. His expression was disbelieving. Faith spoke up. "Do you have any advice for us?"

The farmer snorted a laugh. "This is my land so I'm here till I die. But I'd say take the people and get the hell out." He turned and walked into his house. Ignoring the harvest baskets, he slammed the door behind him.

"Something's not right," Faith remarked. "I've never heard of dark fey ever being in Brigantia, have you?"

"No." Yet Rowan's tone was uncertain. "There have never been dark fey in Brigantia. The stories were just rumors and fairy tales to frighten naughty children."

"How can you be sure? Brigantia is an ancient land," Faith said. Stories of Jabberwock and Bandersnatch circulated, but their existence remained unproven.

Rowan didn't respond, but his expression told her he was considering. He turned to the guards. "We shall return to the palace."

The sudden decision caught Faith off guard. "You're not going to look into this further?"

"I have summoned an alchemist to examine the remains of the creatures you saw," Rowan said. "I'm certain they will be able to determine what is tainting the crops. We will continue from there."

"And depending on what they find?" Faith said.

"I'm certain it has nothing to do with dark fey."

Faith released her breath and crossed her arms while shaking her head. He was avoiding the possibilities. Were the royal family capable of dealing with such a crisis?

"Whatever we find, we will make a formal announcement from

the palace." Rowan mounted his horse. "You should go home. It's likely not safe now. Farewell."

The finality of the word wasn't lost on Faith as Rowan rode away with the guards following.

Argestes approached. "He is afraid."

"He should be." Faith said. "I believe we all should be."

"What will you do, Faith?"

Faith reached into one basket, grabbed a bunch of grapes, and handed them to Argestes. Faith allowed him a few moments to enjoy the treat. "We're going home."

*　　*　　*

Faith had much to consider as she rode home. It wasn't difficult to deduce that the prince, like herself, was frightened of the unknown. If trouble was coming, he had the whole of the Hearts Army at his command, not to mention the warriors of the White and Red Queens. Couldn't they handle this challenge?

When home finally came into view, Faith suddenly recalled what day it was. She certainly didn't feel like celebrating now. The kitchen door slammed open, and Minerva stepped out. "Master Carter! Faith has returned!"

Faith had just dismounted when her father dashed from the kitchen. Faith ran to meet him in a hug. It seemed like a long time since she had last seen him.

"Dearest daughter!" her father said. "Are you well?"

"Yes, Father." She hugged him perhaps a little too tightly, but she needed to hold on to something familiar.

"I hope it's all right," he said as he ushered her into the house. "I canceled the festivities until further notice. I figured you wouldn't want to deal with guests."

"Thank you. It's fine, Father."

"So, tell me all."

Faith did as Minerva set out tea and fruit-filled, sweet cakes.

"I suppose we should all be fearful." Her father shook his head much like Faith had done. "Rowan believes it will be up to him to protect the citizens. He'll likely not ask for help."

Faith said, "I suppose he couldn't admit to being afraid."

"You want to be of assistance to him."

"But he'll never say. He is too proud." Faith ran a finger around the rim of her cup. "I wish I knew what to do."

The Hatter reached over and squeezed her hand. "Protecting the people is the royal family's responsibility in times of trouble."

"But will they?" Faith asked.

"Let us hope."

Uncertainty lingered in Faith's mind. "There has never been true darkness here."

"There is darkness everywhere," her father said. "Perhaps we have been blinded to it all."

They were silent for a few moments, each lost in their own thoughts as they continued to sip their tea. The cakes remained untouched. Faith wasn't very hungry.

Faith spoke up. "Father, I wonder, do you believe the Caterpillar could advise me? I refuse to rely on the royals to act."

"A valid question, my dear," her father said, "but—"

Faith waited.

"Why do you need advice, my dear? What do you plan to do?" The worry in his voice was unmistakable.

"I have no idea." Faith pushed back from the table and stood. She wrung her hands as she paced the kitchen. "Father, I am aware of what I witnessed. I know what happened. Something is wrong and I can't wait idly by while Brigantia is threatened."

She sat down again and took her father's hands in hers and squeezed gently. "I understand your worry. But what happens if I take no action, and the situation worsens? What if I miss the opportunity to protect Brigantia?"

"That is not your job." Her father looked down at her clasped hands.

"Father," Faith muttered, and the Hatter raised his eyes to meet hers. "You took me in when I was a babe. Brigantia is my home. If there is impending danger, where should we seek shelter?"

Faith had never seen her father look so distressed.

"Fine," he finally said, "but promise me you'll come straight home and tell me everything."

"I promise."

It would be night soon, but Faith didn't want to wait any longer. She could navigate in the dark. She tried to convince herself of this as she strode outside into the garden in search of Argestes. Did she really desire to be outside after sunset, when darkness invaded Brigantia? No, she wouldn't falter. She refused to be moved by fear. Faith was determined. She would protect Brigantia.

CHAPTER FIVE

The stench seemed to follow him back to the palace, and Rowan bathed before he presented himself to his parents. Regrettably, no quantity of perfume could eliminate the scent from him.

He found his parents were in the garden playing shuttlecock. His mother stood at one end of the court with retainers surrounding her, whose sole purpose was to hit back any errant birds. His father was completely on his own. A circular table and chairs were arranged beside the court, shaded with an immense blue umbrella. Sandwiches and iced tea in tall glasses were set out.

Rowan sat to wait while munching on the prepared cucumber sandwiches. But as delicious as they were, he couldn't taste them at all. After a time, he became so engrossed in thought, he no longer saw his parents cavorting on the court.

Why hadn't he been honest with Faith?

Because you are a prince of Brigantia. You may not show weakness.

Stupid idiot, coward! Why did they expect him to be sane in a land filled with nonsense? Yes, his parents were quite serious, especially his mother, but still they indulged. The sandwich was sawdust as he forced it down his throat. He wished he wasn't the oldest. He recalled his time in the nursery, first by himself, with the occasional visit from his cousins; then came his other brothers and sisters. He hadn't minded sharing. It was lonely in the nursery.

When his parents finished their game, with his mother winning, of course, but no thanks to her own skill, they joined him at the table.

"Goodness!" The queen waved her hands in front of her face. A servant rushed up with a large feather fan. A second servant placed damp chilled towels on a tray and the queen took one, patting it over her face. His father had to fend for himself.

"So, my firstborn, what have you to tell us?" The queen drank tea.

"Your Majesty —" he always addressed her as such in public, "— I found no creatures at the Sea of Tears." His throat suddenly dried, he poured himself a glass. His mother lifted one manicured brow, but Rowan figured he could do the simple task himself. He told her about the farmer and the tainted crops, carefully omitting what the farmer said about dark fey.

"The White Rabbit said you instructed him to seek out an alchemist?" the queen asked.

Rowan blew out his breath. "There was the gold residue, as the Hatter said, and I believe an alchemist may have some insight once they examine it and the crops."

His mother nodded before picking up a sandwich. She waited for him to continue as she chewed. Rowan knew he had to tread carefully with Faith's dream.

"You believe the Hatter's daughter? About these creatures?" she asked, taking another sip, gazing at him above her glass.

"I—"

Surprisingly, his father spoke up. "Faith has always been truthful, if flighty."

Flighty? Faith? Did his father really believe that?

"Well, an alchemist cannot determine the meaning of her dream," the queen said. "Only a diviner can do that."

There was only one diviner in Brigantia. The Caterpillar.

"What about the Caterpillar?" his father offered.

The queen looked at him, annoyed. "Caterpillar?"

"You recall, my love? She lives in the Grotto."

The queen's brow furrowed. She turned to Rowan. "Oh, yes, you and the Hatter's daughter used to play there. I thought she'd gotten squashed or something."

"She fell asleep," Rowan said. "That is, she is in her chrysalis."

"That doesn't do us any good!"

"It's been six months," Rowan said. "She may be ready for her rebirth."

"I suppose we should see about it." The queen picked up a cloth napkin and dabbed at her lips. "Rowan, tomorrow you will take some soldiers and visit the Caterpillar."

"Yes, Your Majesty." Finally, something he could do, hoping to find answers. "If I may, I would like to continue my research."

"Well…" The queen hesitated.

"Rowan is doing well at his studies," the king said, "so it should do no damage."

The queen huffed. "All right then, but I want results."

"I will do my best, Your Majesty."

★ ★ ★

The queen had given him permission to continue his investigation, so he wasn't required to attend to his studies. It wasn't until a thought occurred to him that Rowan paid a visit to the palace library.

Despite everything, trying to convince himself that the farmer was just paranoid, Rowan studied on his own. He hadn't been honest with himself about dark fey in Brigantia. He just didn't know for certain.

One thing he admired about his mother was that she insisted everyone in the palace learn, even the lowest servant. "I won't have ignorance in my presence." The library was open to everyone in all their kingdoms, and anyone could use it. So, it wasn't surprising when Rowan found others within. When they saw him, they came out of their seats and bowed. Rowan tried not to look annoyed. He smiled and motioned for them to take their seats.

The library was circular and three stories high. A wrought-iron winding staircase stood at the room's center. Rowan climbed to the third floor. That was where the oldest known history of Brigantia rested. Unsure of where to begin, he opted for *The History of Brigantia*. He couldn't help but smile. He took the tome and selected three others and carried them to a nearby table. The wonderful thing about books in Brigantia was that they moved. The words appeared on the page as he read them, and illustrations were animated, as though some swift painter worked with an invisible hand. A man named Charles Lutwidge Dodgson wrote it. It was an unusual name, certainly not something you heard in Brigantia.

It started with a child who loved nonsense and was of precocious intellect. He rejected the world of order and logic because it did not want him. His imagination was beyond what most people comprehended. He desired a place where individuals like him could live, embracing their nonsensical and liberated nature. And from that came Brigantia.

It wasn't much of an explanation. But the illustrations showed him a skinny boy of maybe seven years, although it was difficult to tell since the art didn't present his face. He walked across the page with a red-gold fog swirling around him and he moved his hands in what seemed to be awkward motions. On every page the boy's movement made a new creation. Nothing much was familiar. Rowan supposed it was just the beginning.

The next pages listed the myriads of strange creatures brought to life. Some Rowan was not familiar with, and he wondered what happened to them. Perhaps they were still somewhere nearby. He read about the Jabberwock, which seemed as close to dark fey as anything. Rowan wondered where the Vorpal Blade was. He asked the book and all he got for his trouble was a picture of the blade and beneath it in capital letters: LOST.

Rowan rolled his eyes and huffed in annoyance.

Next, he asked the book to show him any instances of dark fey in Brigantia. Surprisingly, the pages swirled with fog, revealing vague shapes that concealed the book's secrets. He watched for a few moments, tapping the page with one finger. Now what? He couldn't guess why the book behaved this way. Unless it was merely reiterating Rowan's thought that there were never any dark fey in their world? Rowan put it aside for now and went to the next one, aptly titled *Children of the Vine*. He was deep into the book when he got that familiar tickle in his nose.

"Perhaps you should ask Faith for help?"

Rowan pretended to ignore the voice.

Cheshire appeared, stretched across the desk on his back, exposing his furry belly. Rowan resisted the urge to scratch it. "I can do this on my own."

"The smell lingers on you."

"What?"

"The stench. Surely you haven't forgotten?"

"No, but how is it on me?" Rowan asked, his attention fully on the cat.

The cat rolled over onto his stomach and stretched to his full length. "I suppose from the farmer's crops or the Sea of Tears."

"Why is it staying on me? No one else has noticed."

"Couldn't say." Cheshire yawned hugely, showing all his pointed teeth. "I can only say dark magic is involved."

"Damn it all," Rowan muttered. He steepled his fingers and continued to look at the pages.

"What are you looking for?" The cat padded closer to him and stuck his nose into the book.

"I'm checking for records of dark fey in Brigantia," Rowan stated. "You wouldn't know about that, would you?"

Cheshire chuckled. His body vanished and all that remained was his head and tail. "I believe you should learn more about the dark fey. You have the book for it."

"I'd like to return to it, please," Rowan said, voicing his annoyance.

"Honestly," Cheshire said. Both the head and the tail vanished.

Rowan reshelved the books except *History* and *Children of the Vine*, choosing to take them with him. Rowan descended the stairs and opened the book again when he hit the landing. Some creatures on the pages he knew, but many others were unknown. That made him further wonder – *why?*

He returned to his chambers. Once he was alone, Rowan sat on his bed, tossing the books beside him. He thought of the Caterpillar again. Rowan thought to leave early in the morning but realized he'd never get a moment of sleep, while pondering. He decided then. Dark or not, he was going to seek out the Caterpillar tonight.

CHAPTER SIX

The Grotto marked Faith's northernmost journey in Brigantia, nestled in a place of perpetual shadows, with shafts of light finding their way through the canopy. Cliffs surrounded it where a waterfall cascaded from above into a crystal pond. The Grotto was silent and calm. Birds sang softly, frogs croaked lazily, their sounds mellowed. Sunlight shimmered through the lush canopy, casting silver shafts.

While Faith rode down the familiar path, a subtle change seemed to happen around them.

"Something is not right," Argestes said.

"Do not falter," Faith said quietly. "We're almost there."

The sun hadn't broken the tree line, so full daylight had not yet touched the area. It was hard to tell what exactly Argestes was feeling. Faith couldn't help but be relieved upon finally witnessing the unnatural light that illuminated the Grotto regardless of the time.

"Someone is coming," Argestes said unexpectedly. He spun around to face the road behind them. Faith realized that he was right. Someone was riding on the path.

"Friend or foe?" Faith asked, knowing Argestes would sense a threat.

The gryphon continued to dance nervously. Faith's grip tightened on the reins as she gathered her power.

"It's Rowan!" Argestes said, a moment before Faith recognized him.

Of course, the prince was not alone. Three of the queen's guards accompanied him. Faith tried to hide her slight smile from Rowan's view as he got closer. "Your Highness."

"Lady Carter."

She hated how formal they'd become, but she decided not to show it. "I suppose you're here for the same reason I am?"

Rowan slid down from his horse and approached, reaching out his hand to her. Only common courtesy had her take it and allow him to help her down from the gryphon's back. He then patted Argestes on the neck.

The lush green grass cushioned their feet, quieting their footsteps. The center clearing held a tall mushroom with a sparkling green chrysalis. It appeared to float, yet if they looked closely, they could see a fine thread keeping it upright, although they couldn't see its attachment.

And something moved from within it.

"Is that…?" Faith dared to hope.

It was amazing, watching as the life inside the fragile cocoon struggled to free itself. Fingers pushed through the thin membrane and were the same green as the chrysalis. A second hand came forth and gripped the edges of the small hole, tearing it further open.

"Should we be here?" Faith whispered, although her gaze never left this rebirth. It seemed personal, not for prying eyes. Rowan didn't answer, still captivated, and Faith couldn't help but join him in his awe.

When the ritual was nearly done and the being almost free, Faith glimpsed her smooth skin and the curve of her spine. Rowan squeaked and looked away. The being stepped completely from within the chrysalis, and her gaze met Faith's. Realizing she was staring at her nakedness, Faith felt the warmth of a flush and cast her gaze downward.

"Hello, little Faith, I am glad to see you."

Faith swallowed, not knowing what to say.

"And Prince Rowan. Yes, I know it is you. Look at me, both of you."

Faith took a deep breath and raised her eyes. The being wrapped herself in a chrysalis piece.

"I am now Jade."

"The name fits your beauty," Faith said.

"Rowan, why won't you face me?" The prince still had his back turned.

"It's all right," Faith said, amused, "you can look."

"No."

"Rowan, it's fine. She's dressed."

He still hesitated before turning to face Jade. "Um…my Lady Jade?"

"No need to be so formal. Come closer and sit with me as you used to do."

Faith wasted no time but sat on one of the gigantic mushrooms in front of Jade's. It seemed smaller than she recalled. Rowan climbed onto the one next to hers.

"We are happy to see you again," Faith said. "We know it's been a long time."

"And I am happy too, although I wish it were under better circumstances."

"We have come for your advice," Rowan said. "Are you aware of the goings-on in Brigantia while you slept?"

"Certainly," Jade replied. "I represent the green of Brigantia and I have felt the darkness." Jade motioned with her hand, and the hookah mysteriously appeared. "Ah, I have waited for this."

She paused, likely expecting them to fuss, but they had more important matters. After preparing it, she took a long drag and blew out a cloud of smoke before continuing, "I witnessed the darkness and the souls that lived within it."

"Souls?" Faith and Rowan said in unison.

Jade took another long drag and blew out three separate smoke rings. Instead of dissipating, they joined and coalesced into a single large ring. A vision formed at the center. It was a scene of war.

"Do you know of the war fought against dark and light fey? This was long before it tore our land asunder and Brigantia didn't exist."

They had both heard the stories of how the Isles had once been a single nation until the Farm Boy had felled the Vine. They nodded.

Jade continued. "Dark and light fey both lived Above Ground but the dark fey terrorized humanity. Mortals fought back, but it wasn't enough, so they called on the light for help."

The scene changed, showing many mortals and light fey advancing on the combatants of the dark fey. They shed much blood on both sides. The scene dissolved, alongside two other rings. They melded, but everything was smoke and fog.

"It is unclear exactly what happened after the Vine fell, but we know this." Unseen force propelled smoke and earth into the air, which then descended in sizable chunks, enveloping the sight in darkness. "Despite their long lives, many of the fey who were present have passed on." The next scene started off in darkness, but then...

"I saw that!" Faith exclaimed, pointing at faces in the smoke. "Awful faces. They looked human but..."

For a moment, Jade cast her eyes downward. "So much grief and misery."

Faith and Rowan exchanged glances, waiting for her to continue.

"They're people?" Rowan asked.

Jade nodded. "That joined with the misery of the dark fey."

"What do you mean?" Faith asked.

"The light imprisoned the dark deep within the earth, in perpetual dusk. A cursed place with the stench of rotting corpses. They were to remain there for eternity."

"But the dark fey have other plans," Rowan said.

"That's what he meant," Faith said, "the sad man in my dream. He mentioned their longing for sunlight and the fresh air of the surface."

"You dreamt of a dark fey?" Jade was staring critically at her.

"I don't know if it – he was a dark fey. His face twisted as well, but I would swear he was a Dokkalfar."

"Despite their name, they are not dark fey," Rowan said.

"I know that," Faith said, slightly annoyed. "But—"

"If he was once flesh and bone, surrendering to darkness makes him darkness." Jade adjusted her legs on the mushroom cap.

"But why would anyone do that?" Faith said.

"That I cannot say." Jade retrieved the pipe, partook of it again, and blew out another ring. Darkness filled the center, then a presence emerged, indescribable but unified in darkness. No face, only a smiling presence.

"Stop!" Faith said, "Don't let it see us!"

"What in the nether hells is that thing?" Rowan demanded.

The hookah hose fell from Jade's grasp and her eyes were unfocused before they filled with a black liquid, much like the waves at the Sea of Tears. Her voice was unfamiliar as she spoke. "We are Rot."

"Jade!" Faith leapt from the mushroom.

Rowan cried out, "What in the bloody nether hells!"

Faith scrambled up onto the cap and reached for Jade, although uncertain what she could do. Fortunately, Jade's eyes were normal again. Faith grasped her shoulders. "Jade? Jade! What was that?"

She blinked, momentarily unable to speak. "You are correct. I should not have called it. I am fine now."

"You said, 'We are Rot.'"

"That is the name," Jade said. "It truly has none, but it is as fitting a description as any."

Rowan had climbed up beside her. It angered Faith to see he had his dagger clutched in his hand. "Rowan!"

He straightened. "My apologies, I didn't know what... I was worried..."

Jade smiled at him. "Understandable," she said. "I hold no malice against you, dear Rowan, for your caution."

He was worried. About her? Faith's cheeks warmed. "Why did this Rot come to Brigantia?"

"You said the man in your dream wanted you to free them?" Jade said.

"Yes. I won't release them, even if I knew how."

"They may not give you a choice."

Rowan frowned. "Are you saying this Rot may try to force Faith to do so?"

"Yes."

The single word caused Faith's heart to drop to her stomach. "I won't!"

"The Rot took hold of you." Rowan nodded to Jade. "Could it do the same to Faith?"

Jade sighed. "Yes."

The thought of that thing invading and warping her mind – Faith trembled and wrapped her arms around her waist. "What can I do?"

"I would suggest leaving Brigantia."

"No!" Faith and Rowan had spoken in unison again.

Was that a slight smile on Jade's face? "But of course, that's not agreeable to either of you. And it may not stop the Rot from pursuing you."

"Is there nothing we can do?" Rowan asked.

"Well…perhaps I can supply you with some protection." Jade stood on the cap and gathered up the discarded chrysalis. When she finished, she laid it in a pile, then sat again, taking up the hookah once more. "Are you familiar with the tale of the Spinner Queen?"

"Yes."

"Of course."

"Did you realize she is a living person?"

"You jest!"

"Surely."

"Her name is Queen Sylmare Daeric, of Tidaholm."

"Tidaholm," Rowan repeated. "I've seen it on maps in the palace."

"You must go to her and take my chrysalis. Tell her I have sent you to her so she may create the finest armor her Gift can produce."

"Armor?" Faith said.

"It may afford you some protection from the Rot, although I cannot guarantee it, but there is magic in my chrysalis."

"Thank you, milady," Rowan said.

"Yes, you have our gratitude," Faith said.

"Wait," Rowan said. "It's in the Underneath though. How do we get there?"

"The Hall of Doors," Faith whispered.

"Say again?" Rowan asked.

"Is that how we can get there? When the Heroine entered Brigantia, she fell into the White Rabbit's Burrow, then through the door to the garden."

"I haven't been through any of the doors." Rowan's tone was uncertain.

"Truly?"

Rowan shrugged. "Why should I have? I'm quite content here in Brigantia. At least I was until—"

"Rowan?" Faith laid a hand on his shoulder in a gesture of friendship.

He rewarded her with a smile. "Sometimes I wonder – or at least as of late – if we were wrong to keep ourselves so cut off from the rest of Underneath and Above Ground."

"That is a wise question," Jade said, causing a flush to rise on Rowan's cheeks.

"Then perhaps this is the opportunity you need to bring Brigantia out of our fortress." Faith smiled at him. "Who better?"

Rowan's blush deepened into scarlet. "Then that is what we shall do." He hesitated. "Um – milady, which door?"

CHAPTER SEVEN

"Certainly not!"

Rowan flinched at his mother's tone. His father briefly glanced up from his book before turning his gaze downward.

"Mother, Jade said—"

"And who is this Jade again?"

"The Caterpillar." Rowan tried to keep his voice steady. Although he'd had a feeling this conversation would not go pleasantly.

His mother was currently indulging in what she called her beauty regimen, which first was soaking in a tub of goats' milk, then having her muscles worked by the skilled hands of a burly young man as she lay prone on a cushioned table. Apparently, his father had nothing to say about it, which Rowan supposed wasn't surprising. Afterward, maids would work on the queen's hands, feet, and hair. She was currently having her nails clipped, filed, and painted. She normally took no callers during this process, but when she learned it was Rowan, having returned, she had him ushered into her chamber immediately.

Rowan and Faith had parted ways back at a crossroads, she to the left and he to the right. Rowan had offered one of the guards to accompany her, but she refused. Faith had said she wanted to speak to her father. But before she left, Rowan told her of his worries.

"I'm unsure how my mother will react to our journey," Rowan admitted.

"She will surely understand the necessity and our need for armor."

"She may," he said, even though he was still uncertain. "I'll attempt to emphasize its importance to her."

Now he was certain, as he tried rather unsuccessfully to convince his mother that they needed to travel outside of Brigantia and that they should form alliances. At that point, he just wasn't certain if she was disagreeing with one part of the plan, or both.

"Mother," he continued, "I have no information other than what I have told you. Let's assess the extent of this Rot's spread and others' efforts against it, if any."

"And you believe in this Rot?"

"I saw it with my own eyes, Mother."

"And Lady Faith? Do you trust her?"

"Yes, I do."

His mother was silent, longer than he liked.

"Very well," she finally said, and Rowan breathed a sigh of relief, which was short-lived.

"But you will have the Spinner Queen make the suits for you and me."

"Say again?"

"Did I not speak clearly?" she asked in an aggravated tone.

"Yes, Mother, but Jade said—"

"I care not for what Jade said, whoever she is." She was just being contrary now.

He was taking a mighty big chance when he continued. "I've said how the Rot wants Faith to obey its commands. Faith does not want to. She is loyal to the crown and Brigantia."

"What of it?"

She was his mother and the Queen of Hearts, and he loved her like any son would love his mother, but sometimes he wanted to shake some sense into her royal self. "She needs protection to fight the influence of the Rot. If what she dreamt is true, and what happened on the beach at the Sea of Tears and to the crops is any indication of what is to come, without Faith, the Rot could enter Brigantia."

"Then perhaps," his mother said, "if she is the key to the Rot's entry, we should put Lady Faith where she can do no harm. The cellars would work nicely."

"Mother!" Rowan protested. "Perhaps I am being unclear. Faith has done nothing wrong. She does not warrant punishment, but protection! Hence, the need for the armor."

"It matters not what she has done or not done," the queen said. "The safety of our kingdom is more important than one girl."

"She is a friend of mine and of this house."

His mother rolled her eyes. "Very well, my son, travel to Tidaholm and form these alliances. I trust you with this as my firstborn, but they will make the armor for you and me."

"Mother, Jade specifically said—"

"Say one more thing about this Jade, and I will take her head."

Rowan bit down hard on his lower lip. Then he tried a different tactic. "What about Father?"

"What about him?" The maids had finished their tasks and now stood, trembling, and clutching the silver trays on which they carried their cosmetics. They looked terrified as his mother examined their work.

"Yes, very good," the queen said.

The maids visibly relaxed.

"Walk with me, my son."

Rowan considered asking his father for help, but the man acted as if he hadn't heard a word, pretending to be engrossed in the book. His mother wasn't the only one Rowan wanted to shake.

Rowan crooked his elbow in hers and allowed her to lead. The chamber had a balcony, which faced the palace gardens. Out on the lawn, guests were indulging in the queen's favorite sport, croquet. Although without his mother there, the flamingoes were being rebellious, pecking and kicking as they saw fit.

"Do you see them, my son? We as royals handle them. We must not fall in battle. That is why we lead no troops. We must not allow any outside influences to overwhelm us. I insist they make armor for us. To protect the ones who will protect them."

"Mother, please—"

"We'll speak of this no more, my son." There was a clear warning in her words. "While you are on your journey, I will send word to the Red and White Queens to see if this is also happening in their lands.

Depending on what they say, we will come together and form a plan. Now go about your task."

Rowan sighed in defeat. "Yes, Your Majesty."

"That's a good boy."

"With your permission." He didn't stop walking as he said, "Father." If the king heard, he gave no sign.

It was only after the queen dismissed him and Rowan was away from her chambers that his anger truly took hold. Fearing regret, he retreated to his rooms and forcefully slammed the door, causing pictures to fall.

"Damn it!" He paced fiercely around the room. "Damn it all! Damn it to the fucking nether hells!" He raged, kicking over chairs and sweeping things off surfaces, including whatever was in striking distance on the floor. It wasn't until he came to the mirror, which he fully intended to shatter with his bare hands, that he saw his reflection.

His eyes were coal-black in their sockets.

Rowan cried out, filled with fear and surprise. However, upon a second glance, his eyes had returned to their normal state. "No." The single word was a haggard whisper on his lips. He remembered Jade's words about the Rot's attraction to misery, sorrow and now...anger. Was it in him already?

"Calm yourself." Rowan walked away from the mirror and sat heavily on his bed, taking several deep breaths. He must manage his emotions. However, the problem of informing Faith persisted. Speaking to her and trying to make her understand would be pointless. If he didn't do as his mother said, his mother would look at his action as betrayal, and if he obeyed his mother, then Faith would do the same.

Maybe she won't. Maybe Faith will understand.

He laughed bitterly at his hubris.

★   ★   ★

The queen ordered four guards to accompany them. One led a pack mule with enough supplies to feed a small army. Rowan doubted they would need a fifth. The doors in the hall might hinder their mounts' passage. If Jade's assumption was accurate, the Hall of Doors would connect to Underneath, enabling them to journey to Tidaholm. Rowan also had the map of Underneath. Tidaholm was a day's travel, perhaps two if troubles arose.

What he needed was an idea of how to tell Faith of his mother's edict.

When they came upon the Burrow, Faith was waiting for him. She stood with her gryphon, patting his mane affectionately. She wore baggy brown leather trousers, belted at the waist with a gold buckle, and thigh boots, a black silk shirt speckled with gold threads, and a brown greatcoat. And, of course, a brown top hat, with a gold lace ribbon tied around the base. A gift from her father, no doubt. She had a tanned leather backpack slung over one shoulder.

She looks lovely and daring.

"Hello, Faith!"

She turned and grinned at him. "I see the queen insisted on protection and luxuries?"

It was the happiest – no – the most hopeful he had seen her since talking to Jade. He thought she'd be angry with the guards and said so.

"Why would I be angry? They are loyal citizens of Brigantia and are here to protect us. Also," Faith added, "neither of us has been outside Brigantia before." She then pulled out an unusual-looking key from the inside pocket of her greatcoat. The key had a regular skeleton key shape, but it was brass, with a skull encircled with interconnected gears, and two green gems set within hollow circles.

"What is that?"

"The key to Underneath," Faith said. "Jade gave it to the White Rabbit to give to me."

What if the White Rabbit had brought it to him? How would his mother have reacted to such a unique object? His mother had a love for eclectic baubles and knick-knacks. She might have insisted on keeping it, even though they needed it to leave Brigantia. Perhaps Jade had known that.

"And now to our mounts," Faith said.

"I thought we were leaving them behind and continuing on foot?"

"No, no." Faith moved her pack from her shoulder and set it down.

"I don't know if you've heard..." he began. In a land where even the flowers and trees talked, secrets were hard to keep. "The queen is sending messages to the Red and White Queens."

"The March Hare told my father." Faith dug around in her pack. "Now, I just had them—ah!" She held a tiny, stoppered bottle with a clear red liquid inside. A white label on it was printed, *Drink Me*.

"Are you certain you have the right kind?" Rowan asked with a wry grin.

"According to Minerva, it better be. Argestes?"

The gryphon stepped forward. Faith put a few drops on her open palm. "Ready?"

"I'm a little scared," Argestes said.

"Of course you are," she said, "but you trust me?"

"Yes." Argestes lapped it up with his tongue.

Faith handed Rowan the bottle. "Give this to your horse and the mule. The same amount." Rowan watched with amusement as Argestes shrank. When he was about the size of a figurine, Faith held out her palm and Argestes climbed into it. She placed him in the outside pocket of her vest. "Comfortable?"

"Very!" His voice was high-pitched and tinny.

Rowan made sure he did exactly what Faith said. He had one guard hold on to his horse while he fed him the potion. His horse was not as patient as Argestes with the results, and Rowan ended up placing his horse in his own coat pocket and wrapped in his very soft – and costly – silk handkerchief.

The donkey was another matter since it carried the supplies. They would either send it back with one guard, and Rowan could imagine how incensed his mother would be, or shrink the donkey and have the guards carry the supply packs instead. Rowan decided on the latter.

"Are we ready?" Faith said.

"Yes."

When one looked at it from the outside, the Burrow was within the trunk of a massive willow tree, its roots half in, half out of the earth, making it look like it could pull itself up and start walking. It stretched upward, reaching for some unknown light, its branches spread out and thick with cascading leaves. The tree's top hid in a cloud. No one had ever seen where it ended.

The single heavy wood door was rather plain, with no carvings or decorations. It seemed strange such an ornate key would be the method of unlocking it, but Faith brandished the key and inserted it into the lock. She turned it and Rowan heard the click. The door, after Faith grasped the knob, opened inward.

Previously, Rowan had only ever entered the Hall of Doors to study library books. Still, it fascinated him the way they'd set it up. When he'd asked the White Rabbit about its power, he was told it was eternal and nothing more. When Rowan had pressed, the Rabbit cowered and said he didn't know. Rowan then apologized. He didn't want his subjects to believe he was like his parents.

Upon first seeing the Burrow, anyone would realize it was divided into sections that floated above one another. The room Faith and Rowan stood in had circular levels, and the center's round glass table fit perfectly. There were several silver trays on it, with an assortment of vials, bottles, and cakes. Usually, they appeared with no known origin, or at least no one confessed to placing them there.

Between two of the tiniest doors and to their left, a fireplace crackled peaceably. Why no one seemed concerned about the dangers to the library was a puzzle. Two armchairs sat facing the hearth. The second level was the library, with shelves going around the circumference of the Burrow. And no one asked how square books all fit on round shelves. Books didn't always stay on said shelves and floated freely until someone came in and requested a specific tome. There was also a tea tray on a smaller round table draped with a white tablecloth.

The farther one looked up, the darker it became. You could only see up to the fourth level. Supposedly, there was more floating furniture, cabinets with dishes, and a dinner table with ever-lit candles that remained on the table even when it floated upside down. And things did that frequently. Yet nothing ever came crashing down.

Somewhere above them, in the darkness, was Faith's world of origin.

Rowan's attention returned to Faith, who drew a second key from her greatcoat and stood before the door that Jade had shown. The second key, less ornate, had an amber gem with open wings on each side.

"Faith?"

"Yes?"

"Do you wonder—" He stopped and couldn't help glancing upward.

"What goes on up there, you mean?" Faith shrugged. "No. Brigantia is my home. It's all I remember."

She placed the key in the door and turned. The lock clicked. "Although I remember the journey down."

Faith pulled the door open. "After you, Your Highness."

"How could you possibly recall? Weren't you an infant?"

"Yes," Faith said. Her father and their tea companions were the only ones who believed her. Faith disregarded those who didn't pay attention anymore. To forestall any other comments, she stepped forward into an enormous cavern, so massive that, like it did in the Burrow, darkness hid the ceiling. Ghost light filled it. It made her fearful at first until she realized the light was from hundreds of mushrooms, ranging from thumbnail size to ones that were several man-heights.

A thick carpet of grass covered the floor of the cavern. The walls glistened with thousands of tiny stars, which Faith realized were minerals interspersed on the surface. She wondered what they were. Silver? Diamonds?

"Magnificent," Rowan said in awe.

Even the guards, who never broke protocol by speaking, muttered their amazement. Faith agreed with them all.

"We don't even need the lanterns!" Rowan, obviously excited, added, "The map."

One of the guards who carried a pack rummaged around inside before withdrawing a rolled paper, which he handed to Rowan. "Have a look." Rowan moved to one of the shorter mushrooms, which made an imperfect table. "As you can see, we're here. There —" he pointed to the north-east portion of the map, "— is Tidaholm."

Faith could read maps, although she had trouble telling the distances. "How long will it take?"

"A day, if nothing occurs, perhaps two."

Faith reached into her other back pocket and pulled out a watch. She pushed the release, and the lid popped open. "It is half past eight now, Saturday, so we can assume that we should arrive before Monday." She removed her backpack. "I'm glad it's big enough in here for us to ride." She withdrew a small square, wrapped in a handkerchief, just like Rowan's. When she unwrapped it, Rowan saw the small square cake. Written in cursive on the label was *Eat Me*. Faith broke off a corner. She gently lifted Argestes out of her pocket.

"There you are." The gryphon climbed onto her outstretched palm and bent his head to eat. It didn't take long for him to regain his full size. Just as Faith handed Rowan some cake, Argestes danced nervously, his head swiveling back and forth. "Where are we?" His voice was rising in panic.

"Underneath." Faith's brow wrinkled. "Argestes, you knew—"

"No, no," Argestes said, shaking his shaggy mane, "I didn't know it was like this!"

Faith reached to grab his bridle, but Argestes jumped away. "It's here! It's all around us!"

"What is?" Faith said.

"The darkness! It's all around us!"

Rowan and their guards drew their swords and moved into a defensive stance. Faith didn't see or hear anything.

"Argestes, please calm down, I promise—"

The second time he pulled away, he jerked Faith forward so harshly she tripped over her own feet and fell hard. The grass cushioned her fall, but it still took her breath away.

"Vile beast!" She heard Rowan cry out and he went for Argestes. Faith reached out and grabbed him by the ankle.

"Stop!"

Rowan hesitated, then stopped and instead helped Faith to her feet.

"He attacked you!"

"He did not," Faith said. "It was an accident."

Faith approached the gryphon, cooing softly to him until she could take the bridle again. She continued to stroke his mane. "Can you see anything, or is it merely a sense?"

"I'm sorry, Faith." Perhaps he realized he'd hurt Faith by his action, for he'd stopped trembling.

"Don't apologize. Tell me what you sense."

"Just like at the beach," Argestes stated. "It's so sad."

"I know." Faith patted him gently on the head. "But we – I need you now to be brave."

"Yes," Argestes said. His voice had more strength. "Let us go."

"You can put your swords away now," Faith said. While she focused on Argestes, she sensed the others standing, tense and ready for a fight. The Cheshire Cat was right. *Boys.*

CHAPTER EIGHT

"Tell me about it," Rowan requested.

They had traveled in near silence. Faith didn't know if it was her imagination or not, but she was sensing something herself and she had to keep reassuring Argestes. He remained calm overall.

Faith didn't pretend she didn't know what Rowan meant. "I have no memory of the world above."

"Nothing at all?"

For a moment, Faith closed her eyes, drawing on her memories of that night. They hadn't faded, which was incredible. She recalled it as though it had happened this morning. "The only thing I recall is bright flickering lights. Yellow and red. I recall smoke, thick and black."

"It sounds like you were in a fire!"

"That is possible, but I don't recall." Faith pushed that memory away. "I have no fear of fire." Her father and his tea companions had gone camping many a time, and sitting around the fire telling stories was one of her favorite things to do.

"Then?" Rowan encouraged.

"I was falling – no, floating, down the Burrow. I recall looking around and seeing all these wonders. The books, the furniture, campfires! There were tree branches and vines growing out of the walls. I heard a voice speaking to me."

"A voice?"

"Well, not a voice exactly." Faith recalled the words, soft and reassuring, and she smiled. "It's hard to explain. I experienced the words and understood them."

"What did the voice say?"

"She told me about the Hatter."

"She?"

"Yes. She said the Hatter would wait for me."

"So, a mystical force told you the Hatter would be your father?"

"Just that he would be there." Faith smiled to herself. "I was placed on the rug in front of the fireplace, and suddenly, the Hatter was there smiling at me. I liked him immediately, and I reached up to him." Faith recalled how the Hatter had snuggled her cheek and she'd giggled in delight. "He picked me up and carried me out."

"Incredible," Rowan said. "How did the Hatter know you were there?"

"He dreamt it." Faith grinned. "He said he was at his worktable and the voice came to him. He wasn't afraid. In fact, he said the voice made him feel rather content."

"I'm glad he found you, Faith."

He'd said it so quietly, she wasn't certain she'd heard it right. Tugging the reins, she turned Argestes to face Rowan. "I want to say—"

Something behind them drew Faith's attention. Movement. Rowan pulled up his mount.

"What is it?"

Faith didn't answer immediately, trying to focus on what she was seeing. Rowan turned his mount, and the guards followed his lead.

"What in the hells—"

Argestes took steps back. "It's coming."

It was obvious something was coming, but they were unaware what it was. It seemed like the floor itself moved, except it was coming toward them at an alarming rate. Rowan's horse danced nervously, backing up to stand beside Argestes. They would have perished if Argestes hadn't cried out, "Basilisks!"

"Ride!" Rowan shouted and before Faith could protest, Argestes reared with a scream and turned, and then they were galloping across the cave floor.

"No, wait!" Didn't he know a gryphon's tears could kill a basilisk? Faith heard one of the guards yell, "Highness!"

But Argestes was barreling forward.

"Argestes, whoa, gods be damned!" Faith pulled back violently on the reins. She hated doing that, but Argestes would have kept going. "We must help them! Would you weep for them alive or dead?" He trembled, continued to dance, and Faith took control, guiding him to turn and go back the way they'd come. The guards stood still, and Faith realized they'd already succumbed to the basilisk's stare. For one horrified moment, Rowan didn't move either, then Faith noticed he'd tied his handkerchief around his eyes. He stood facing the beasts, his sword raised.

Faith didn't hesitate. She squeezed the gryphon's sides with her heels.

"Faith!" How Rowan knew it was her wasn't her concern. Faith squeezed her eyes shut and rode Argestes straight into the fray. The surrounding air abruptly changed from a cool wetness, with the scent of moss, to a sudden acrid heat as Faith tried to breathe. It scalded her mouth, throat, and filled her chest as her stomach lurched. She could only grasp tightly on to the gryphon's neck as she twisted the reins around her hands.

Argestes was screaming. Whether a cry from pain or fear, Faith couldn't tell. The burning silenced her, leaving only a hoarse whisper. "Argestes, continue."

It was then that the voices began.

Mere whispers carried on the sulfurous air:

Open your eyes.

Look at us.

Fear the darkness.

How can you continue to fight?

Someone or something leapt upon Faith. One of the creatures latched itself on to the back of her greatcoat, its wings wildly beating against her head. Its fetid breath burned her neck. Faith screamed as she blindly reached behind her, only to have the basilisk sink its hooked beak into her palm. The pain was almost unbearable, as acidic saliva entered the wound. Somehow Faith called on her Gift, putting all her pain behind it. There was a hideous shriek as the beast fell away.

Now, with the poison coursing through her blood, Faith had to concentrate. She let loose the reins and slid from Argestes' back and, thankfully, landed on a reasonably soft spot. She expected to be set upon immediately, but Faith realized the cackling of the basilisks was fading.

"Faith!" Rowan exclaimed, "Dear gods, you've been poisoned!"

Faith shook her head, which ached. "Wait."

"But Faith—"

"Silence!" Faith hadn't wanted to do that, but she needed to focus. Needed to feel her blood as it moved through her veins, needed to separate the poison from her life's blood, to turn it into something that would not hurt her, that would move through her body without injuring her further. When the burning ceased, Faith worked on the wound, mending her skin. It would scab, but it couldn't be helped.

"Faith?"

She sat up. "Is it safe?"

"Yes, you can open your eyes."

Rowan had not come out of the battle unscathed. The fight had left him battered and bruised, and he was bleeding from several superficial wounds. But he grinned at her.

"I'm sorry for being snappish," Faith said, "but I needed to concentrate on removing the poison."

"Gods, you can do that?"

"To be honest, I wasn't certain if I could. The last time I tried it was when I got a wicked splinter." It hadn't been bad. She'd changed the splinter to dust, then sucked it out of her finger and spat.

"Argestes?" Faith looked frantically about until she saw him cowering against the far wall. Faith dashed over to him. "Are you injured? Let me see!"

His eyes darted around in his sockets. "They're gone, they're all gone?" Argestes said.

"Yes, they are."

"They fled before you," Rowan said. "Didn't you see?"

"You're a hero," Faith said.

"And a great warrior," Rowan added.

"Me?" Argestes said, his fear forgotten. "I did what I thought was right." He knelt before Faith. "Let's leave this awful place before something else comes after us."

It was the strongest she'd ever heard his voice.

"We must attend to some matters first," Rowan said.

Their escort was dead. Their bodies were frozen in grotesque poses, with their dying screams etched on their faces. Tears welled in Faith's eyes and tracked down her cheeks. Rowan plunged his sword into the soft ground and went down on one knee, his hands grasping the pommel. He remained quiet and motionless. The only sounds were his heavy breathing and Argestes pawing at the moss.

He finally stood and Faith wiped away her tears.

The mounts had long since fled, so they were without food and water.

"Argestes, can you carry us both?"

The gryphon ate mushrooms growing on rocks. "Yes, Faith."

"Then we'll just have to pray nothing else attacks until we get to Tidaholm." Faith mounted, then held Argestes, waiting. Rowan stood there for a moment. Faith cocked an eyebrow and leaned her head aside a bit. What did he expect? For her to dismount, then allow him to mount first and help her on? Like a true gentleman. Or a haughty prince.

He finally realized that she would not do that and climbed on behind her. Faith urged Argestes forward. Although they encountered no one as they continued along the Underneath corridor, Faith couldn't shake the feeling that their journey was, in fact, being observed. They continued until Argestes asked for a rest and Faith agreed. They dismounted and sat right where they were in the dirt. Faith looked around. The walls here were smoother, as if humans had carved them. They seemed... smaller to her.

"This part of the cavern seems man-made."

"Or dwarves," Rowan said. "This is more their domain. I've read they command earth magic."

She'd read about dwarves too, and how they found wealth with the help of mythic beings called knockers, who signaled when large deposits of metal and gems were nearby.

Despite his wandering, Faith could still see Argestes near a stand of rocks. "I'm going to gather some of those mushrooms for us."

Rowan smiled slightly. "No dessert?"

"What?" Faith said over her shoulder as she crossed the space. Argestes pointed out mushrooms, allowing Faith to pluck a few.

"Don't you recall? That time we had lunch at your home and Minerva served those awful cabbage things. And I suggested you change them into something else?"

"Sugared cherries." Faith sat down, smiling at the memory. "I know it was disappointing."

"Don't worry over it," Rowan said. "Were you ever able to figure out why?"

Faith thought on it for a moment. She had tried to figure it out over the years and had recently concluded, "I can't change things that have...*life* in them."

Of course, he was confused. His brow furrowed. "What do you mean, life in them?"

It had always been difficult to explain. Faith picked up one of the mushrooms. "You see this mushroom? I can't change it into anything else. Say an apple. Now, I can cause this mushroom to grow until it reaches the natural time to expire or sprout others. I can alter inanimate objects like elements due to their distinct aura."

Unfortunately, that only confused him more. "I still don't understand."

"Have you ever heard the word *organik*?"

"Yes. Doesn't it mean *to live* or *things alive*?"

"It's a bit more complicated than that," Faith continued. "Things organik, like foodstuffs, that are grown or bred, have their own distinct makeup." Faith dug into the moss next to her until she found a small stone. She held it in her open palm and laid the other over it and called on her Gift. When she lifted her hand, the stone was gold. "And I can also do this." Again, she pressed the metal between her palms and when she showed him again, it was a small pile of gold dust. "Do you understand better?"

"A little." Rowan mused. "But what about the poison? I mean, I understand it's not organik, but you healed yourself after."

"I'm not sure you would call it healing," Faith said. "I just sped up the process of natural healing. Using my power on my person, well, I wasn't sure it would work."

"Either way, I've always thought your Gift was amazing." Rowan grinned.

Faith smiled for the first time. "Thank you."

"We should get going." Rowan stood and offered her his hand, which she took, and he pulled her to her feet.

"Argestes, time to go."

"Yes," Argestes said, "that stench is returning."

"Then we must leave. Put some distance between us and whatever it is." Rowan mounted behind her again. As they continued, they saw other denizens of Underneath. Wil-o-wisp floated gently in their wake. They came upon a troop of brownies, whose friendly nature eased their nerves, and the brownies gladly gave over some fruit. Rowan offered to pay them, but Faith scolded him, reminding him that brownies consider any form of payment for their deeds an insult.

So, they munched on a strange fruit that they'd never had before and didn't grow in Brigantia. The fruit had a dark red and leathery skin, and its insides contained pockets of tiny *arils* that glistened like rubies. The brownies instructed them on how to eat them, although Argestes ate the fruit whole.

They didn't always come upon good fey.

Argestes caught its stench first, and when Faith and Rowan saw what created it, it raised gooseflesh. A Black Agnes sat against the opposite side of the cave wall. Rowan drew his sword, perhaps just as a precaution. The old witch watched them as she sat atop the pile of bones that were her victims. Her single piercing eye followed their progress as they passed. She clutched a ragged, filthy dress around her front, the ash color almost blended with her bluish skin.

"Don't look at it," Rowan warned. "I'll keep an eye."

The thought of Brigantia being invaded made Faith shudder. They reached a point in the cavern with many offshoots. Some entrances were huge, while others were too small for a cat. And from one of them, shrouded in darkness, came a group of goblins.

If Agnes was ugly, these things were repulsive. Their bodies were squat, twisted things with putrid green flesh. They had pinched and mean eyes. They each carried a bottle of what Faith supposed was hard liquor and with the way they swayed and stumbled, guffawing at nothing, it was obvious they were all drunk.

They spotted the two riders. The goblins initially peered at them, unsure of what they saw. Then they started dancing and whooping and hollering, showing their jagged rotting teeth, but when they attempted to charge the two, they stumbled over each other then started fighting amongst themselves. Even after Argestes had taken Faith and Rowan away, they could still hear the noise.

Luck accompanied them on the journey, despite their not finding the other mounts and nearly running out of food before reaching Tidaholm's gates.

Two immense gryphons perched on top of pillars. They were motionless. Their massive chests moved with each breath, the only sign of life.

"Now what?" Rowan said.

"Climb down," Faith said. "Argestes?"

The one thing Argestes wasn't afraid of was his own kind. He approached the two and bowed his head. He spoke in calls and squawks. They leapt down from the pillars and approached. Faith bowed, and after a few moments Rowan followed her lead.

The gryphon on their left, his whole body, fur, and feathers the color of onyx, stepped forward. "Welcome, Lady Carter and Prince Rowan. Welcome to Tidaholm."

CHAPTER NINE

Tidaholm was a bustling city, nothing like Brigantia. Such a place was beyond Rowan's imagination. The Three Queens' realms were less full than this. The first thing Rowan noticed was how bright and colorful everything was. Not that things weren't bright and colorful in his kingdom, but here he would have to say it was in grave excess.

Still, Rowan couldn't help but stare at the surrounding wonders.

It took both gryphons to push open the massive doors, causing both Faith and Rowan to squint as sunlight poured through the opening. Stretched out before them was a lane made of multicolored stone. The lane itself ended at a massive building, taller than either Rowan or Faith had ever seen, and constructed of the same color bricks. Arched windows and circular balconies dotted its façade. Turrets extended out halfway up the building, including one that was topped with what appeared to be a rectangular open-air arboretum.

An immense clock hung between two balconies at the center of the façade. It was a quarter to three. As they stepped farther onto the lane, they saw it was lined with smaller buildings, just as colorful, their façades decorated with flower boxes. The sweet scents tickled their noses. People moved along the lane, entering and exiting shops, some carrying many packages. Others just seemed to stroll by, walking pets on leashes. Not only dogs, but cats, foxes, and others Rowan didn't recognize, and he was certain Faith didn't either.

No one seemed surprised to see two strangers and their gryphon.

Well, that's understandable, Rowan thought. Both human and fey beings walked the streets. Some Rowan had only read about in fairy tales. Yet here they were, existing just as easily as humans and animalia in Brigantia. Rowan was so in awe that he didn't notice a young woman had approached them, dressed in an official uniform of black and gold.

"Cadet," the black gryphon, named Nyx, addressed the woman. "You will escort our guests to the queen's house and present their letters of introduction to your superior."

"Yes, sir."

She bowed to Rowan and Faith. "Please follow me."

Faith turned back to the gryphon. "What about Argestes?"

"Look at the sky," Nyx said.

They did so and saw the rock face itself contained actual dwellings. They could see people moving within the structures through windows and lounging on balconies. The rooftops had a covering of flowers or moss. Rowan heard Faith draw in a surprised breath and he had to admit he was just as astonished as she.

"At the top of the cliff is the gryphon aerie," Nyx said. "Argestes is welcome to come with us and visit with our people."

"May I, Lady Faith?" Argestes had such a hopeful expression that Rowan was certain Faith would allow it. He wouldn't have disappointed Argestes by saying no.

"Of course," Faith said. She hugged him around the neck. "We will see you later."

"Thank you both for allowing us entry," Rowan said. "May fortune favor you." He faced the cadet as the three gryphons soared above. "Lead on, please."

As they walked, Faith asked the cadet questions about the sights and the city, and the cadet answered each with knowledgeable patience. Rowan, however, was aware of their surroundings. He didn't quite trust all of this...activity. He missed the quiet of Brigantia even after such a short time, but something else caught his attention, the myriads of scents coming from the various eateries on the lane. He'd forgotten how hungry he was.

Faith shared the same sentiment, marveling at the delightful scents. "We haven't eaten decently in a couple of days and everything smells wonderful. May we stop for a moment?"

"Yes, of course," the cadet assured. "We can expedite it to avoid any delay."

"Thank you," Faith said. "What do you recommend?"

The cadet smiled. Her face flushed. "Follow me."

They came upon a small food vendor on the avenue. The eatery face was open, with a crude wood counter set atop molded stones of various sizes and shapes, held together by a grayish substance that neither Rowan nor Faith recognized. A plump man stood behind the counter. His face was pleasant, and he smiled at them with even white teeth. Rowan was unsure if his face's copper hue was innate or from the sun. He had a twinkle in his dark eyes and wore a flour-dusted apron around his ample waist. He spread his arms wide in welcome as they approached.

Unfortunately, when he spoke, it was in a language that neither was familiar with. It was the cadet who stepped forward and spoke for them. The two had a rapid-fire conversation. The man nodded and called out their order to the bustling kitchen.

This place was unlike anything Rowan had seen before. He seldom, if ever, entered the palace kitchen unless it was to pilfer a snack. That's what the servants were for, to bring him whatever he desired. The man returned to the counter with a tray, leaving Rowan puzzled about its contents.

They were rectangular, with deep ridges covering their light brown surface. When Rowan took a closer look, he realized they were corn husks tied by strips keeping whatever was inside – well, inside. As the cook set the tray before them, he also included a small ceramic dish filled with a chunky red sauce. He said something in his native tongue as the cadet translated. "You want to be very careful when they're hot," she said as she lifted one herself and dipped it into the dish of sauce. "Go ahead, try them." She motioned with the strange food.

Rowan picked one up and Faith followed. The cadet's warning proved true as he tossed the hot item between his hands. Still, he tried it, and he dipped it into the sauce and took a bite. A burst of unfamiliar flavors surprised Rowan. The dish combined spicy, sweet, and savory flavors, along with seasoned meats and vegetables. And after a few moments, Rowan was relishing it until he noticed his tongue growing hot.

"What?" Rowan stuck out his tongue and waved his hand in front of it. It didn't help.

He looked at Faith and saw her expression of surprise as she took several breaths through her mouth.

"What is this?" Rowan demanded.

"I'm sorry," the cadet said through a mouthful. "I should have warned you." She dipped the food again, seeming to have no problem with the heat. "Haven't you ever had masa before?"

"How could we?" He could swear his tongue was on fire. "How do we stop this?"

The cadet took a moment to have their food wrapped in paper before paying the cook. "Follow me!"

Then she was off at a fast walk. By then, both Rowan and Faith had tears streaming down their cheeks. The cadet stopped in front of another building that wasn't wide open, although its façade displayed colored stones. The entrance was through a metal door. The door had a hideous, almost demonic iron knocker attached to it. The cadet grabbed it, slammed it down repeatedly, stepped back, and waited.

Shortly, the door swung open, and a girl emerged, wearing inappropriate clothing for the season. She smiled, seeming to recognize the cadet, and again they spoke in a language unknown to both Rowan and Faith. The young girl shut the door, and the cadet faced them again. "Again, I apologize," she smiled. "It will only be a few moments."

The door opened, and the girl brought two small bowls with Rowan's favorite dessert.

"Iced cream?" Confused, Rowan turned to Faith and shrugged. The girl supplied two flat pieces of wood, which were rounded at one end.

"Eat," the cadet commanded.

They did. Rowan hesitated before devouring the entire thing, but soon noticed the burning sensation fading. As upset as he was, he was very relieved that the burning had stopped. Faith surprised him when she asked, "Can we take some masa back to Brigantia?"

"Absolutely!" the cadet said.

Rowan looked at them both, thinking they'd lost their minds, when he realized that before the heat, he was enjoying the masa too.

"But," Faith amended, "we'd rather not have that sauce."

*   *   *

Now that they were moving toward the queen's house again, Rowan discovered he was eager to explore this strange place and taste more of its food. They'd finished off the masa as they walked, and the cadet dropped the papers into a nearby trash receptacle. The clock indicated that an hour had passed since they arrived, and he was anxious to have a conversation with the queen. As they approached the palace, Rowan saw the entrance consisted of two immense open arches. Beyond those was a short hall that ended in an open space. There was a fountain in the middle; three unfamiliar creatures spat out streams of water. Rowan kept going, hoping to get a closer look, but he heard the cadet call, "Your Highness?"

When Rowan turned back to the inner hall, he saw something that fascinated him. There appeared to be doors, eight in total, with four on each side. Yet, Rowan had never seen anything like them. The doors were adorned with golden embellishments that created intricate patterns over a dark base, possibly metal. The design included an arched top, contributing to its elegant appearance.

Flanking the doors were wall panels in dark blue with gold trim, echoing their opulence. Ornate lamps on either side cast a warm glow, enhancing the rich colors and detailed workmanship.

As Rowan approached, the cadet stepped aside and reached for a handle affixed to the door. The surface of the handle was etched with delicate filigree, patterns that swirled and looped to form the shape of some unknown mythical creature. The cadet lowered the lever and pulled open the door and motioned him into a very small room, no more than an enclosed box. Inside was a woman – *no* – a giantess. She had to be. She could reach up and touch the ceiling. Rowan hesitated. Although he'd never been claustrophobic, he wasn't too keen on entering the small room. "What is this thing?"

"It is called an *elevare*."

Its walls were lined with wood panels, each meticulously painted with scenes of mythical creatures. Ornate copper railings, polished to a warm sheen, were attached to the three sides of the box, their elaborate swirls and patterns reminiscent of the Vine. They provided not just safety, but a touch of elegance and artistry.

Beneath their feet, the floor was a masterpiece in itself – a mosaic of tiles intricately fit together that depicted a spinning wheel, complete with threads, and the young Miller's daughter spinning straw into gold, which paid homage to the device that the kingdom was built on.

"What is the purpose of this room?"

The cadet glanced at him with a knowing look. "This will take us below the house to the queen's workshop."

"How?" Faith asked. "Are you saying the queen is farther underground?"

"Yes," the cadet said. "I don't understand how it works. I know it involves wheels, pulleys, weights, and such. Upon entry, the door is closed, and you'll descend to the queen's work area."

The door is closed. Rowan liked that even less. "Isn't there another way?"

"I'm afraid not." The cadet looked confused. "It's safe."

If someone hurt Rowan, his mother would unleash fire and brimstone upon the responsible party.

"It doesn't appear we have a choice," Faith said, although Rowan heard a catch in her voice as well.

Not wanting to seem impolite, Rowan stepped in first. He inclined his head to the giantess. "Good afternoon, milady."

A faint smile appeared as she nodded back. Faith stepped in and repeated the greeting.

"Fare thee well." The cadet bowed as the doors closed.

The giantess grasped a lever attached to the wall and pulled it down. There was a rather loud and uncomfortable jolt, which made Faith gasp, and the sensation that they were indeed descending. It wasn't smooth. Faith grasped on to one of the handrails. Rowan moved beside her, placing his arm around her and laying his hand on hers. The other hand he placed on her back, hoping to steady her. He couldn't see her face, but she didn't step back.

The trip took longer than Rowan liked, but he kept his wits about him. However, relief flooded in as the box stopped. The giantess pulled the lever back, and the doors opened. They were indeed underground, but here the walls were smooth and even. The stone was full of tiny jewels that sparkled like stars in the dark sky, reflecting the light of floating wil-o-wisps.

Faith gasped in delight and was careful not to tread on or kick them. They seemed to take a liking to them as they gathered around their ankles. Rowan believed the giantess would guide them, but she only leaned out of the elevare and pointed right. Then she moved back inside, and pulled the door closed.

"Well," Faith said, "I suppose we're on our own." She strode forward and Rowan had no choice but to follow.

The endless tunnel echoed with increasing sounds as they walked on. It also became cooler, not too uncomfortable. Noises persisted, including striking metal and steam releasing from a kettle. The tunnel opened to the most fantastic workshop either of them had ever seen. Although it was underground, sunlight streamed through large windows carved into the stones that circled the room. The high ceiling held rafters from which hung a variety of weapons. There were several long tables littered with tools and scraps of metal and gems. To their far right was a wall of shelves filled with books. A round stone table with four chairs, a tea set, and snacks sat there, waiting for lunch to be served.

To their left was an immense forge, black with soot, flames showering sparks from the wood as it split under the heat. A cauldron filled with water reflected the shapes of its surroundings. And standing at another long table with a hammer grasped in her slim fingers and her muscles bunching as she brought it down against hot metal, was the Spinner Queen.

Rowan didn't know what he'd expected. A beautiful young girl, sitting at her spinning wheel, dressed in homespun, with a fresh face and long flowing hair, surrounded by straw? This was far from his expectations.

In fact, the Spinner Queen stood tall and muscular, with her hair shaven close to her head. She was attractive, Rowan had to admit, with high cheekbones and full lips and those eyes – the darkest he'd ever seen – like obsidian pools, but they held a fierceness that even rivaled his mother's. She wore blacksmith leathers and an apron. What captured his attention most was the intricate tattoos that traveled the length of both arms, although some were broken by scarring.

Rowan was just wondering if she'd noticed them when she spoke. "Welcome to my forge. Please sit at the table and help yourself to some coffee and tarts. I shall be with you shortly."

Her manner of speaking surprised him as well. He'd expected her to be gruff and crude in her mannerisms, but she spoke like a true queen.

"Thank you, Your Majesty."

Amid the swinging, she paused, glanced up at him, and erupted in laughter. Then she went back to work. Rowan felt his face warm. What had been so amusing? He kept silent and followed Faith to the table. They removed their packs and set them against the wall. Faith allowed him to pull out her chair. They both sat and Faith went about serving them, much to Rowan's surprise.

"Did you hear her?" Rowan said as Faith sliced the tart. It had mascarpone filling topped with a mixture of berries covered in a sweet glaze.

"What do you mean?"

"When she laughed at me."

"Oh."

"Oh?"

Faith offered him the sugar bowl, which he waved away. "Are you asking me why she did it?" She spooned a generous amount of sugar in her cup, then added cream.

"Well…" How would she know? "I thought it rather rude."

"I suppose it was," Faith said, eating a slice of tart. "Just remember why we're here. If it comes to it, we can take a bit of joking at our expense."

"Yes, of course." She made sense. Besides, after this, it was likely they wouldn't see the Spinner Queen again.

The whooshing – which was the queen dunking the metal in the water – alerted them to the fact that she'd finished her project and strode over to the table. She grabbed one of the chairs, spun it around, and sat astride it like a warrior and rested her arms on the back. "So, you are Lady Faith and Prince Rowan."

"You were expecting us?" Rowan said.

"Of course." She grinned, her teeth even and white. "I received word from Jade. She told me you were coming and what you needed."

Rowan was relieved that they didn't need to explain themselves, although he wondered how the Spinner Queen had received word.

"So," she continued, "let me see the chrysalis."

As Rowan went to retrieve their packs, Faith said, "Thank you, Your Majesty, we appreciate this."

"Sylmare," she said. "I come from humble beginnings and never cared for formalities."

Rowan sat again and pulled the cloth from his pack. Sylmare grasped a corner and pulled it toward her. "Magnificent." She examined it for a time, turning it over in her hands and running her fingers along the material.

She sat back, satisfied, and instructed, "Both of you, please go to our seamstress for measurements. It shouldn't take long."

"Your pardon, Your Maj—Sylmare?" Rowan reached into his pack again and pulled out a piece of paper. He'd been dreading this moment their entire journey. He couldn't look at Faith as he spoke. "I have here measurements for my mother, Her Royal Highness, the Queen of Hearts. She ordered you to make the armor for her and me. She will accept no other."

CHAPTER TEN

After Rowan's declaration, Faith felt as though she had been gut-punched. Although she'd not expected this, it came as no surprise. The Queen of Hearts' wants were clear, and no one, not even her eldest son, dared refuse.

Faith was damned tired of it.

She longed to convey a multitude of things to him, but despite her overwhelming emotions, all she uttered was, "Coward."

Faith saw the tensing of his jaw, but he didn't contradict her. It was Sylmare who spoke next. "Before I have my guards drag you out of my home and my kingdom, you had better explain yourself." Of course, if the Spinner Queen had been in touch with Jade, it was likely she knew of Jade's instructions.

"What I said," Rowan began, "what I mean is my mother, the Queen of Hearts, requests—"

Faith snorted.

"That you create the armor for both of us."

"And nothing for Lady Faith?"

He looked at Faith for the first time. "I'm sorry."

"And were you ever planning on telling me?" Faith demanded.

Rowan cast his eyes down. "I didn't know how." He looked at her, his expression pleading. "Please, you know how my mother is."

"And what do I care about your mother's temperament?" Sylmare answered instead.

"I thought, I didn't know—"

"Have you lost your wits?" Sylmare demanded.

"What the prince avoids saying," Faith interjected, "is that the Queen of Hearts might get offended and retaliate against you and your kingdom."

This time Sylmare's laugh was mocking.

"But neither of us knew," Faith continued, "that your kingdom was so formidable. I assume you have massive military forces?"

"So, you're saying –" Sylmare directed the question at Rowan, "– that your mother is so sanctimonious that she would go to war over something she can't get? That doesn't belong to her?"

He didn't answer, so Faith did it for him. "Yes."

Sylmare pushed back from the table and stood. "Lady Faith, I wish to discuss this with you further." Sylmare pointed an accusing finger at Rowan. "As for you, be grateful I don't throw you out as it is. I'll have guest quarters set up for both of you. I do not care about how you spend your time."

Faith could see Rowan's anger threatening to boil over, but he knew better than to allow it to take hold, or at least Faith hoped. Despite Sylmare's indifference toward the Queen of Hearts, the woman would go to great lengths to fulfill her desires. And Faith didn't want to see anyone else die.

There was a strange device resembling a brass horn attached to the wall behind Rowan's seat. Next to it was a small lever, like the one in the elevare. Sylmare approached and grasped the lever, turning it several times. The horn emitted a tinny voice, much to their surprise. "Yes, Your Majesty?"

"Have two rooms prepared for our guests." She glanced back at Rowan, then said several sentences in an unfamiliar language, which Faith thought was very soothing. There was a response in that language, then Sylmare approached the table again. "Someone will escort you to your rooms shortly."

Rowan seemed to find his voice. "Shouldn't I remain here, Your Majesty? If we're going to discuss—?"

"We will discuss nothing," Sylmare said. "You tell your mother whatever you like. I will make the armor for you and Faith. Be grateful I am allowing you to have any."

Rowan stood. "Now see here—"

Neither Faith nor Rowan had seen the giantess approach. Faith was uncertain if she was the one Sylmare had been speaking to, but she appeared behind Rowan with a spear drawn and rested the tip of the blade on Rowan's shoulder. The prince went rigid.

"Sylmare." Faith hoped she sounded respectful.

The queen spoke to the giantess in the lilting speech. The giantess nodded and stepped away. She motioned Rowan to move ahead of her. When they were out of the room, Sylmare said, "Well, now that unpleasantness is over."

"Queen Sylmare," Faith began, standing, "Rowan spoke the truth. It will go badly if the Queen of Hearts doesn't get her way."

"Hmm." Sylmare stroked her chin with one finger. "The Queen of Hearts may find it difficult to even enter my kingdom. There is much occurring here in Underneath."

"Basilisks attacked us when we started out," Faith said, remembering the guards in their death state. "We lost some good men and women." Realizing what had happened was catching up to her, and she wrapped her arms around her middle and trembled. "It's strange. I was so fascinated by your kingdom that I'd almost forgotten—"

"Come here." The queen held out her arms and Faith went into her embrace. Against that powerful shoulder, Faith cried for the first time since they'd started on their journey.

"I'm sorry," Faith sniffed as she shed tears. She wiped them away with her hand.

"Don't fret." Sylmare smiled at her. "Come over here. Bring the cloth."

Faith noticed Rowan hadn't taken his pack, so she retrieved both swaths and followed the queen to her work area and handed them over.

"I will try to be as quick as possible," Sylmare said, "but it may take a good two weeks."

This worried Faith. What would happen in Brigantia while they waited? Should they return home and come back later? "I'm worried about leaving Brigantia for too long," Faith explained. "Could you perhaps send a message to Jade, letting her know what's happening?"

"Yes, of course," Sylmare said. Her words eased Faith's conscience a bit.

"Now, since His Royal Ass—"

Faith tried to stifle a giggle.

"—already supplied us with his measurements, you'll still need to visit the seamstress. Afterward, you may retire to your rooms or explore my city a bit more, but dinner is promptly served when the clock strikes five. You'll hear it no matter where you are."

"All right."

"Now before you go…" Sylmare strode over to the bookshelves and chose three tomes. "Here is some reading for you. One relates to our history, while the other two hold more importance. They were helpful to me when I was working to master my craft and my power."

Faith looked at her, shocked. "You know?"

"Of course I do," Sylmare said. "Although I am confused why you hide your power."

"I don't, not really," Faith said. "I just have little occasion to use it in Brigantia." *Until now.* "I don't need to create things like gold or jewels. I have everything I want."

Sylmare displayed an expression of admiration. "You are a remarkable young woman."

"Oh…" Faith felt her cheeks warm and she cast her eyes downward. "Thank you."

"Don't be modest." The queen lifted Faith's chin with one finger so Faith could meet her gaze. "You will do great things, I know." Sylmare stepped back and approached the wall horn, turning the crank. "Esther, please show Lady Faith to her rooms."

Faith was in awe of the queen and her words filled her with such delight that she didn't notice the return of the giantess. "Lady Faith," Esther said, "please follow me."

"Thank you, Your Majesty. I will see you soon."

"Indeed." Sylmare was already examining the cloth.

Faith followed Esther back to the elevare. She became shy alone with the imposing woman. Still, Faith felt she should say something.

"Your kingdom is beautiful, and the queen is wonderful."

Esther looked at her with that slight smile. "Thank you."

Another giantess, identical to Esther, stood waiting as the door opened.

"Good afternoon, Lady Faith," she said in a deep baritone. "I am Esther, head of the queen's house."

"What?" Faith looked back, "but I thought—"

"I am Esther," the other woman said. She nodded at her twin. "She is Damara."

Her face warming, Faith said, "Pleased to meet you both."

Was there a knowing look between them when Faith stepped out? Well, she supposed she could stand being the subject of their private joke. As Esther turned and walked into the hall, Faith hastened to follow. Unlike her sister, Esther was very amiable, telling Faith about the history of the city and how the queen made her palace. Sylmare had discovered the sisters roaming the realms, trying to avoid humanity unless necessary. During a tour of the kingdom, Esther had engaged in a fight to protect the queen from bandits.

Damara, a quiet and introverted person, preferred working in solitude. She assisted the queen in her workshop as required. Faith wondered about the sisters' origins but hesitated to ask, considering it impolite. She'd read stories about the giants and what happened to them. Rumors told of their kingdom of Brobdingnag, which was where the Farm Boy found himself after climbing the Celestial Vine.

Instead of one giant being at the top of the Vine, the Farm Boy found an entire civilization and, despite the reservations of their king and queen, they began visiting and trading with the people Down Below. But once the Farm Boy killed the giant, some people started calling him Jack-in-Irons, and he brought down the Vine. There were giants who were Down Below when it happened, and they got trapped forever.

Faith couldn't imagine being cut off from your home forever. It made her lonely for Brigantia and her father. For everyone and all she knew. The Queen of Hearts, selfish as always.

"And the queen," Esther was saying, "helped to shape the look of our city."

"Amazing." Faith went back to the conversation. "Everything here is so lively and beautiful."

"It is, isn't it?" Esther smiled. They had stopped in front of a second set of elevares. A young girl, around fifteen, dressed like a cadet, ran into the room. They ascended for what Faith believed to be hours, until the doors unveiled a hall adorned with carpets. Outside, vibrant wallpaper covered the walls, while hanging pots overflowed with blooming cacti and succulents. Faith knew them because she had visited the Red Queen's land, where she had seen them scattered throughout the city and palace.

"Here you are." They stopped in front of a door, which Esther opened with a key. Faith found it strange that someone had locked it. Thoughts vanished as Faith entered the room. Esther opened the door, revealing a room done up in various shades of green, although it wasn't too much. Complementary colors, from bedcoverings to curtains to upholstery.

"It's lovely. Thank you."

"You're welcome. Feel free to go out, but please be back when the clock strikes—"

"Five." Faith grinned.

Esther laughed. "All right then."

She departed, allowing Faith to survey the room. They provided separate facilities for the washroom and dressing room. The washroom had an immense tub, made of green marble, and shelves filled with fluffy towels and bottles of oil. A bath would be divine right now. Faith frowned at it as she approached. Should she call someone to bring up water? That's the way they did it in Brigantia. She noticed two star-shaped handles. When she touched one, she knew they were brass. In the center, there was a mysterious curved oblong tube with an unclear purpose.

Faith wondered. She reached for the handle on the left and pulled. No, that wasn't it. She tried to turn it one way, but it wouldn't budge.

When she ventured in the opposite direction, a powerful tremor that emanated from deep below the floor shocked her. Faith moved back from the tub's edge as water gushed from the middle tube. She stared as steam rose and the tub filled at too rapid a pace for her liking. She turned the handle again, and the water ceased. Obviously, the water was too hot. So, she wondered again. Faith turned the handle on the right, bringing back the shaking, roaring, and water. Faith touched her finger and discovered it was lukewarm, if not cold.

Now understanding, Faith worked the handles and filled the tub, then she selected one of the bath oils and the rushing water caused the oil to froth. She couldn't read the writing on the oil's bottle, but it smelled of lavender and lemongrass. Faith undressed and immersed herself in the water after testing it with her toe. She made a mental note to ask the queen how this was even possible.

By the time she completed her bath, it was dinner time. Unsure, Faith pondered her clothes. Visitors to any Brigantia palace could leave their dirty clothes outside the door for the laundress assistants to collect. She followed suit. Clothes filled the closet, just like in the palace. They were big, but since she was dressing for dinner, she chose a simple blue gown, rather modest.

A cadet operating the elevare provided Faith with directions to the dining hall. She met many colorful people while walking through the hall. Humans and fey interacted, even amid heated debates. Respect was always present.

Upon entering the dining room, she discovered a crowd had gathered. Upon entering, the clock chimed, drawing her attention to Rowan's presence on her left. People noticed her and greeted her, leaving how they recognized her a mystery. But then again, she was the queen's guest. Faith sat in an empty chair several seats away from Rowan and didn't even acknowledge his presence.

Sylmare entered, using the door at the opposite end of the room. Faith wondered as to the king's whereabouts. But her attention returned to Sylmare as everyone stood, then waited until she sat. However, unlike earlier, the queen's troubled expression showed on her face.

"Thank you all for joining me this evening." As always, she commanded the room. "I have some disturbing news from His Majesty."

Faith drew in a breath. She never imagined trouble in this land.

"There is a beast never seen before in our world – nay – in any world. His Majesty believes someone may have stolen it from an unknown place and brought it here to aid our enemies," Sylmare said.

Whispers and mutterings of excitement and worry filled the room until the queen raised her hand. The guests quieted.

"The beast lacks a name, but the harpies control it."

Faith felt a sick feeling in her stomach upon hearing the word *harpies*, even though she didn't know what it meant.

"This beast," Sylmare continued, "can spit a blast of fire which incinerates anything in its path."

This time, the muttering increased in its shock and urgency.

"Remember," Sylmare said, "it is crucial that we maintain the confidentiality of this information within the confines of this room until it becomes necessary to announce this disturbing news to the populace."

"You have our word, Your Majesty."

"Yes, of course."

"By your command."

Should they be here, listening to this? Faith had no issue keeping this a secret, but it was her experience that people discovered secrets no matter how well they were kept. And now talk of some unknown beast that spat fire?

Faith's eyes met Rowan's for the first time. His expression was one of panic. Why was he panicking? They would be gone before anything happened. Was it right to leave amid such turmoil outside the kingdom?

Rowan pushed back from his chair and stood. Faith suspected what he was going to say, and he didn't disappoint.

"Your pardon, Your Majesty," Rowan said, and he nodded at Faith, "but what does this mean for us?"

CHAPTER ELEVEN

Perhaps it wasn't an appropriate question to ask. But if there was trouble brewing in Tidaholm, Rowan wanted no part of it. His priority was Brigantia. All eyes were on him now, with expressions of anger and offense on every face. Faith wasn't even looking at him. She had her palm over her face, her head tilted as she moved it back and forth. She made her point with no confusion on his part.

Sylmare glared at him, her hands folded before her, as she said, "And what do you mean, Prince Rowan?"

"Will there be an issue with creating the armor?"

Sylmare didn't answer at first. "Don't fret, Your Highness, you'll get what's yours."

Someone made a noise. He thought it sounded like Faith drawing in a sharp breath. Had Sylmare just threatened him? Rowan decided not to push it. He muttered, "Thank you." And sat down.

Sylmare continued with her report of the goings-on far away from the city. At times she assigned tasks and gave orders to those gathered. The atmosphere relaxed – well, Rowan couldn't say relaxed. There was an air of urgency surrounding the group. Despite the ongoing conversation about city matters, Rowan still felt like an outsider. And he was. Everyone ignored him. While Faith was the center of attention, being complimented and peppered with questions, which she answered with patience. How did she do it? Dinner was served, things familiar and foreign, but Rowan had long since lost his appetite. His thoughts were on how he could salvage the situation. It was obvious that Sylmare planned to ignore his request, and she wasn't concerned about his mother's wishes in the least.

Well, since no one was speaking to him, he figured he'd better listen.

It wasn't easy, but Rowan caught a few words and snippets of conversation. Someone mentioned the harpies again. Rowan made a mental note to ask where he could purchase some books on the subject. There was one harpy that was mentioned many times, *Uryphe*, the leader of the harpies, although there was also talk of her taking a *mysterious council*. Rowan figured her a puppet but wondered who controlled her.

People spoke of the king and his soldiers forming a line across the Sands. Rowan thought it sounded like a desert. It gave him a clearer picture of how large Tidaholm was. Although they had Wasteland in Brigantia, which bordered the Red Queen's land.

Dinner seemed to end as dessert was served, and Rowan realized he'd not eaten a thing. The servant seemed disappointed by this, asking Rowan if the food wasn't to his liking. To avoid upsetting someone, Rowan made an excuse of feeling unwell, leading the servant to offer stomach relief in his room. Rowan thanked him and found he was able to slip out as the dinner guests were preparing to leave.

He remained upset by the queen's treatment when she removed him from her workshop. He'd almost protested but realized it would be pointless. He doubted the giantess would care. In silence, they rode the elevare and he followed her to a door.

When she opened it, Rowan couldn't help but flinch. The rich decorations were a bright pink, from the furniture to the bedspread to the wallpaper. And Rowan was certain he'd never seen this many frills and lace in his entire life. Not even his mother or sisters had their rooms decorated in this manner. It was clearly a joke on him.

Still, Rowan bit his tongue and said in the most civil tone he could, "Thank you."

"Restful night," was her response, and she left him.

Now back in his room, Rowan pulled off his boots and flopped on the bed, which smelled of a heady perfume that tickled his nose. He lay there, gazing at the veiled canopy, unsure of what to do.

"Well, now this is an interesting room."

"Damn it to the nether hells!" Rowan shot up at the voice.

Cheshire stretched across the foot of the bed, relaxed in a white silk dressing gown. "Did I startle you, oh Prince of Hearts?"

"Do not start with me. I am in no mood!"

"Do you have any right to be upset?"

He didn't, and he knew it.

"What is the matter with you?"

A scathing remark formed on his lips, but instead he said, "What is a harpy?"

Cats might seem expressionless, but Rowan knew Cheshire was an exception. "Why?" His eyes went very wide, his dark pupils drowning in the brilliant green, and his fur stood on end.

Rowan told him about the conversations he heard. "Is this something we should worry about?"

"Indeed," Cheshire said. "They are evil, screeching things, part woman and part vulture."

Rowan couldn't imagine. He wasn't certain he wanted to.

"Their claws can rend a bull to pieces, let alone a man," Cheshire went on, "and their gaze may not turn you into stone like the basilisk, but it will paralyze you with fear, and then they strike before you can react."

"Enough," Rowan said. "How do you kill them?"

Cheshire turned on his stomach and stretched. "I stay away from them, so I couldn't say."

"You've seen one before?"

With that, Cheshire dissolved into smoke, leaving Rowan both confused and worried. Rowan growled in frustration. He loosened his shirt from his trousers before flopping back down on the bed. He wanted to lower the wall lanterns but was unsure how. If it were even possible. A small copper house-shaped lantern sat by the bed. That would suit him better. Rowan pushed himself off the bed and approached where one of the lamps hung. After a cursory examination, he found a tiny lever attached to its base. Turning it had the desired effect. With only the copper lantern for light, he felt better and returned to bed.

Although he lay there for a while, sleep eluded him. A small bookshelf sat across the room. Recalling his desire to study harpies, Rowan wondered if there was a book he could use. He found a tome about mythological creatures. After retrieving the lamp from the nightstand, he sat down at the dressing table, pushed the many bottles of perfumes and powders to one side, and opened the book.

Surpassing Rowan's expectations, the book contained details of many creatures, such as harpies. He wondered, if he asked, would they let him keep the book or at least say where he could buy a copy? As for the harpies, they were nothing like he expected. Half woman, half vulture, they had a – what was that saying? Dreadful beauty? They had no arms but a massive wingspan with claws on the shoulders. The face was the most humanlike part of them if you discounted the cruel predatory gaze that the artist somehow captured.

Despite the torso being covered with feathers, the sight of the large breasts still brought heat to Rowan's face. It was the hooked claws, larger than daggers, that made Rowan shudder. The king had battled these monsters. Rowan didn't envy the man. He threaded his fingers and laid his chin atop them, staring at the pictures, but was uncertain what he was looking for.

It took him a while to notice the shadows in the corners. He doubted his eyes until he tried to turn his head to observe. Rowan found he couldn't. The shadows moved, gathering in the room's center, forming a dark pool.

Rowan's body refused to respond to his rising panic. A shape formed, resembling twisted snakes, taking on a human form. A face with prominent cheekbones, a straight nose, and plump lips. But it was the eyes that made his chest squeeze tight. They were full and black in their sockets.

To Rowan's surprise, the thing looked confused. It raised its hands to its face and examined them as though they were unfamiliar. "Still cannot get right."

A soft voice, hinting at deep sorrow. The apparition seemed unaware of Rowan's presence and the Prince of Hearts found solace in it. To his horror, the thing lowered its hands and looked straight at him.

"Sometimes I wonder," it said. "Did I make the proper choice?"

The thing drew in a hoarse breath and moved to stand next to Rowan. In denial, Rowan wanted to scream as the thing approached him. It leaned against the desk, and the prince's stomach roiled at the stench.

"All I wanted," it continued, "was what was mine."

It was a battle, forcing the bile down that threatened to come up, and it burned his throat.

"The witch took everything from me."

What witch? Who or what was this figure standing beside him, as if it belonged?

"I suppose you don't know about her," the thing continued, "her and that damnable prince. I would have given him everything he desired."

Rowan struggled to move, to speak, to act.

"You'll meet her soon." It was silent after that, lost in its own thoughts. It was several minutes before it spoke again.

"I am – was Prince Serval of the Dokkalfar," he said, "until..." He crossed his arms. "But they have promised me glory again. Now that I have given myself over, I'm ready to prove myself."

They?

"Long journey," Serval murmured, glancing away. "The queen has many protections here. I don't know if I'll be able to return."

He had to mean Sylmare. Did she even notice someone – no – some*thing* had broken through her defenses?

"You helped me in this," Serval continued, "for that, I am grateful."

Now it was Rowan who was confused. What had he done to help this thing?

"Oh, you don't understand, do you?" Serval asked. "It's anger, sadness, jealousy – anything to feed on. It's like a beacon."

Did he cause this thing to be here? Serval turned to face the mirror and Rowan couldn't help but meet that frightening gaze. "For what it's worth, the woman shouldn't have treated you that way. Don't fret, we'll take care of her, but right now, she's of little consequence."

Rowan's muscles coiled like springs, yearning to be released. Serval's words stirred up the bile once more.

"We've come for the girl."

Girl? He couldn't mean— "No." Rowan forced the word out. "You won't hurt her."

What resembled Serval's brow creased. "Of course not," he said. "We have no intention of hurting her. We need her."

"Then why?"

"The barrier that separates Underneath from Deep Earth is weak in some places, which is why we've escaped," Serval explained. "It's at its weakest at the Sea of Tears."

"What barrier?" Rowan said.

"You never crossed the Sea of Tears," Serval stated, "but its end holds a massive barrier. Like veils that separate the ethereal from the living, but stronger."

"That's how you entered," Rowan said, "but if the barrier is already breached—"

"It's not large enough," Serval interrupted, "and it seals itself. It falls off into the ether, creating two obstacles."

Rowan was about to inquire, but Serval explained, "Faith's powers could transform the barrier, enabling us to move without hindrance."

"She won't!" Rowan was able to flex his fingers, although it took all his concentration.

"What makes you say that?" Serval said. "Besides, why do you even care?"

Rowan's fists clenched. "Because—"

"Didn't she humiliate you? Doesn't she expect you to disobey your mother's orders for her own benefit?"

"That's not—"

"And then that insult with the queen," Serval went on. "I know you want her punished for how she treated you."

Rowan wanted to deny it, but he couldn't. As much as he tried to hide those feelings, they emerged, filling his head with angry whispers and visions of what he would have done. So many ways to lash out at Sylmare repeated themselves.

"See?" And Serval knew. "Let's agree. You bring us Faith and I will ensure that the queen pays, and she will know that her tortures are in your name." He straightened away from the desk. "Lure Faith from the city to the harpy encampment. There is no need to be afraid. They will know your arrival."

Serval turned back to him and laid two fingers in the center of Rowan's forehead. The touch burned him with icy fire. Rowan screamed in his mind.

"I've rooted the directions in your mind. It won't be difficult," Serval said. "Although I should warn you, lingering too long will compel you."

"I – won't – do – it!"

Serval reached for him again, saying, "I suppose I'll need some of that free will."

An explosion of smoke appeared behind them, drawing their attention, and at first Rowan wasn't certain what was happening. Like the inky blackness that had formed Serval, something was created amid smoke and white fire. From its heart, a beast with glittering emerald eyes and unsheathed silver claws leapt, emitting a low guttural hiss from deep in its throat.

Not the Cheshire Cat that Rowan knew, yet he recognized the fey cat in this beast. Rowan had never seen this side of the creature before. It ripped into the putrid flesh as Serval struggled to break free, but eventually faced its adversary.

For a few awful moments, all Rowan saw was the smoke and fire, tangling with the inky blackness, and one of the snakes, wrapping around Cheshire's throat until it became smoke again and pushed its way into Serval's torso. The man, whatever he was, turned himself inside out. The whole of his body plunged into the center. Gray and black continued to intermingle, but it wasn't until Rowan heard Cheshire howl, that he gathered all his strength and pushed back from the desk, spilling the chair onto the stone floor. Just as the blackness threw the cat across the room, where he lay unmoving.

Rowan cried out and grabbed the lantern, hurling it at Serval. It smashed at his feet, spraying oil all over him, and the flames burst from within his center, racing up his filthy body. He shrieked and tried to crush the flames away, but they continued to devour him. Rowan picked up Cheshire and hurried out the door. He needed help, and he needed it now.

"Fire!" Rowan yelled at the top of his lungs. And individuals arrived, as expected. Servants and guests alike rushed toward him. "Fire in my room! Please, I need help!"

It was then that the giantess appeared. With a glance at Rowan and Cheshire, she urged, "Come with me."

"Beware!" Rowan called to the servants who entered the room. "There is something evil about!" Then he ran, trying to keep up with the giantess.

The descent within the elevare seemed slower than normal and grated against Rowan's patience, but it stopped and when the giantess opened the door Rowan was greeted by a corridor of alabaster stone. The gathering was sparse, yet among them, the healers stood out in their robes of unblemished white, embroidered with runes. The giantess strode down the corridor, forcing Rowan to follow. She halted before a door painted blue. After a knock that resonated like distant thunder, she pushed the door open without waiting for an answer.

After that moment, everything seemed like a blur. A woman, draped in a gown of deep sapphire, gently convinced him to entrust Cheshire into her care. With a soft hand, she led them to a different chamber – a room dedicated to examinations. It was a clinical space, with a bed and an array of instruments neatly arranged on tables and tucked away in cabinets. There, she carefully placed Cheshire on the bed and began her assessment, methodically alternating between gentle taps and meticulous palpations.

The giantess was saying something to him. No, asking him questions. His responses were methodical. He wasn't even certain what he said, his attention on Cheshire. Sometimes, he felt annoyed by the magical cat dismissing or insulting him, but tonight Cheshire saved him from something he didn't want to consider. Now there he was, lying still, his eyes closed, or sometimes he spat out the black ichor that was Serval.

The blue-robed woman addressed him. Rowan's response was a shake of his head, a silent admission of his confusion. Redirecting her attention, the woman conversed with the giantess.

Rowan interrupted. "What is it? Can you tell me what's being said?"

The giantess met his gaze, her eyes brimming with compassion. "I am so sorry," she said, her voice a somber echo, "the little one is dead."

CHAPTER TWELVE

The frantic knocking at her door brought Faith abruptly out of her studies. With an annoyed hiss between her teeth, Faith pushed back from the desk where she'd sat to peruse the books Sylmare had given her. She strode across the room and yanked the door open – then halted when she saw the young cadet, whose name escaped her. She was pale and disheveled, and Faith knew immediately something was very wrong.

"What is it?"

"Please come with me, Lady Faith. The prince needs you."

Oh, no, what has Rowan gotten himself into now?

"Is he injured?"

"No, no," the cadet said. "I'm afraid the poor creature—"

She didn't finish as they stopped by the elevare. When the door opened, Esther was there.

"I'll take it from here, cadet."

The girl was obviously grateful for the chance to escape.

"Esther, what is it? What happened to Rowan?"

"Someone attacked him in his room."

"What? But she said—"

Esther said, "He is not injured."

Faith's relief was short-lived when Esther said, "The cat – I am sorry – perished while fighting the prince's attacker."

"Cat?" Realization dawned, the weight of the truth settled on Faith like a stone in her stomach. "The Cheshire Cat?" The very thought that Cheshire could be the subject of their conversation was as devastating as it was horrific.

"I don't know his name, but what we gathered from the prince is that a beast invaded his room, and the cat bravely defended him."

"No," Faith whispered. It couldn't be Cheshire. She had never seen him be more than mildly annoyed in her life, except when he lost a mouse he had been chasing. But Cheshire didn't eat mice. It was just a game he played. Faith had often scolded him about it since she found it cruel. Not to mention one of her father's best friends was a mouse.

Faith resolved not to form any conclusions until she saw Cheshire for herself. She tried to ignore the feeling in her stomach that threatened to spread through her body. When the elevare finally stopped, Esther led her down a hall, pristine white, and there were people moving around in uniforms of the same crisp white, blue, and gray. Faith guessed healers and doctors. Esther led her to a room with a blue door, where she found Rowan seated.

He didn't look at her, but Faith could see he'd been crying. Another woman, in blue, a healer perhaps, stood before a long table.

"Oh, no." It was Cheshire. Faith reached out, wanting to touch him, to convince herself he was there. Tears blurred her vision. She turned on Rowan. "What in the nether hells happened?" Faith never cursed, but this…it was unbearable.

Rowan looked up at her, his expression defeated. "He saved me."

"From whom?" Faith demanded.

"An excellent question." Sylmare stood at the threshold of the room. "What has happened in my home?" The question was aimed at Rowan, but his gaze was downcast again.

"I want an explanation!"

"Rowan!" Faith said.

Slowly he lifted his head and then his eyes went wide, seeing something over Faith's shoulder. The healer gasped and Esther said something in her language that from her tone Faith guessed was some type of swear word.

Faith turned, expecting the worst, and found a cloud of gray floating in the air, swirling and pulsing, shaping itself and taking a form.

"Oh, dear," Cheshire said. "Well, I wasn't expecting this."

Faith let out a cry of joy. "Cheshire!" She grabbed him, pulling him down and against her chest. "Cheshire, dear Cheshire, you're alive!"

"Oof!" Cheshire said, "Gently, my dear Faith."

"Oh, I'm so sorry!" Faith buried her face in his fur. "What happened?"

"By the Vine," Sylmare whispered, "is the beast fey?"

"I suppose you could say that, Your Majesty." Cheshire had that mischievous gleam in his eyes. "Your Highness?"

Rowan was staring at him, his mouth agape. "Cheshire." He seemed not to believe the cat was alive. "How?"

"Sacrificed a life, did you?" Sylmare grinned.

Cheshire looked at the ball of lifeless gray striped fur. "Yes, I'm afraid so. But –" Cheshire amended quickly, "– you must not feel guilty about that. I have eight more."

Faith believed the reassurance was for Rowan. The prince continued to stare.

"We will discuss this further in the morning," Sylmare said, and Faith was grateful. It was clear to her that Rowan was still in shock.

"We will have guards in your room, and we will heighten the security," Sylmare said. "Esther, if you'll come with me so we may make further arrangements."

"Yes, Your Majesty."

Sylmare approached Faith and whispered, "Stay with him. See if you can bring him from his trauma."

"Yes, Your Majesty."

Faith knelt before Rowan. "Let's get some rest."

Rowan nodded, still not speaking, as Faith took both his hands and pulled him to stand. She draped one arm around his shoulders. "Cheshire, please come with us."

"Of course. I will meet you there. Confirm nothing questionable is happening." Then he vanished. Faith figured he likely knew where her room was. Rowan was silent during the walk to the elevare and the whole ride up, which suited Faith fine. It wasn't until they were standing in front of her door that Rowan spoke. "Faith?"

"One moment." Faith opened the door. She guided Rowan to sit on the bed then went back to close the door. Cheshire appeared in the middle of the bed, stretched out full on his back, exposing his furry white belly.

Faith sat down beside Rowan and reached over to tickle Cheshire. Unlike normal cats, Cheshire didn't mind a little tummy tickle.

"Now, what did you want to say?"

"That…" Rowan said, "…I'm sorry for being such an ass."

Faith couldn't help but giggle at his use of the word *ass*. He raised an eyebrow. Before he could say anything, Faith gave him a peck on the cheek. "Apology accepted."

Rowan sighed, releasing whatever was trapped inside of him, and he leaned against Faith's shoulder.

"Get some rest." Faith gestured to the bed's other side. Rowan looked at her, his expression comically shocked.

"It will be fine," Faith said. "Cheshire will be right here."

"Like I said, I'll make certain nothing untoward happens."

Rowan grunted before slipping off his shoes and crawling over Cheshire. Once he settled himself, he fell asleep almost immediately. It wasn't until Faith saw his steady breathing that she got off the bed and turned down the lights, leaving on one lamp that sat on the nightstand. She removed her own shoes and lay across the bed. She rested her head on the crook of her arm and watched Rowan slumber. He was a handsome man. She smiled.

"Have you forgotten me?" Cheshire remarked quietly.

She had. "Sorry, my sweet Cheshire." Faith scratched him behind the ears. "Now, softly, tell me what happened."

"An intruder forced its way in." Cheshire began. "It was like oil bleeding from the stones. I watched from the canopy in my incorporeal form. I didn't know what it was, and it's always good to inspect things."

"Of course."

"It held Prince Rowan in some kind of charm. He could not move from what I could see, and it spoke to him."

Faith found that odd. What would prompt a dark being to engage in conversation with Rowan?

"I'm afraid you will not like what it had to say."

Faith certainly did not. This – *thing* – this *apparition* wanted her to help them break some barrier?

"This barrier," Faith said, "have you ever seen it?"

"Yes," Cheshire said, stretching to his full length, and his claws unsheathed. "I didn't get too close. It did not seem safe."

"Was it as the apparition described?"

"He was surprisingly accurate," Cheshire said. "A waterfall rising from a deep canyon. While the Sea of Tears fell off into oblivion."

Faith shuddered. "That sounds so terrifying."

"Oh, it was," Cheshire said. "It pulls you forward until you can't escape. The one time I went there was the last."

"Rowan fought for me?"

"He did," Cheshire said, "for both of us. I am embarrassed to admit that our enemy completely outmatched me. Had Rowan not intervened, it would have taken all my lives."

Faith reached out and pulled Cheshire against her. "Make certain you tell him. He likely feels guilty."

"I shall."

"And next time, don't take on a battle you can't possibly win."

*   *   *

A soft knock on the door woke Faith. It was morning. Cheshire lay between them; he lifted his furry head at the knock. Rowan muttered in his sleep and turned his back to them. Faith silently rose and cautiously moved toward the door. She cracked it, then opened it wider upon realizing it was a young servant girl. "Good morning, milady," the girl said. She presented a tray of small jars and tins. "The queen asked me to deliver this to you for your friend, Sir Cat."

"Ask the young lady to come in." Faith heard Cheshire behind her.

As Faith opened the door all the way, the servant continued, "The queen asks that you join her for breakfast in the arboretum in one hour. Please be prompt." She set the tray down on the bed in front of Cheshire. "Please enjoy, Sir Cat."

"Thank you, lovely lady."

Faith sat back on the bed in time to witness the girl blush. "Merely take the elevare to the top floor." She bobbed a quick curtsy and left.

"What do we have here?" Cheshire inquired. He nodded his furry head and one of the jars rose into the air. The lid unscrewed itself.

"You should save your strength." As Faith reached for the second jar, Rowan suddenly came awake, lifting himself up on his elbow.

"Cheshire?" He sounded panicked.

"Right here."

Rowan turned his body around to face them. "Faith?"

"Good morning," Faith said. "The queen wants us to meet her for breakfast soon."

"Yes, but—" To Faith's surprise, Rowan grabbed Cheshire like she had done and hugged him, burying his face in Cheshire's fur.

"I'm sorry."

Rowan was crying. Although she couldn't see the tears, she heard them in his voice.

"Why are you sorry?" Cheshire washed Rowan's face with his rough tongue.

"You sacrificed a life for me!"

"You would have done the same if you could," Cheshire said, "but since you cannot, I wouldn't recommend you try."

Faith chuckled. Rowan smiled slightly.

"But I must say," Cheshire continued, "that you saved my lives."

"I did? How so?"

"I am embarrassed to admit, as I did to Lady Faith last night," Cheshire said, "that I was far outmatched. Had you not intervened, I would be without any of my lives!"

Rowan inclined his head. Then his expression changed, and Faith could see the walls coming up. Rowan pushed himself off the bed and turned away. Even so, Faith observed him wiping tears with his hand. "I shouldn't be in here. It's improper. I will see you at breakfast."

He strode from the room, pulling the door closed behind him.

"Honestly, that boy!" Cheshire leaned his head to one side and back, the cat equivalent of shaking his head. "Now what is this?" The first jar was brimming with tiny, glistening spheres that resembled delicate pearls. "Interesting." Cheshire lowered his nose to one. "It smells divine." With a mischievous grin, Cheshire poked a paw into the jar and scooped out a cluster of the pearl-like objects, lapping them up with his tongue. "Exquisite."

The second jar caught the cat's eye next. It was filled with ruby-red beads, each one a tiny gem that promised a new flavor. Cheshire's grin widened as he sampled these. Next, the third jar, glinting like a pot of gold under the sun, beckoned. These golden orbs were the rarest of the bunch, and Cheshire tasted them, licking them off his paw and purring his delight.

Faith watched while Cheshire enjoyed his treat and smiled indulgently. She reached for one of the tins and pulled back the lid by grasping and lifting an attached ring. "It's tiny fish." Faith dipped the tip of her pinky in the yellowish sauce. "It's mustard."

"Hmm." Cheshire moved over to them and sampled the sauce with his rough pink tongue. "Spicy."

The fourth and largest jar had an acrid scent, somewhat like sour pickles. Faith couldn't quite figure out what it was. It looked like tiny squid tentacles. Not that she'd ever seen one in real life, just in drawings, so she wasn't certain. Faith made a face as Cheshire slurped one up. "Tasty!" Cheshire went to his washing. "You'd better wash up. The queen is expecting you."

Faith did so, though she wanted a bath. Like the tub, you could have fresh water in the basin to wash up. Faith still couldn't figure out the mechanics. Having freshened up, she returned to the bedroom, only to find Cheshire and the food tray gone. She decided not to change clothes and did her best to smooth down her blouse and pants. She hoped, feeling a bit embarrassed, that it was enough.

Faith didn't see Rowan as she walked toward the elevare. The young man operating it was talkative, but Faith didn't mind. When the doors opened and Faith entered the garden, something completely drew her attention away.

Faith was enveloped by a symphony of fragrances. The rich aromas of various herbs and spices were immediately apparent. A path of stones twisted ahead, leading to a gazebo entwined with fine spiderwebs. It was nestled among beds of flowers and vegetables, with tall trees overhead. Chrysalises dangled from the branches by the hundreds. Nearby, a beekeeper tended to hives while bees and butterflies danced in the air, adding to the garden's vibrancy. The melody of birdsong complemented the scene, where sunflowers, morning glories, zinnias, grapevines, and an assortment of herbs stood in neat rows, dominating the landscape. At the garden's heart, a table with four chairs awaited, and servants moved diligently between the plants, picking herbs and spices.

The queen awaited her under the gazebo. A servant was pouring what Faith hoped was coffee into her cup because she could really use it. Surrounded by beauty, Faith wished she had changed clothes, but it was too late. She approached the gazebo and bowed low. Faith wasn't for curtsying, and she always had trouble doing it. "Good morning, Your Majesty."

"Why so formal?" The queen waved her toward the chair across from her. "Sit. Breakfast with me."

Faith slid into the other chair and a servant quickly approached. She bobbed a perfect curtsy. Faith felt slightly envious. "What may I get for you this morning?"

"Oh…" No one had ever asked what she liked to eat. Minerva always knew Faith's cravings – griddlecakes, always. "Do you have blueberry griddlecakes?"

"Absolutely." The servant grinned. "And would you like coffee or tea?"

"Coffee, please."

The queen had chosen scones and took her time, slicing and spreading them with butter before she spoke. "So, where is the prince?"

"He said he would join us," Faith said. "Rowan was extremely upset last night, and I thought…well, as a friend, you know."

This time, the queen waved her explanation away. "I understand," Sylmare said, "not that it would be any of my business, anyway."

Faith lowered her gaze, her cheeks on fire. "No, I mean—"

"Calm yourself, Faith, I jest." Sylmare gave her a mirthful smile. "Although he is quite handsome, isn't he?"

"Yes, of course." Faith couldn't meet her gaze.

Sylmare called over one of the servants and instructed him to find Rowan and escort him to the arboretum. The servant who had taken Faith's order returned with the steaming griddlecakes.

"Hmm, I should have gotten those instead."

They both chuckled.

"Honestly, I wanted to talk to you privately without Rowan. Today, I'll work on the armor. I want you there."

Faith stopped eating and laid down her fork. "Me? Why?"

"I want you to witness transmutation," Sylmare stated. "Do you recall when I said you needed to use your powers to keep them sharp? While you are here, I want to teach you."

Faith gasped. "Really?"

The queen chuckled. "Yes. You will assist me in creating the armor."

Sylmare went on to discuss the tasks required for a perfect fit and sufficient protection. Faith was almost finished with her cakes when Rowan joined them. Unlike her, he'd bathed and changed clothes.

"Honestly," the queen muttered.

Apparently, her clothes did not cause the queen any distress. Rowan, like her, bowed and wished Sylmare a good morning.

"Sit and eat," Sylmare said. "I want to know about last night."

She pushed back her chair. "Come with me please, Faith."

Guided by the queen, Faith walked to the right of the gazebo and followed a stone path into a grove of trees. Countless chrysalises hung from the branches, requiring her to tread carefully to avoid touching them. In the heart of the grove, she encountered a surprising scene – a large green chrysalis, like Jade's, was affixed to a tree and stood taller than Faith herself. Faith gazed at it in awe.

The queen smiled with secret knowledge. She almost reminded Faith of Cheshire. "This is how I spoke with Jade. I thought perhaps you would want to speak with her to ask about your family."

"Thank you." Faith did. She needed to know her father was all right.

The queen touched the chrysalis with one finger and, to Faith's utter shock, portions of it peeled back, opening like the petals of a flower to reveal a chamber within.

"Step inside," said the queen, gesturing with both hands.

"But—?" How was she supposed to speak with Jade? How did this work?

"Once you are inside," Sylmare said, "you merely ask to speak with Jade, and she will hear you."

Faith hesitated. She didn't understand how this worked. Some form of sorcery or witchcraft evidently, but it was completely unfamiliar to her. She wasn't normally claustrophobic, but still... "I know you are nervous, but trust me," Sylmare said. "Neither I nor Jade would ever put you in danger."

Faith drew in a deep breath. "All right."

She moved forward and slipped between the open petals. As she turned to face Sylmare again, the petals rejoined, sealing her in.

CHAPTER THIRTEEN

Faith's expectations of the chamber were far from what she experienced. Instead, she encountered a familiar and comforting atmosphere. A faint yet pleasing aroma filled the space, but she couldn't quite put her finger on the scent. A soft, emerald light illuminated the walls, revealing the intricate veins of gold that ran throughout. They appeared to undulate, as if the walls were a living entity with golden blood flowing through its veins.

She had no idea what to do next. She pressed her palms against the wall before her. To her surprise, the soft folds enveloped them. A vibrant green light illuminated her surroundings and Faith found herself back in Brigantia. She felt overwhelming joy as she returned home and reunited with her father, the White Rabbit, and the Dormouse once more. However, there was a sense of wrongness about her. Despite everything appearing as it had been, there was an unusual scent in the air, and as she stood there, the surroundings fell into dusk. Faith moved forward, but something seemed to smother the sound of her footsteps. Faith approached Jade, who sat perched atop her mushroom. "Jade, I'm home," she said, her voice filled with uncertainty, her happiness draining away.

A cold breeze whispered through the flowers and tall grass, making the tree leaves shiver. Jade's look was haunting, shifting between a spectral presence and profound sorrow.

"Jade, please tell me how things are at home," Faith pleaded.

Jade struggled with each word before responding, "They are close."

Faith knew what this meant. "How much time do we have?"

Jade responded, "Do not worry, focus on your task."

"But—"

"Be swift, but also be careful."

"I understand. We have already faced an attack." Faith saw the world dimming around her, like a flame snuffed out. She asked, "My father, is he well?"

Jade's head rolled back, and her body went rigid. When she straightened and met Faith's gaze again, her eyes were as black as pitch. Faith remained frozen in place until a sweltering wave surrounded her and pushed her back into the chrysalis.

Faith struggled to draw air within the cramped space, tearing at the fabric as she gasped for breath. A hand burst through, grabbed her arm, and yanked her out. To her astonishment, Rowan, not Sylmare, drew her closer. "Are you all right, Faith?" he asked, as she buried her face in his shoulder.

Rowan turned to Sylmare. "What did you do to her?"

"Step away, Faith," Sylmare commanded.

As the tension rose and the surrounding space filled with heat, Faith refused to let things escalate any further. She detached herself from Rowan. "Stop," she said with gentle force. "I'm fine." Faith reached out with both hands between them, keeping them at an arm's distance. "Rowan, you should know better."

Rowan's mouth opened as though to speak, then he clamped it shut.

"Faith," Sylmare said, "what did you see?"

"I spoke with Jade," Faith said. "I was in the Grotto where she sat atop her mushroom, but she seemed unable to articulate. It was a struggle."

Faith moved from between them, ravenous. She didn't wait to see if they were following. "We're running out of time," Faith continued as she approached the breakfast table. She took the coffee cup between her palms and took a fortifying sip, the heat warming her hands and quieting her shivering. Rowan and Sylmare were waiting. Sylmare took her seat again, but Rowan remained standing. When Faith was able to collect herself, she told them of what she had seen.

Neither Rowan nor Sylmare spoke. They didn't have to. Their expressions voiced their thoughts. Rowan slammed both palms on the table.

"We have to go back."

The queen raised an eyebrow. "And do what?"

"I'll convince the queen we need to prepare our armies. If we can convince the White and Red Queens to join us—"

"And what of the armor?" Sylmare steepled her fingers before her face, but her eyes flickered with fire.

"Fuck the armor!" Rowan said.

Rowan's use of such a vulgar word took Faith aback. It was the first time she had heard him speak like that. Only those who were of low character and lacked proper manners used the word.

"Rowan!"

"No!" Rowan paced. "We don't need the armor. Faith won't be fighting. I will lead our armies. Why did I even journey here?"

"You?" Sylmare asked.

Rowan was quick to assert his authority. "I am the firstborn son of the King and Queen of Hearts," he stated, his anger subsiding. "The sons of the White and Red Queens are not of age. So, it falls to me." Drawing himself up, Rowan took a deep breath. "Faith, I understand your concerns for your father, but I am commanding you to stay here. I promise I will see to it—"

"No," Faith retorted.

"Faith, you'll be safer here," Rowan persisted. "I will send for you—"

"I said no."

"Are you disobeying your prince's direct command?" Rowan asked, incredulously.

Faith moved forward until they were standing face-to-face. "If you are my prince," she said, "I will fight for Brigantia, my home. I didn't come this far to be treated like a fragile maiden." Faith turned away from him. "We need armor. Your Majesty, if you are still willing to create it…"

The queen stood. "I am."

Faith turned to Rowan and said, "You can leave. I will return home once we complete the armor."

Sylmare reminded them, "And don't forget, your royal mother will be quite displeased if you return empty-handed."

Rowan's fists clenched as his jaw tightened, revealing his frustration. Sylmare was correct. He could not afford to return to court with nothing to show.

"Faith, if you will come with me," said Sylmare.

"Of course," Faith replied. She turned to face Rowan. "Think on your decision," she said before following Sylmare.

Once they were in the elevare, Sylmare spoke. "This opportunity is perfect for your training as I work on the armor. Your help will speed up the task."

"Anything I can do," Faith said. She bit her lower lip. "Do you think Rowan will leave?"

"Not now," Sylmare responded. "Tell me, were you close to the prince?"

"I was once," Faith admitted. "As children, we played together. I thought we would be lifelong friends, but…"

They rode in silence as the elevare continued its descent. "Did you have any friends before becoming queen?" Faith finally asked Sylmare.

"I did," Sylmare said. "And many of them are here. I needed trustworthy people, not those who would flatter me only to betray me later."

"I'm glad," Faith replied.

"Rowan is still your friend," Sylmare told her. "Although he behaves like…"

"A royal?" Faith suggested.

Sylmare laughed. "I've seen him show his concern for you, despite his efforts to conceal it. Don't give up on him yet."

"I won't," Faith promised. Perhaps there was still a glimmer of hope in her childhood friend.

Once she was in the queen's workroom, Faith's eyes widened as she witnessed Sylmare's Gift unfold in front of her. The room transformed right before her eyes, morphing from a nondescript workspace into something magnificent. At first, she couldn't remember what the room originally looked like – everything seemed hazy and indistinct. But now, as her focus sharpened, every detail came into view.

Walls stretched and shifted, creating an ever-expanding space that defied the laws of physics. Faith stood rooted in place, mesmerized by the sheer power and elegance of the magic. The transformation was akin to what she'd seen in Brigantia, where rooms adjusted to the presence of those who entered, either expanding or rising to accommodate their needs. Although this wasn't her first encounter with such enchantment, the spectacle left her in awe. The forge itself was a diamond created by the edges of five octagons. Faith noticed all the rooms but one had open doors. The room by the entrance hall, with a locked metal door, held unknown importance for Faith. She did, however, hear noises coming from within, a steady hum of machinery like when she rode the elevare and what sounded like running water.

To her left, she could see inside another room, which resembled one in her father's shop. For a few moments, her sadness threatened to overwhelm her. Drawers lined the walls, filled with various gems that could easily pay a hundred royal ransoms. Tools cluttered a table in the room's center. Her father used the same types when weaving jewelry into his hats.

The door to the room where'd they eaten was also open, with large arched picture windows reflecting Faith as she stared outside. Instead of the city, Faith saw a forest and, in the distance, snow-capped mountains. Why hadn't she noticed that before? Well, considering the condition they were in when they'd first arrived...

Someone had already set up the small round table with coffee and iced cakes. A cool breeze emanated from the room, leaving Faith perplexed about its origin with the closed windows.

The library from where Sylmare had retrieved the books Faith was reading stood right in front of her. Smoke hindered Faith's view of the final room. Instead of filling the space, some force drew the smoke upward, and that's when Faith saw two large circular holes, with metal pieces connected to a circle and twisted at the bottom, going from narrow to wide. They went round and round by themselves.

"Faith?"

Sylmare held the cloth in her hands, twirling and hovering, drawing her attention away. Sylmare's hands and feet moved in intricate patterns more graceful than any dancers Faith had seen, but also powerful, like a warrior readying for battle.

"Faith, can you fetch a few items from the materials room?" Sylmare continued with her floaty dance. "Just place them in the bowls there." Sylmare motioned with her hands. The worktable was smooth and scarred and seemed already cluttered with various tools, metals, gems, and stones, but it was clear that Sylmare needed more. "Please retrieve me the following items…"

Faith knew what to look for by feel, touch, and scent. They were precious metals, although many of them she'd only heard of. Faith ran her fingers over them; some were rough, others smooth, some translucent, others opaque. Some were dull as stone, while others had mixtures of colors that changed when she moved them in her hand.

Faith brought everything back to the worktable and saw the famous spinning wheel in the last room, which connected the library and materials room. Small wood bowls adorned the table. Sylmare directed Faith on the precise placement of each gem or metal. Sylmare guided the cloth between her hands and before Faith's eyes, it came apart between her fingers.

"Faith, now take some of the trine."

"What?"

Sylmare pointed to one of the extra piles. It seemed like gold, but it wasn't. When Faith grabbed a handful, she felt a trembling in the metal, reforming itself into many crystals like flowers blooming on a tree branch. There was something volatile within this material and

Faith had seen an explosion of sparks deep within it. Faith almost warned Sylmare to be careful, but she figured the queen knew the danger of the beautiful metal. Would it even be safe? Even as the thought occurred to her, Faith realized, *Of course it will be.*

The crystals floated among the suddenly glittering threads as Sylmare coaxed them to spread across the table like they were a living thing.

"Beryllium, please."

Sylmare then instructed her to crush the cobalt, a beautiful blue shade resembling gems, into fine powder, filling Faith with regret. Certainly, there was the well-known copper. If one were to describe it, it would resemble red gold.

Bismuth displayed a multitude of colors that rivaled the rainbow. Afterward came piles of gems. Faith had never seen so many in one place, from the rare alexandrite to the familiar tourmaline. Faith asked why Sylmare had two separate drawers for jade. Sylmare explained that, just like their namesake friend, the gem possessed unique personalities. Jadeite and nephrite, one rare and more malleable, the other harder and used solely for statues. Faith had always thought they were the same. Faith thought a third stone was chrysoprase, but it was chalcedony.

Faith also learned that gems, like animals, could belong to different families. For example, people could also refer to chalcedony as jade and agate, but they did not consider nephrite as chalcedony. The situation was confusing. But Sylmare made certain she touched everything in the workshop and used her Gift to fashion them in a variety of ways.

And all this Sylmare spun into the cloth that separated into its base threads and wove the various metals and gems she chose. Faith continued to fetch what she needed, and while the queen continued to work, she continued to teach as well.

"Be careful with iron, of course, even if you aren't born fey," Sylmare warned. "Since we categorize our Gift as witchcraft, iron can cause harm to us."

Faith nodded.

"Certain colored gems have traces of iron, did you know? You can handle these gems, but you must take care."

Faith hadn't known. After some thought, she inquired, "Can I borrow a journal to write this down?"

"I'll have someone bring one to you," Sylmare said. "I must regain my strength, so I will rest. I will send for you when I am ready."

"All right," Faith said.

The cloth looked different now from when they had brought it to Sylmare, but the longer Faith looked at it, the more it changed its appearance, from a myriad of colors to solids encrusted with gems. Then it broke apart into separate swaths. Sylmare hung it up again, where it continued to transform.

CHAPTER FOURTEEN

Since he had nothing else to do, Rowan found his own way to send a message to Brigantia. Riding the elevare down, he rehearsed his speech in his head. He planned to tell his mother the truth, that the queen refused to create the armor for her, but he'd also learned that Brigantia was under attack. He would ask the Queen of Hearts if she wanted him to come home.

Rowan asked around until someone directed him to a shop several blocks away. The person drew him a crude map and Rowan set out. As he made his way through the crowds, he realized he did not like big cities. Despite the beauty and cleanliness, the sounds, smells, and movements overwhelmed him.

Since when have I become so insular?

Then again, that was Brigantia's issue, wasn't it? Upon reaching the designated location, he double-checked the map and building to ensure he was in the right place.

The exterior, cloaked in shades of gray brick, boasted a singular entryway, a set of double doors crowned with golden, frosted-glass panes. These panes, etched with intricate dark lines resembling veins, rested atop an elevated stone arch. At its zenith, a solitary lamp cast a warm glow. Yet, it was the colossal harpy statues flanking the doors that seized his gaze, their stony wings unfurled in silent sentinel.

He must be a raving lunatic to want to go inside.

Yet he reached for one of the iron door handles and pulled it open. What first hit him was a pungent smell that made him sneeze aloud three times. It was dark at first, so Rowan called out, "Hello?"

When the lights flickered on, he stood in a rectangular room with lanterns hanging low from the ceiling. Shelves lined the walls, showcasing an array of glass tubes, bottles, beakers, and jars. Oddities that he had never seen before adorned the walls and dangled from the ceiling, while a wooden counter sat at the far end of the room, with a single decorated chest nestled between dark metal bands. It was clear that he had entered the abode of an alchemist.

"Hello?" Rowan called again.

"May I help you?" a voice said from behind him. He turned but saw no one. Yet, when he looked back, an old woman stood behind the counter. She was tall and thin, her head wrapped in a cloth, and she wore gray robes with white – or at least reasonably white – stripes at the opening. Around her neck was an assortment of wooden necklaces. One looked to be strung with carvings of small skulls.

It took Rowan a few moments to get himself together. "Is it possible for me to send a message from here?"

As she met his gaze, her eyes' green-gold color captivated Rowan. These were the first of that color that he'd seen in any dark-skinned person. With a cryptic smile, the woman inquired, "Do you possess a coin?"

"Yes, of course." He had coins from Brigantia, but the White Rabbit had told him from his travels outside of their home that gold, regardless of its origin, had widespread acceptance. Apparently, the Rabbit was correct, for the woman's eyes lit when Rowan presented her with three gold coins. "Is this enough?"

"Quite right." The woman ran her tongue over dry lips. Probably once beautiful, she now resembled a skeletal figure ready to break free. "Please come with me."

Curtains masked a doorway, concealing a room to the right of the counter. Rowan was nearly certain it hadn't been there before. He understood he should have become familiar with such situations. They happened in Brigantia all the time. Still keeping his guard up, and his hand on the pommel of his sword, Rowan followed.

Velvet drapes of the deepest black enshrouded the chamber's walls, reminiscent of a circular wardrobe in size. Dominating the heart of the space, however, was an imposing cauldron crafted from cobalt glass. It held his fascination, a silent siren in the gloom. The alchemist drew near, trailing a solitary finger through its contents. In her path, a dance of stars and a kaleidoscope of hues came alive, orbiting in the liquid cosmos.

Rowan's eyes widened in disbelief as a cushioned chair appeared out of thin air, leaving him shocked. Another appeared behind the old woman. She sat after Rowan did. "I'm assuming your country of origin minted these coins?" She rubbed the coins between two fingers.

"Yes."

"Brigantia."

Rowan nodded.

"And the name of the recipient?"

Rowan assumed it had to be Jade and stated it.

"Tell me more about this Jade."

Despite the difficulty, Rowan's description sufficed, and the woman dipped her finger in the water again. She chanted in an unfamiliar language, but Rowan disliked the harsh tone. It left him uncomfortable.

An image formed in the water, distorted, but stilled when the alchemist withdrew her hand. It was Jade, sitting on her mushroom. The Hatter, White Rabbit, March Hare, Dormouse, and others gathered around her. Cheshire was there as well.

Rowan's brow furrowed. He didn't recall Cheshire saying he was going home recently. Then how...?

The sound of Cheshire's voice startled Rowan out of his deep thoughts. "It seems I have a twin."

The alchemist's eyes darted back, widening at the sight of Cheshire materializing out of the darkness. A shared moment of mute surprise enveloped them. From the cauldron's depths, a phantom arose, its form barely contained. In haste, the prince seized the vessel's rim, tipping it over in a desperate act that scorched his palms. Yet, as the alchemist stepped forward, he unsheathed his blade in defiance. Wounded, the prince retreated to the shop's end, his senses reeling, his sight dimming. Gritting through the agony, he grappled with the door's iron grip, flung it wide, and spilled into the forgiving embrace of daylight.

Rowan dropped to his knees and clamped his hands beneath his armpits. Onlookers paused and gathered, whispering and gesturing. Rowan, with his eyes shut tight, was aware of someone kneeling next to him. "Do you require help? Are you all right?"

Although it was a simple inquiry, Rowan realized he wanted nothing to do with this individual. "Cheshire?"

"I am here, Your Highness," Cheshire responded.

"Can you help me escape?"

"I…" For the first time, Rowan detected uncertainty in Cheshire's voice. "I've never tried something like this."

"Please try it."

Cheshire must have altered his size, as Rowan felt the furry creature coil around his shoulders. "Hold on."

Rowan might have believed he had stepped through a mirror into another world. He sensed an exhilarating rush, as if he were a leaf caught in a tempest, spiraling uncontrollably. He clenched his eyes tight, dreading the sights that could unravel before him. His stomach churned in protest, threatening rebellion. But soon, the tumultuous journey ebbed away, and he found himself gently alighting, embraced by a tranquil hush, as if the storm had passed and left behind a serene whisper of peace.

★   ★   ★

"I told them it would fail."

The familiar voice caused a moment of cold fear to race through him. Rowan opened his eyes, afraid it would be Serval, but only Faith was there. She was dozing, looking peaceful in her slumber. He wanted information but didn't want to bother her. He wondered how he'd ended up in bed and what time it was. The sun shone bright through the windows, so Rowan assumed it was morning.

"Faith?"

She awakened, at first disoriented, then her expression cleared. "Rowan."

Faith rose up to her knees and grasped his shoulders. Leaning down, she pressed her lips to his. Rowan widened his eyes before allowing them to close as she deepened the kiss. And he was rather disappointed when she broke it.

"Morning." Faith smiled at him.

"It is."

And, of course, nothing further would happen, because someone knocked at the door. A few choice words crossed Rowan's mind.

"Come in," Faith said.

It was the queen. Rowan went to pull himself up, but she said, "No, no, keep still."

"Your Majesty." Rowan inclined his head. "How did I get here?"

Sylmare said, "They found you at the palace entrance, with severe burns on your hands."

Rowan had forgotten. The skin on his palms was red and irritated, but not painful.

"You have Faith to thank for your healing."

"Of course." Not surprising. "Thank you."

Faith lowered her head as she smiled, pleased. "You're welcome."

"Cheshire," Rowan said. "Have you seen Cheshire?"

"No," Faith said. "Did something happen to him?"

"He was the one who brought me here." Rowan furrowed his brow. "At least I asked him to."

"I'm sure the fey creature is fine," Sylmare said. "Such a feat requires immense power and rest."

"I'm hoping."

"Now, tell us what happened," Sylmare said. "How did you reach this state?"

Rowan recounted how he sought directions to the alchemist shop, only to be deceived by the old woman's false promise of contacting Brigantia for him.

"Is the alchemist dead?" Sylmare said.

"I don't know." Rowan couldn't recall much, just the swing that connected.

"Do you recall where this shop is?" Faith asked.

"Someone drew me a map."

"Do you still have it?" Sylmare asked.

"It was in my jacket pocket."

Faith stood and walked across the room. A lidded basket was there for soiled clothes. Faith lifted the lid and rummaged through, and withdrew the jacket. She searched the pockets until she came up with the crumpled map. After examining it, the queen ordered one of her servants to contact the constabulary to bring the alchemist to justice if she lived and to dispose of the body if not. When she returned to the room, Sylmare asked, "Now, who drew you this map and suggested you visit the alchemist?"

Again, Rowan's brow furrowed. He'd spoken to so many people. "I don't recall."

"It will come to you, I'm sure," Faith said with a smile.

"For now," Sylmare continued, "we assume that someone compromised my home and the city."

A thought occurred to Rowan, but he didn't voice it. He recalled the words spoken to him before he woke. Maybe he could leverage that to his advantage. He just hoped he didn't make another mistake. However, he must wait until he was alone.

The queen was saying, "Faith and I will return to my shop and continue work on the armor."

He'd forgotten about the armor. One thing was certain in Rowan's mind: no matter what his mother had to say, Faith was getting her armor.

"We'll inform you if we find the alchemist, assuming she's alive." The queen crossed her arms. "We will need you to identify her. Stay here and rest. I'll have breakfast sent."

"Thank you, Your Majesty." Rowan lay back and closed his eyes.

"Come down when you are able." The queen turned to go. Faith rose from her chair and gave Rowan another of her beautiful smiles before leaving.

When the door closed, Rowan pushed himself up and propped the pillows to sit against them. He waited. After about twenty minutes, when nothing happened, Rowan said aloud, "I know you're here."

A shadow emerged like a splatter, as if an angry hand had shattered an ink bottle on the wall. It coalesced into Serval. However, he couldn't seem to take his full shape, bordering on more of a blob of melted wax worked by unskilled hands.

The look of him sent a shudder of revulsion through Rowan, but he fought to steady his nerves. "What did you mean when you said you told them it would fail?"

If his appearance was revolting, his voice was an attack on Rowan's ears. It was a guttural sound, each word ending with a gurgle, like something clogged his throat. "The deception."

"Why did you believe it would fail?"

"You are…much…too smart." He spoke the words like he had difficulty forming them.

"Thank you." Rowan held his gaze. "Are they planning to strike again?"

"You mean you?"

"Myself, Faith – whoever."

"We won't hurt Faith."

"I'm relieved to hear you say that again," Rowan said. "And the queen?"

"No interest," Serval said.

Knowing that also was a relief. Although he wondered, did they know about the armor? Maybe it wasn't of interest either. Rowan wasn't about to tell his enemy.

"Are you in Brigantia?"

"Can't do," Serval said. "Not full… need Faith."

Now Rowan was confused. "I don't understand."

Serval tried to adjust his form and only succeeded in further degrading his body. "You let me…in here. Someone…let us in there."

Rowan straightened up, leaning forward. "I let you in?"

"Anger, guilt, humiliation," Serval said. "So much."

Dear gods – it was me. How could I not have seen it?

"Go back."

"What?"

"Go back!" Serval was struggling to keep his corporeal form, but what did he mean? His tone grew urgent as his body lost all human resemblance.

And Rowan understood. Recalling his previous experience with Serval, he knew why their enemy had been able to infiltrate the palace and city. "What did you mean by someone let you into Brigantia? Who?"

But Serval was gone. The last of the ink dissolved through the stone.

CHAPTER FIFTEEN

We can't go back to Brigantia. Not yet.

Despite his instincts, Rowan felt compelled to do it. Someone was allowing their enemy into their borders. Rowan tried not to think of the obvious person. Besides, the obvious one was never that obvious. He'd spoken with the giantess, Esther, and asked where the queen was. Now Rowan rode the elevare down to her workshop.

How would the queen react to Rowan's association with the enemy? Well, he hadn't been doing that per se. He reached the lower floor and exited to the left as the door opened. He didn't want to disturb them if they were at anything magical, so he approached cautiously.

The queen was at her spinning wheel, and it filled the surrounding air with a shimmering incandescence as the cloth flowed through her fingers, coming apart in glittering threads and rejoining once it ran its course from the spindle and along the wheel.

Faith fed the cloth to the queen despite her being busy. Rowan didn't pretend to understand what he was seeing. He knew most of the palace weavers started with wool or flax that they spun into thread. Rowan's heart swelled with contentment as he observed the two women gracefully dismantling the fabric. He swelled with pride as he continued to watch Faith handle the cloth that changed form with just a touch of her fingertips. It was a remarkable sight.

His understanding of spinning and the Spinner Queen's legend suggested that the wheel might be a catalyst for Sylmare's and Faith's Gifts. The witches focused on tasks that went beyond the capabilities of the spinning wheels alone. Rowan continued to watch, entranced.

Movement to his left drew his attention to the worktable, where the whole cloth settled on the surface, but it no longer looked as it did when Jade first gave it to them. In fact, it didn't look like anything he'd seen before. It seemed almost liquid. It wouldn't surprise Rowan if it transformed into a puddle on the floor.

Everything calmed. The material came to rest on the worktable. The incandescence faded into a shower of colorful sparks.

"Rowan!"

Faith approached Rowan and drew him out of the dreamlike state he had gone into. "Are you feeling better?"

"Yes, very much." Had she gotten lovelier since he'd last seen her? "I have something important to tell both of you."

"Come sit with us," Sylmare said. "We both need nourishment after utilizing so much of our Gifts."

"Extraordinary," Rowan exclaimed, heading to the table. "I wasn't aware you could use your Gift that way."

"Neither was I." Faith graced him with a smile as he pulled back her chair for her, then hurried to do the same for the queen. "Sylmare is instructing me."

Rowan waited until the servants finished bringing food and coffee. The view outside the window distracted him. An expanse of beach, its sand glistening pink before an ocean that stretched out into the horizon. But hadn't it been a mountain range before? Had the windows even been there?

"First, I must apologize. I have done something that, well, it was idiotic, but it provided us with what I believe is useful information."

As he told his story, Rowan expected both women would be furious with him. Their intense gaze made him uneasy and was unexpected. *Likely thinking how stupid can one man be?*

"That is an accurate assessment."

All three jumped and made surprised noises.

"Cheshire!" Faith scolded.

The fey cat appeared in the queen's lap. "Don't you agree, Your Majesty?"

"Hmph." Sylmare scratched Cheshire behind the ears. "And what do you mean?"

"You found the prince's action foolish, however—"

"It is useful information," Sylmare said.

Faith continued to glare at him, but it wasn't a look of annoyance. Rather, consternation?

"Why were you so angry?" Faith said.

Rowan drew in a breath. "I – the queen – was not showing me the proper respect. Your rapport was remarkable. You seemed unconcerned with my views."

"So, your anger and resentment drew this thing to my home?"

"Yes." Rowan didn't hesitate. "And I apologize." He looked at Faith. "To both of you."

They both smiled at him, disregarding his flushed face.

"Well, now that's settled," Cheshire purred, enjoying the queen's ministrations. "What is our next move?"

"Your next move is off my lap, furry one."

Cheshire rolled over on his back, exposing his stomach. "Must I?"

"Hmph," the queen said again, but stroked Cheshire's belly.

"Faith," Rowan went on, "I know you're worried about your family and Brigantia—"

"But we can't go home. Not yet." Faith drew her arms up around her shoulders.

Cheshire rolled over and vanished in a puff of gray smoke before reappearing, floating above the table. "Perhaps I could do a bit of spying? I love being stealthy."

"Cheshire—" Rowan and Faith said in unison.

"I promise, I will take the utmost care," Cheshire said. "However, I will task you to finish the armor and return home as soon as you can, if you don't hear from me in, say – three days?"

Rowan nodded once. Faith looked stricken but gave three brief, curt nods.

"Very well, it is decided," Sylmare said.

Cheshire disappeared and reappeared on Faith's lap. He nuzzled her face for a few moments and then he disappeared again.

"Your Majesty—" Rowan began.

"Sylmare."

"Sylmare." Rowan was pleased she was inviting him into her confidence. "Did the constabulary provide a report to you on the alchemist?"

"Not as of yet," Sylmare said. "They may not have thought it necessary."

"Would they give us the information if we asked?" Faith said.

"They will with a note from me," Sylmare said. "I take it you're planning on visiting the station yourselves? Very well. While you do that, I'll consult my court sorceress about dealing with the Rot. I take it there will be no other troubles with you, Your Highness?" Her eyes twinkled.

Rowan grinned. "There will be no further trouble, Your Majesty."

The queen stood. Rowan stood after her. "Please continue with your meal while I run my errand."

They agreed. The queen summoned a servant to bring paper and a pen. She wrote a quick note and sealed it with her crest. She turned to Rowan and Faith and gave them instructions on how to reach the nearest station.

"It won't be hard to find," Sylmare said. "And be careful, the both of you."

"We will be," Faith assured her.

★ ★ ★

Despite Rowan's belief that they were safe walking the streets, he still carried his sword. Faith made no comment. The station was close and as the queen mentioned, it wasn't hard to find.

The building was constructed entirely of shimmering blue bricks that seemed to absorb the blue of the sky, its entrance adorned with a charming array of bluebell flowers, their delicate bells swaying gently in the breeze, releasing their subtle fragrance. Faith stopped a moment to take in their scent.

People rushed in and out of the double pane doors. Rowan and Faith stood, unsure of their actions.

"May I help you?"

An older woman who sat at a small wooden desk, carved and polished, drew their attention. She had a no-nonsense appearance and wore a starched button-down blazer of royal blue.

"Afternoon," Rowan said as they approached the desk. "Her Majesty sent us to ask about the incident with the alchemist?" Rowan handed her the queen's order. She broke the seal and her eyes darted over the page.

"You must be Prince Rowan and Lady Faith."

"Yes," Rowan said. "The alchemist. Does she live? Was she questioned?"

Instead of answering his questions, she said, "A copy of the official report was prepared for you in the event the queen requested it. Since it involves her guests." She stood and smoothed down her jacket. "Please wait here."

"She didn't answer your questions."

"Indeed." Which, of course, raised Rowan's suspicions.

When the woman returned, she handed Rowan a rather thin sealed envelope. "Here you are."

Rowan knit his brows. "The alchemist's interrogation is in here?"

"There was no interrogation."

"She was dead then," Rowan said.

"No." She didn't look at them, apparently engrossed in her paperwork. "But, please ask the queen to forgive us, but this is beyond our purview. She needs to inform us of her desires."

"Wait." Now Rowan was confused. "What do you mean, not in your purview?"

"There are no Gifted here," the woman said in an exasperated tone. "We have no experience with dark magic."

"What happened?" Rowan demanded.

"Read the report," she said. "Our people won't enter, despite the shop being cordoned off with a warning." The officer continued working, disregarding their presence.

Rowan broke the seal, hoping the queen wouldn't be upset. He held the paper so Faith could read along. Unfortunately, neither Rowan nor Faith understood the language. They'd both assumed, since many of the citizens spoke the same language they did, that their writing would be the same. However, hearing Brigantia spoken didn't imply everyone else understood it. Before Rowan could ask the woman to translate, Faith touched his arm.

"Let's get this back to the queen."

Rowan nodded as he flipped through the papers. The map he found was easier to understand than the one he had. "Look at this." He showed it to Faith. "It tells where the shop is."

"You're not thinking of going there? You don't know what happened."

"We should find out."

"The queen could tell us."

"I know, but what next?" Rowan said. "I must find out because the constabulary refuses involvement."

"Yes," Faith said. "In truth, I must know as well."

They followed the map, checking the street signs and comparing them to what they had. When they got lost, they inquired about the restricted shop. Many people knew about what had happened there. It was the latest gossip. Apparently, something like this seldom happened in Tidaholm. Petty crimes and occasional mediation for neighbor disputes were common, but dark magic incidents were rare.

"It seems much too perfect here," Rowan commented as they walked.

"We could say the same about Brigantia," Faith said.

"Perhaps that is why the Rot wants our home so bad. Perfection, peace. What entity filled with sorrow or hatred does not want it?"

They remained quiet until they reached the shop. The officer had mentioned cordoning off the entrance, but the door remained open, as though welcoming the next patron, but both knew better. They noticed a group of boys gathered across the avenue. Their attention was on the shop and a few times they tried to push the smallest one of them off the sidewalk, likely trying to dare him to enter.

The boys stopped when they saw Rowan and Faith approach. Rowan rolled up the paperwork as tight as he could and stuffed it into his jacket. Unable to be stealthy, Rowan unhooked and dropped the cord that roped off the entrance. "Stay close," he told Faith. Across the street, the boys began to whoop and holler.

The lanterns burned. However, a film of dust covered everything. They both had the same thought. When had the officers been inside? A sour smell was coming from the next room, and Rowan felt reluctant to allow Faith to follow him.

He drew his sword. "Stay here."

"No."

"Faith."

"Wouldn't you rather face whatever is within with a Gifted at your side?"

If it were any other Gifted but you. "Very well, but please stay close."

Rowan moved into the next room. The table was still overturned, and the empty cauldron lay where it had fallen. Like the other room, it appeared undisturbed.

"What did they see that scared them?" Faith asked.

Rowan walked to the cauldron, noticing the oily substance that spread across the stones. So, what had happened to the alchemist? Had she escaped? Or dissolved into that vile-smelling puddle? Despite hearing stories, he knew for certain that water did not make the Gifted melt.

"Nothing appears to be here," Rowan said.

Faith looked at him, and Rowan noticed a flicker in the corner, as if darkness moved. At first, he assumed it was Faith's shadow. However, a voice soon infuriated him by uttering, "Faith."

Even though he expected it, the sound startled Rowan. Faith spun to confront the approaching form.

"Thank you for bringing her."

"What in the nether hells!" Rowan cried. Was he trying to make Faith think he'd betrayed her?

"You!" Faith said. "The man from my dream! How did you—?"

Rowan's throat closed and his breath caught in his chest. This presence was the one who had tormented Faith. Why hadn't he realized? It was so damned obvious!

"I am Prince Serval of the Dokkalfar." He'd taken his full form and stepped away from the wall, yet not out of the shadows. "And I have asked for your help. I have told the prince why we need you." Serval nodded at Rowan. "Well done."

"You bastard!" Rowan rushed forward, reaching for Faith, who had not moved. Rowan soon found out why.

"Help me!" Faith's voice was filled with anguish, unlike anything he had ever heard.

Rowan wrapped his sword arm around her torso, holding the blade flat as a meager shield. He went to pull her away – and couldn't.

The shadow was creeping its way over Faith, up her legs, rooting her to the spot.

"No!" Rowan cried. "Let her go!"

Serval said, "I assured you we will care for her. She will join us in the Deep—"

Rowan could listen to no more. He released Faith, wishing he didn't have to, and leapt for Serval, swinging his sword. It swung toward his throat – and passed through. Rowan almost lost his balance.

"Stay out of our path," Serval cautioned. "We are grateful for your help."

Rowan swung again, and again. Each time it passed through Serval, but he wouldn't give up. "You'll have to take me first, vile demon!"

"How dare you!" Serval reached out his hands. "I am not a demon!"

His arms stretched out across the space separating them, and Serval closed his hands around Rowan's throat, snatching him forward until he was face-to-face with horror. Rowan dropped his sword and clawed at the shadow's hands, but he couldn't get a grip. He tried to push away, but his hands sank into Serval's chest. Rowan's legs were giving way, and the world was going dark.

Faith, forgive me.

Then Serval screamed.

Rowan was free. He fell to his knees in a fit of coughing and struggled to take in air. Through watery vision, he saw Faith, her hands moving in patterns much like she had done while working with the queen.

"You won't hurt him anymore!" An immense shard of stone burst through the floor, first creating a barrier between the two of them, then, like the shadow trying to consume Faith, the stones grew and surrounded Serval, freezing him where he stood.

"No, no, no!" Serval screamed.

Rowan scrambled to his feet just as Faith turned and reached for him. They both half ran, half stumbled out without looking back. The boys were still there, mouths open in shock. Who dared to enter the cursed place?

"Rowan." Faith stumbled, and Rowan couldn't see why at first. He glanced downward and exclaimed, "Oh, gods." The shadow had dissolved Faith's boots and stockings. Rowan looked around until he spied a stone bench nearby, and he helped her over to sit there.

"How do they feel?"

"Cold," Faith said. "Freezing."

Unsure of what to do, Rowan knelt and massaged her feet.

"Rowan—"

"No arguments," Rowan said. "Thank you. You saved me yet again."

"You shouldn't take such chances," Faith said. "But I will always come to your rescue."

Her declaration brought comfort to Rowan, even though it might have embarrassed other men, she knew. He continued his ministrations until a new sound caught their attention.

They looked up in wonder and saw the sky filled with powerful beats of wings and raucous cries as dozens of gryphons flew overhead in tight formation. Rowan and Faith forgot everything for a moment as they watched the show. They weren't the only ones, of course. Everyone had stopped whatever they were doing to watch.

Another shock awaited them as a gryphon veered left, breaking formation. It circled, searching for someone or something. Rowan thought it seemed familiar, then it dove and landed on the avenue.

"Argestes!" Faith went to get up, but Rowan admonished her, directing her to stay seated.

"There you two are!" Argestes said. "I went to the palace, but they said you weren't there. I've been looking all over!"

As Argestes came close and Faith reached out to hug him and snuggled her face in his feathers, Rowan noticed something different about him. Did he seem more muscular and confident?

"I missed you," Faith was saying.

"I missed you too."

"Argestes," Rowan said. "Are you traveling somewhere with the gryphons?"

Argestes pawed at the stones. "No, although I wanted to. They said it's more important that I find you." Still, he looked up at his passing brethren with longing.

"But where are they going?" Rowan asked.

The gryphon's eyes held an uncommon expression. An almost dangerous glint. He spoke two words that left them both troubled.

"To battle."

CHAPTER SIXTEEN

Upon seeing the flight of gryphons, Faith asked, "Argestes, what else have they told you?"

"The king has requested reinforcements. The harpies are gathering, ready to make their advance."

"Where are they coming from?"

"From Deep Earth." The gryphon's face showed fear before returning to his hardened expression. "Nyx said to find you and make certain you returned to Brigantia. He was quite adamant." Argestes dipped his head. "Faith, what happened? Are you injured?"

Rowan was still working at her feet, although they felt better now. Faith gave Argestes an abbreviated version of the incident in the alchemist shop. "But I'm fine now."

The sky was clear of gryphons. They were mere dots on the horizon. A single black feather, the only testament to their passing, floated down to rest on the walkway. Argestes moved over to it, picked it up in his beak, returned to Faith and dropped it in her lap.

"Perhaps this will bring us all luck. It belongs to Nyx."

Faith couldn't have been more impressed. "You seem so different, my friend."

"Agreed," Rowan said.

"I can't explain," Argestes said, "but being with my family, witnessing their bravery and strength. Perhaps a part of me wanted the same. Wanted to do them proud?" He spread his wings, testing them a few times. "Climb on. I'll take you both back to the palace."

Rowan helped Faith up, then mounted behind her and Argestes took to the air. They arrived in no time. Once they alighted on the palace steps, much to the shock of the citizenry gathered, Faith asked, "Will you return to the aerie?"

"Yes," Argestes said. "Send for me when you are ready."

"Be safe, Argestes." Rowan laid a hand on the gryphon's shoulder, which anyone could see pleased him. They stayed a few moments to see him off, then entered the palace. The air held no surprise, only urgency. After asking one of the nearby cadets, they were informed that the queen was at the war council but no one would say where that was. Without knowledge of her whereabouts and no one willing to disclose them, Rowan and Faith felt lost.

"We should find you some shoes," Rowan said.

The cool stones felt good on her bare feet. "I'm fine." Although she figured she looked rather silly. People were glancing at her with raised eyebrows. "It's more important to find the queen."

Sadly, people refused to take them to the queen for unknown reasons.

"This is ridiculous." Faith placed her hands on her hips in exasperation. "This way."

She walked to the elevare, with Rowan following. There wasn't anyone minding the device, but Faith saw a lever. She grabbed it and pushed it down. From somewhere in the distance came the sound of a bell ringing. After a time, the doors came open and a bespectacled young man whose uniform didn't quite fit his slender frame stood there. Faith spoke before he asked. "We must reach the queen's war council."

"I'm sorry?"

"Do you know where the war council meets?"

"Well, yes, but—"

"We are the queen's special guests. I am Lady Faith Carter, and this is His Royal Highness Prince Rowan. You know about us?"

"Oh, yes, yes, of course!"

"Then if you would, please?"

The boy swallowed, his Adam's apple bobbing up and down. "Yes, milady."

They climbed into the elevare, and the boy worked the lever. It rose, then the boy lowered the lever to stop it. When he opened the door, they faced a corridor paved with stones of muted gray, illuminated by lanterns mounted on the walls at even distances. Simplicity reigned, with no call for windows, adornments, or furniture. At the corridor's end stood twin iron doors, reinforced by six sturdy bands that lay across their breadth.

Esther and Damara stood guard before the doors, clad in leather armor and each wielding a spear. "Lady Faith, Prince Rowan." Esther stepped forward. "It's good you're here. The queen was about to send for you." Esther nodded to Damara, who knocked at the door before opening it. "Your Majesty, Lady Faith and Prince Rowan are here."

The queen looked up from where she stood, leaning over a raised table. "Excellent."

The chamber bore the unique geometry of a heptagon, its walls in hues of earthen brown. Above, the ceiling was held aloft by robust beams of aged wood that crisscrossed into an intricate vault. Light danced through the chamber, spilling from a frosted-glass dome. At the heart of the room, a heptagonal dais cradled a map of Tidaholm, its topography alive with a subtle animation. Surrounding lanterns, twins to the glass above, bathed the chamber in a honeyed glow, weaving a spell of warmth and wonder. Yet, it was the cartographic masterpiece on the left wall that seized Faith's gaze; a tapestry of their entire realm, each detail unfurling before her in breathtaking clarity.

Sylmare straightened to face them. "Did my messengers find you?"

"Our gryphon brought us. We were outside," Rowan said.

"Then you saw the others," Sylmare said. "Come closer."

Faith gasped and covered her mouth with her hand. The figures *were* moving, like the chess pieces in the Red Queen's palace where the Heroine entered through the Looking Glass. She'd never seen them in person, but her father had described them to her. The Heroine had gained the spell to vanquish the Jabberwock and encountered both the Red Queen and her chess soldiers.

Sylmare introduced all those present. Her court sorceress was an ancient woman, wrinkled and bent over, her spindly fingers grasping a staff, yet there was a fire in her expression that belied her age. A bearded man, tall and muscular, dressed in a pressed uniform, was interim commander of the Tidaholm military. There was a scholarly woman dressed in long robes who carried a bundle of books in the crook of her arms. A strategist by training and position, obviously.

There were others in the room, rushing about, working at desks, and passing papers among themselves and every so often approaching the council and providing them with information. Servants were there, delivering food that remained untouched, except by the commander, who deemed it necessary to take several swallows from a flask, which Faith found inappropriate.

"We've received word from my royal husband." The queen was looking at the map again. "The beast is dead. Killed by my husband's hand."

"Thank the Vine," Faith said.

Sylmare looked up and smiled. "Thank the Vine, indeed."

She looked back down. "The harpies advanced," the queen continued. "They were in a rage after their beast was killed. They called other foul beings trying to make a push farther into our kingdom."

Faith looked down at the map. The fighters resembled tiny figurines, moving across the intricate landscape as if gods were observing from above. A blue stretch divided the factions. On the far side were figures of darkness, and a wave of oily black followed in their wake as they moved to the shores and spread their forces along the banks.

"Your Majesty," Rowan said. "I offer myself to fight alongside the king and his troops."

"Rowan!" Faith cried.

Rowan moved next to her and touched her elbow. "It will be all right."

"No," Sylmare said.

"Majesty?" Rowan said.

"Both of you need to be able to return home once the armor is complete. You must ensure the safety of your people. Your responsibilities are to them and your country."

Faith said, "Yes."

"I will finish the armor tonight." Sylmare straightened and stretched her back. "You will have to travel alone when you return to Brigantia. I'm afraid I can't spare anyone."

"It's all right. We'll be fine," Faith said. "Cheshire will return soon. Hopefully, he will have some news for us."

"And it is my hope it is good news."

"Your Majesty, are you certain you can finish the armor that soon? You must preserve your energy," Faith said.

"I will have you to help me."

"Yes."

"May I ask a favor of you both? Please do not leave the palace beforehand. I can concentrate on things if I know you are safe."

"We won't," Faith said. "Another thing, Your Majesty, you must know."

Rowan approached the queen and pulled the report from his jacket. Despite being crushed, it remained readable. He handed it to Sylmare. "We got the report from the constabulary, but we couldn't read your language."

"So, we went to investigate the shop," Faith said.

"You did what?" Sylmare said. "Why, by all of Underneath?"

"Our apologies. It was my doing," Rowan said.

"No," Faith replied. "We both agreed, and Serval was present."

This drew everyone's attention. "You mean that foul being is still within our borders?"

"I'm afraid so," Faith said.

Sylmare leaned over the map again, planting her hands on the edge of its surface. She expelled a frustrated breath as her shoulders slumped. Faith wanted to comfort her but wasn't sure if it would be appropriate. Her sorceress did lean forward and whispered something. Sylmare straightened again.

"Please wait for me to summon you," Sylmare said. "I will have guards placed at your doors. Please, give me your word if this thing comes to you again, do not confront it."

"You have it," Faith said.

"Yes, of course," Rowan said.

It wasn't a difficult thing to promise. Neither of them wanted to deal with Serval again. As they left the room, Faith heard someone remark, "Why is she barefoot?"

As they rode the elevare back, Faith looked down at her feet. "I suppose I will need new shoes."

The same cadet was in the elevare, and he said, "Beg pardon, milady, but my sister is the shoemaker here. I will have her visit you."

Faith turned and graced him with a smile. "Thank you very much." She blew him a kiss, causing his face to flush. The doors closed, and Rowan chuckled. "You flirt."

"Quit it!" Faith hit him on the head.

True to her word, Sylmare had guards at her door.

Rowan took her hands before they parted. "Be safe." He kissed her. Just a quick peck.

She noticed the guards were trying their best not to smile. Relief washed over her as they confirmed the room was secure. The shoemaker arrived and conversed with the guards, gaining permission to enter. She carried the tools of her trade and a few pairs of shoes. She measured Faith's feet and commented on how ladylike and delicate they were, which made Faith uncomfortable. The shoemaker gave her three pairs to try on.

"I'll take these." Faith displayed vibrant boots, crafted from gleaming black leather with colorful lines painted in a swirling pattern.

The shoemaker thanked her as she gathered her supplies.

"No, thank you! These are beautiful."

The shoemaker nodded and bowed with each step out.

Faith must have fallen asleep soon after because an insistent knocking woke her up. "Just a minute!" Faith slipped on her new boots and went to answer.

"Her Majesty is ready for you now." It was another young female cadet. "She asked me to escort you into her presence."

"Of course."

Rowan met her at the elevare. "Are you ready?"

"Yes." Faith had never been surer about anything.

When they arrived at the queen's workshop, they found she had already started. The forge was hot, and the material was laid out on the worktable. As always, Sylmare looked magnificent with her leathers, apron, and hammer in hand. "Your Highness, please make yourself comfortable. However, I have another favor to ask."

"Anything, Your Majesty."

"To finish the armor, we may need to draw from your own quintessence." Sylmare's gaze was severe. "That means it may take time off your life. I won't do it without your consent."

Rowan drew a deep breath. "You have my consent."

"And mine."

"Cheshire!" Faith said. "We're so glad to see you!"

"Indeed," Rowan said.

"You bring news of home?" Faith asked.

Cheshire took on his full form and floated before them. Faith had never seen him so serious. For a moment, he appeared as a regular cat, exuding wisdom and mystery, before reverting to his usual self. "I am glad to see that you are determined to finish the armor today. Things are not going well at home."

"Oh, gods," Faith breathed.

"What is it? What's happening?" Rowan demanded.

"The Rot has been encroaching deeper into the land," Cheshire said. "The Three Queens have agreed to meet, and your royal mother is awaiting their arrival. Many people are falling ill, not being careful what they eat," Cheshire continued. "The Rot has ground itself deepest into the farmland."

"No!" Faith said. "How many?"

"Only a few dozen farmers have come. Most people are cautious, but some…" Cheshire turned to face her. "I am sorry, Faith, the Hatter is one of the ill."

"Oh, gods, no!" Faith reached out.

Rowan came to stand beside her and touched her elbow like he'd done the night before.

Faith fought to still the tears that threatened. She shook, although she wasn't cold, and wrapped her arms around her middle.

"Faith." Rowan stepped in front of her, taking her by her shoulders. They were all waiting.

This time it was Faith who drew herself up and took a deep breath. "All right then," Faith said. "Let's get started."

CHAPTER SEVENTEEN

Faith struggled to stay focused on the task. She wished Cheshire had not told her about her father, on the one hand. But on the other, she might have been angrier if Cheshire had withheld that information.

Prior to starting, each of them received a gambeson made by the queen. She'd taken their measurements and used them well. Faith and Rowan changed in the library. When they were ready, they approached the forge. Cheshire diminished his size and wrapped himself around Faith's shoulders. He was a comforting presence, and his soft steady purring relaxed her somewhat and helped clear her troubled mind.

Someone dragged a chair over for Rowan to sit nearby. Despite his clenched fists, he maintained a composed expression.

"Faith!" Sylmare raised her hammer. "Call on your power!"

And Faith did so. She felt a humming warmth in her veins, always the true sign. Sylmare brought the hammer down, but instead of it hitting soft cloth there was a metallic ring, which reverberated across the room with sound and luminescence. The hammer came down again.

Faith realized after a few moments the glittering green surrounded her, interspersed with the many gems she'd gotten to know. Cheshire made a growl of protest and jumped down from her shoulders. The fey cat chose instead to curl up on the workbench.

"Faith, withdraw, allow me to feed off your power."

Faith obeyed. She realized Sylmare was forming the armor on her, right then and there. Faith closed her eyes and steadied her breathing. She could sense Sylmare, like a soft touch on parts of her body where she molded the armor.

First came the helm. It was lightweight, which was no surprise to Faith. She could feel it as it alighted on her head. Next came the section that would protect her neck and throat. A gorget, Faith believed it was called. She glimpsed the forming pauldrons from the corner of her eyes. She could see the multiple panels shaped to cover her shoulders. They were shimmering with translucent images, green with glittering spots going in rows where one piece of the metal joined the other.

With the breastplate, Sylmare couldn't attach the material. Faith tried to hold still. Although she knew there was nothing untoward about Sylmare's touch, still – what was Rowan seeing? *Then again –* she tried not to chuckle – *how will he react when it is time for Sylmare to fashion his—* She cut the thought.

Then came the vambraces and finger gauntlets. Again, Faith wasn't sure what the leg coverings were called. Greaves, maybe? Or was she thinking of something else? She'd had little reason in the past to study armor parts. She'd only read about them in stories, and when the queen was having one of her tours of the kingdoms and her soldiers accompanied her. Faith realized she'd forgotten to take off her new boots, but they didn't seem to be a deterrent. The magic and the material were integrating into the design.

"Faith, be still," Sylmare uttered, fatigued. Faith almost apologized, but she didn't want to distract the queen further. And then Sylmare finished her task. Sweat was making rivulets on the queen's brow and dripping off her chin. Her skin was flushed, and her breathing labored.

"Sylmare!" Faith went to move to her, but Sylmare put her hand out to stop her.

"No!" Sylmare said. "Don't move. The spell must settle."

Faith stepped back again.

"Your Majesty, perhaps you should rest," Rowan said.

Sylmare rested her head on her folded fingers, which settled at the handle of the hammer. She shook her head. "Faith, move away. Take the seat. Rowan, take her place."

Watching it from afar was both awe-inspiring and worrisome. Sylmare could barely keep the hammer aloft. Her whole body shook, but she pressed on. Faith had to admit she was feeling drained herself. But for Sylmare, she would continue to give of herself and her Gift.

Sylmare forged the armor, sent the Gift through it, and, in a sense, presented it to the wearer, and the armor went to rest on the correct part of Rowan's body. As the hammer fell, armor floated around Rowan, like Faith's.

"Faith, would you mind calling for help?" Sylmare's voice was a hoarse whisper. "You should be fine now." Sylmare managed a slight smile. "It's perfect." The queen then fainted.

Rowan moved, but Faith said, "No, your armor isn't ready. Let me."

Faith went to the horn and called for help. She returned to where Sylmare was lying. Faith moved her away from the forge, then laid the queen's head in her lap, much like she'd done with Rowan. Esther and Damara rushed in. They halted when they saw Faith, and looked intently in what seemed like awe, which confused her. She had expected anger or shock. "She fainted!"

The two came to themselves. "Yes, we were told to expect this. If you please, Lady Faith."

Faith moved away, lowering the queen's head. Esther lifted Sylmare into her arms. Upon seeing Rowan, Faith realized why the sisters had stopped and stared.

If he looked handsome before, he was stunning now.

The prince's armor combined dark green and burnished copper, with a unique helm designed as a crown. At his forehead was an enormous emerald, surrounded by a band of green with gold swirls. Like Faith's, the pauldrons were two separate plates, raised and topped with triangular shards. The breastplate had two layers of metal, one wide at the shoulders, narrowing to a point. The surface was spiderwebbed with burnished copper, and the center of the breastplate featured a raised arrow-shaped patch with another large green gem at its center. Faith noticed that a tempest, a storm of swirling, angry gray clouds that appeared to be moving, adorned the sides of the breastplate.

The knight's sword belt sat low, which made it ideal for drawing a weapon, and it had etched living scenes depicting the battle against the Jabberwock. His vambraces started wide and narrowed at the tips, like the pauldrons, and cut to sword points. The bottom split, providing extra protection for his legs. The knee braces were copper with gold, raised embossing, and the boots, which were knee-length, held the braces secure. They were the same color as the storm on his breastplate.

Captivated, Faith tried to put into words the wonder she experienced but instead she could only say, "Rowan – Your Highness – you—"

"Yes," Rowan said in a whisper. "As do you."

Time allowed Faith to view her armor. Esther focused on the queen and escorted her to the elevare.

"Are you certain she'll be all right?" Faith asked.

"Oh, yes." Esther gave her a reassuring smile. "She's just asleep."

"There's nothing we can do to help?" Faith asked.

The sisters exchanged a glance. "The queen left explicit instructions for you. Ride with us."

It was a bit of a tight fit, but Damara operated the elevare.

When the elevare doors opened, they stepped into a corridor that exuded grandeur, surpassing any splendor they had encountered since their arrival. It was evident they had entered the domain of royalty – the king and queen's private residence. The hall was adorned with ivory panels and walls gilded with the finest gold leaf, a testament to the regal opulence. Majestic portraits framed in intricately carved wood graced the walls, each telling a story of lineage and legacy. They proceeded to the left, their footsteps echoing softly, until they arrived at a pair of imposing white doors at the corridor's end, standing like silent guardians to the royal chambers within.

"Please wait here," Damara told them. She opened one of the doors and Faith and Rowan got a glimpse of the furnished and decorated interior as Esther carried the queen in and Damara shut the door behind them.

"You look wonderful," Rowan told Faith.

"Thank you. As do you."

Esther came out of the room. She held two envelopes sealed by the queen's crest. "She wanted me to give you these in case something like this happened." She handed them to Faith.

Then, to the shock of both, Esther bowed low before them. "We appreciate your unwavering loyalty to the queen," Esther said. "We will meet again someday."

Before any questions could be asked, Esther disappeared into the room.

"Shall we have a look?" Rowan said.

Faith broke the seal of the first letter and pulled out two pages. Thankfully, Sylmare had written the pages in their own language.

My Dear Friends,

It was a great honor and pleasure meeting you. Apologies, I couldn't see you off due to uncertainty about my availability. Not to take a chance, I prepared this correspondence for you.

Faith, I once advised you I wanted people near me whom I could trust. I now consider you and Rowan one with them. You will always be welcome in my kingdom. Feel free to come and go as you please, no explanations or permissions required. It is, I believe, the least I can do. I am overjoyed to have been able to assist you in nurturing your talent. Helping such a smart and enthusiastic student brings me great joy.

Rowan, I've seen remarkable growth in you as royalty and an individual. You will be a fine leader some day and convey Brigantia into greatness. I would ask one last favor of you. Please take care of Faith. She is special and will impact your life.

We both have many trials ahead of us. We may need to unite against the Rot, to banish it from our realms, from Underneath, forever. Farewell for now, as the armor is ready and available to you. We will meet again.

Return home. Use your armor in your quest to save Brigantia and if you need help, call on me and my kingdom. My soldiers and my people are at your disposal. Take care as you journey home.

Regards,

Her Royal Majesty,

Queen Sylmare of Tidaholm

The second letter was to Rowan's mother, explaining why Sylmare made the armor for the two of them, and that it was her decision.

Sylmare also offered her military might to the Queen of Hearts if she so desired and needed their aid. She saw Rowan's mother as a powerful ally. She hoped the Queen of Hearts would understand the importance of providing armor for those fighting on the front lines to protect Brigantia.

"If that doesn't convince my mother, nothing will," Rowan said.

"Queen Sylmare is so wise," Faith said.

"Agreed."

"Let's prepare," Faith said. "Get supplies and send a message to Argestes at the aerie." Faith glanced at the doors. "I wish I could say goodbye to her, face-to-face."

"Not goodbye," Rowan said.

Then why did Faith feel it would be goodbye?

★   ★   ★

Upon Faith's return to her room, she discovered a pleasant surprise – someone had packed for them. She realized that one pack was stuffed with travel rations, while the other contained a bedroll and tools needed to make camp. The queen had thought of everything. Guards positioned themselves at her door once more. *Were they waiting all this time?* And Faith requested they send the message to the aerie. She also found out the queen had supplied a gryphon for Rowan, a female considered too young to join the battle.

Inside her room, Faith examined her armor.

Like Rowan's, hers had the same polished green and burnished copper. She knew she had a headdress, but when she saw it, she squealed in delight. Not only did it protect her forehead with a diamond-shaped plate that lay over the bridge of her nose, but the remaining part was in the shape of a top hat. It almost brought tears to her eyes.

The double pauldrons were green metal surrounded by burnished copper at its edges. Of course, her breastplate took the shape of her form, with nothing prominent except for etched motifs of two gryphons facing each other on their hind legs, their claws up as though ready to battle on either side. The spaulders and vambraces ran the length of her arms and were a combination of metal and leather bands, melded together by disks.

Her armor didn't have a belt for a sword, although the vambraces stopped at the backs of her hands so she could use her Gift. Two triangular plates adorned her upper thighs with intricate embossing. The cloth produced a long, tapering piece that had an arrow shape at the end. Underneath were green tights, and they had transformed her new boots to combine their old design with additional metal embossing in the burnished copper.

A wide smile spread across Faith's face as she reveled in her satisfaction. "Thank you, Sylmare. Thank you for everything."

Faith didn't know what would happen next, unsure if Tidaholm would repel invaders or not, but she knew she had a tool to save Brigantia. Their trials would not be in vain if they endured.

It was time to go home.

CHAPTER EIGHTEEN

As they departed from Tidaholm, Faith couldn't help but look back at what they were leaving behind. They were not just abandoning the realm, but also its inhabitants and Queen Sylmare. However, it was Sylmare who had urged them to return home, insisting that their people needed them. Faith's thoughts drifted to her father, her heart heavy with worry. Cheshire had no clarity about the Hatter's illness. Despite Rowan's selfless offer of help, Faith was burdened with guilt for leaving at this moment.

"Do you feel as guilty as I do?" Rowan's words broke into her thoughts.

"Yes," Faith said.

"I can understand," Rowan said. "I feel like we're abandoning them. Betraying them."

"You shouldn't," Argestes said. "It is important that this Rot gets no farther."

The female gryphon was Epione, who seemed shy, answering questions in a whisper. However, she appeared to be a pleasant creature.

As Rowan and Faith rode through the city, people stopped and looked astonished. They came upon the group of boys who had been playing their game of dare. The boys cheered and hollered, waving. Faith and Rowan waved back. Faith wagered that the boys would brag about what they had seen for months to come.

A crowd surrounded and followed them down the avenue. Some reached out and touched the armor or tried to stroke the gryphons' heads, which they both took with extreme patience.

The group stopped on the outskirts, a few hundred yards before the doors. Faith believed no one wanted to be near the entrance, even the fey. Yet they moved forward, through the great doors, leaving Tidaholm behind them.

Faith noticed the eerie silence right away.

There was no sign of anyone or anything. They worried about running into basilisks again, or goblins, but there was nothing. Even the Black Agnes was gone, leaving behind the telltale pile of bones that she rested upon.

"Is it crazy to think the atmosphere is unsettling?" Rowan commented.

"Not at all," Faith said. "I fear that the creatures have turned their attention elsewhere."

"Brigantia."

And their entire journey seemed that way, with neither dark nor light fey finding them. Nothing accosted them when they first camped. A few times they heard scurrying feet or a plaintive cry echoing through the cavern, but nothing they ever saw.

"A thought occurs," Rowan said. "Argestes, Epione, there's something we need to tell you."

"The Rabbit Burrow," Argestes said.

"Oh, dear." Faith hadn't realized. "How will we get you both back in the Rabbit Burrow? We need you to wait while we retrieve the *Drink Me* potion."

Epione was looking at Argestes in confusion. The male gryphon went on to explain their dilemma.

"Could you both stay here while we retrieve the potion?" Faith asked.

"No trouble thus far," Argestes stated. "Don't worry, we'll be fine, won't we?"

Epione bobbed her head in agreement, although she pawed at the ground whenever they stopped. Argestes would stand close to her, and his presence seemed to calm her.

Unlike their journey to Tidaholm, returning to Brigantia didn't seem to take as long. But of course, they didn't encounter anyone during this trip. That did not comfort them.

They dismounted, both relieved and guarded.

Faith had held on to the keys. She drew them out of her pack but hesitated to look at Rowan. A sudden sense of misgiving filled her.

"Let me," Rowan said, taking the key to the door from her hand.

Things were normal in the Burrow. The potion sat on the table. Faith grabbed it and left. She tried not to spill the precious liquid, but her hands were shaking so she could barely hold the bottle. Still, she completed the task, and after stowing their mounts in their pockets, Faith and Rowan stepped into Brigantia once again. Relief filled Faith when she saw the Burrow was – or at least seemed – normal. And the *Eat Me* cake had appeared on the table. Rowan picked it up and Faith used the other key to the outside.

They believed it would be early afternoon, with the sun above. But the land was in dusk. Had they guessed wrong? Thick gray clouds obscured the sky, with weak silvery light breaking through every so often, only to be swallowed again as the clouds joined to snuff it out. The sun, when it appeared, was a pale version of itself.

Faith looked back at the Burrow. "Rowan, look at that." Faith pointed. The tree that held the Burrow had sprouted several extra limbs. Vine stems had wrapped around the trunk or hung down low, burying themselves into the dirt. Or perhaps they had grown up from the dirt? It was impossible to tell.

"It's the Vine," Faith said. "This isn't a tree. It's part of the Celestial Vine."

Faith stepped forward and laid her hand against one of the offshoots. Contact made, she felt herself being pulled forward into another world's center. No, it was Brigantia as she had seen it in the first dream. But Faith had the impression the Vine struggled to keep its roots where they grew deep beneath the realm, farther than anyone had ever gone, pushing against the Rot, which took advantage of every crack, every dark recess to push forward.

Faith cried out. When she felt a presence next to her, she feared they would trap her. *Rowan.*

Faith? She heard him in her mind.

I'm all right.

I saw you go into some type of waking dream. I feared for you.

His presence was comforting. *How?*

I touched the tree like you did.

This is the Celestial Vine. Calling out to me.

Once Faith thought those words, the scene before them changed, shrouded in a sudden fog. As though two separate tapestries were being presented before them, images appeared, but they were alive. To her left, she saw a shrouded vision of a dark-skinned woman. Faith couldn't quite tell where the woman was, but she saw the staff she held raised above her head. The woman spoke, but Faith couldn't hear the words. Another woman sat to her right, hands moving over cards in a cross pattern.

Faith had never seen either woman before, but she knew them. Yet she couldn't explain how. To her shock, they both stared at her. The woman to her left maintained a neutral expression, while the woman to the right smiled at her. She picked up one of the cards and held it up. Faith leaned forward and squinted, trying to see, but she realized that it wouldn't work. Her eyes saw, but the fog hindered Faith's vision.

Who are they? Rowan asked.

I don't know. I've never seen either of them before.

The two women vanished into the fog as quickly as they came. However, something caught Faith's eye, just out of her line of sight. As she turned her head, she noticed two figures amid the fog but couldn't discern their identities. She assumed they were women.

Faith wondered, *Are they a part of this too? Why can't I see them?* A thought occurred. Maybe the Vine didn't intend for her to see them yet. But she would meet them, perhaps soon. It wasn't time, and one shouldn't know too much about their future, she'd once read somewhere. They vanished, and the vision faded. She and Rowan stood in front of the Burrow.

"Faith, look at your armor."

A fresh pattern had been etched into the metal. Verdant tendrils of vine crept across her right side and palm, seamlessly blending into the existing tapestry of engravings. "What do you suppose it means?"

Rowan rubbed the stubble on his chin. "I'm uncertain, but I think it's a good sign?"

"Perhaps it is," Faith said. "It's getting dark – or darker than it was. Feed the cake to the gryphons and we can go."

Once they had their mounts again, they led them at a trot down the path, now overgrown with alien weeds and puddles of coal-black water. The living flowers that spoke and lined the path bowed their heads as though the weeds had cowed them. Faith considered clearing the unsightly objects, but time was limited.

"Prince Rowan, Lady Faith!" a frantic and familiar voice called to them. They turned their mounts to find the White Rabbit bounding toward them. He did not look well. His fur had splatters of black mud, and his ironed waistcoat seemed on the verge of coming apart.

"Thank the queen's mercy, you're home!"

"White Rabbit!" Faith said. "Are you well?"

"As well as I can be. Or as any of us can be. Oh, dear! Rowan, they sent me to fetch you! The queen wants you by her side. The other monarchs are here."

"Not surprising," Rowan said. "Rabbit, we will ride for the palace. Faith is going home. Cheshire said the Hatter is ill."

"Oh, yes, I'm afraid." The Rabbit checked his watch. "We must make haste, young prince!"

"Of course." Rowan turned the she-gryphon, so he was looking at Faith. "Once I discover the situation, I'll summon you."

"Agreed," Faith said.

"Give my utmost respect to your father."

"I will."

Rowan rode off. Faith patted Argestes. "Let's ride, my friend."

"No," Argestes said. "We will fly."

And before Faith could voice her shock, Argestes took to the air. Beneath them, the landscape was a blur of subdued tones, as if all vibrancy had been leached away, leaving a world devoid of color. Yet, Faith's resolve was unshaken; she was steadfast in her quest to purge the darkness from her realm. At this moment, her father's call beckoned her – his need for her eclipsing all else. Although she felt relief at the sight of Brigantia again, a mix of happiness and trepidation consumed her as her home approached.

She jumped off the gryphon's back before he landed, and opened the back door. Pots simmered on the stove, yet the kitchen remained vacant. "Minerva, where are you?" Faith called.

"Faith? Faith, is it you?" Minerva approached the kitchen but stopped short at the threshold. "My word!"

Faith had almost forgotten she was wearing the armor. It had molded to her skin so well. She hesitated, unsure of what to say.

Then Minerva whispered, "The queen will make you a knight."

Faith moved forward and Minerva met her halfway. They embraced and tears welled in Faith's eyes.

"It's so good to see you safe, child!" Minerva's voice contained a sob. When she drew away, Faith saw her tears.

"And I am glad to see you," Faith said. "Minerva, what about Father?"

"He's abed. Go to him, child."

Faith didn't hesitate. She rushed through the parlor to the staircase, calling to the Hatter as she climbed the stairs.

"Faith? Darling Faith?" the Hatter responded.

Faith came to his room. She found the Hatter in bed, as Minerva had said. His face was pale and there was a sheen of sweat on his skin. His hair, no longer trimmed, had grown long and tangled.

"Father!" Faith rushed to him and threw herself across his chest. "Father, I'm so glad to see you!"

He wrapped his arms around her. "And I you, welcome home, my child."

Faith was loath to let go of him, but she sat up wiping away her tears, then her father's.

"By my hat, what is that magnificence you're wearing? Is that the armor?"

"Yes, Father." Minerva was right. Upon seeing her, the Hatter seemed to perk up, regaining his strength.

"My compliments to the Spinner Queen."

"She was wonderful," Faith said. "Father, how long were you ill? I'm sorry I stayed away for so long but—"

"Now, now." The Hatter waved her apology away. "You had important business." His expression fell. "The Rot seems to poison our food and water. Many like me are falling ill. The White Queen brought supplies, but of course she can't feed the entire kingdom."

"Rowan returned to the palace. The White Rabbit met us on the road. Apparently, the Queen of Hearts was growing impatient."

"I suppose we can't blame her."

"Father, what else has been occurring?"

"Besides this illness that saps our strength, there have been strange flora choking out the living flowers."

"I saw them," Faith said. "It was as though these horrible weeds had taken control of the flowers."

"Most of the animals have fled, although I don't know where they went." The Hatter's expression became pained. "The Dormouse and the March Hare took their families to the Red Queen's kingdom."

"Oh, no." Two of her father's best friends had fled. It angered Faith. "How could they leave like that? Knowing you are ill?"

The Hatter laid his hand over hers. "I told them to go. They were afraid for their families. I told them I would wait for you."

How often did they gather around the table, drink tea, and do silly things? Faith's favorite thing to do was make faces underneath her father's hat, and when he lifted it off her head – because, of course, it didn't fit – they would all laugh. Dormouse, who slept most of the time, did so too. Would she never have that again?

"Faith," her father interrupted her thoughts, "do you know why we named you such?"

"I just knew that was my name when I first arrived," Faith said.

"Because you must always continue to trust. In yourself and the surrounding people. I believe your mother knew that someday your name would show who and what you are."

"What is that, Father?"

"Someone who will not allow herself to be lost. Someone who will instill confidence in others. That's why you came to Brigantia's Wonderland," said the Hatter. "I have confidence in you."

"Father." Tears welled again. Faith wondered if she merited such confidence. Doubt had no place at that moment.

"Tomorrow you will stand before the queen and offer her your service," the Hatter said. "She would be foolish to refuse you."

They heard Minerva clear her throat. They both looked toward the doorway. She stood there holding a tray with a tea set.

Faith stood. "Minerva, when you have seen to my father, will you help me remove my armor?"

"Of course," Minerva said.

"Thank you," Faith said. "Tonight, I will rest as well as I can. Tomorrow, Rowan will send for me, and I will face the queen."

CHAPTER NINETEEN

Epione tore up the ground beneath her as she dashed down the muddied path. It would soon be too dark for her to see. However, the waning light didn't keep Rowan from seeing several misshapen beings standing lined up across the road.

"Slow, Epione," he said. She came to a stop and flapped her wings nervously.

"What shall we do, Highness?" Epione asked.

"Are you a fighter, Epione?"

"Yes," she said with confidence. Her supposed shyness did not equate to inexperience or fear. Rowan drew his sword. "Onward!"

Epione rushed forward and Rowan gave a war cry, catching the beings off guard, so it was a small thing to cleave his way straight through their line. Rowan didn't hesitate or look back. He was too close to his goal. He'd send a hunting party out later.

When the palace came into view, Rowan was relieved to see the lights chase away the darkness. It had not yet encroached on his home. A line of guards stood at attention on either side of the pathway. At first, they didn't recognize him. Four of them stepped forward in a line like apparitions and blocked his path.

"State your business!" the lead guard demanded. Rowan dismounted and stepped forward. Recognition dawned. "Your Highness!"

Things moved after that. The guards broke protocol and welcomed him home. He accepted the many compliments on the armor. Rowan would not admonish them for that. He was glad to be back. One saw to Epione, saying they would take good care of her. The lead and two others ushered him into the palace.

"The queen demanded your immediate presence when you returned."

"Where is she?"

"The war room, Your Highness."

Rowan knew its location, but he had never visited. It was on the palace's highest floor, in a turret room, offering a view of all Brigantia. Rowan ascended two flights of stairs, only to find the room's open doors unguarded, an unusual sight.

The room was like Sylmare's. Rowan figured all war rooms were that way. Standing around the realm map were his parents and the Red and White monarchs. Their retainers were at their business.

"Your Majesties."

The king caught sight of him. "Rowan, you have returned at last!" He'd never seen his father so animated. "I was worried."

Rowan approached, and bowed to the fellow monarchs. Queen Millesant Remont, also known as the White Queen, and Queen Taira Kameko, also known as the Red Queen, gathered with their kings. Unlike in other monarchies, it was the Three Queens who held sway. The women of Brigantia issued the commands and strategies that everyone followed, while their husbands supported and led their armies in battle. That is, if his mother approved.

Compliments flowed and fawning over his handsome armor continued. The other kings nodded at his father, displaying their strong admiration. Rowan dared hope he had their support.

His mother commanded their attention. "Rowan, where is my suit of armor?"

Rowan had forgotten about his mother's edict with everything that had occurred during their journey to and from Tidaholm. Everything that had happened in the land of the Spinner Queen.

"Mother—"

"I asked you a question!" Her voice was shrill. Before Rowan could respond, she said, "That girl has it, doesn't she?"

"If you mean Faith, Mother, yes, she does."

"Bring her here!" The queen slammed her fists on the map, disrupting the stationary figures there. "She will turn the armor over to me or I'll have her head!"

Rowan had had enough. "You will do no such thing, Mother!"

All the attention was on him now, yet no one dared speak. The only one who seemed amused was his father. His mother, however, appeared on the verge of combusting.

"How dare you, insolent boy!" The queen strode around the table until she was facing him, so close that Rowan caught the scent of the familiar perfume that once had brought him comfort as a young lad. He had always laughed when his mother was going about in one of her fits of temper because she never directed it at him. How things had changed.

"Mother, the Spinner Queen said—"

"I don't give a rat's damn what the Spinner Queen said. Bring me that armor or—"

His father spoke up. "My dear."

"Silence!"

"No."

Rowan's jaw dropped in disbelief. He couldn't recall a time when his father had defied his mother. The other monarchs realized this was not the best place to be. His mother simmered with rage, but his father held her gaze, and the rest left the room, along with all their retainers.

"So, you both betray me? Disrespect me?" Her voice was deadly soft.

"No," his father replied, "but let's hear Rowan out."

"Mother," Rowan said, "please."

She turned back to him, and he could see she'd calmed somewhat. Before she could change her mind, Rowan told her of everything that had occurred. The attacks they'd suffered. The creation of the armor. Their encounters with Serval and the battle that even now raged against the harpies to protect Tidaholm.

"Mother," Rowan said, "I believe Faith was called to protect us and all Brigantia. She has the power our enemies seek. That she will use that power to fight against them is quite admirable, don't you think?"

Rowan waited. He could see his mother mulling things over.

"All right," she stated, "but remember, if she deceives us, I'll punish her severely."

"She won't," Rowan said. "I trust her."

"You should trust no one." She walked back around to her former place at the table. "Tell the others they may return. Honestly, a petty squabble and they run with their tails between their legs." The queen examined the map as if nothing had occurred.

"Rowan," his father said. "Have something to eat and rest. In the morning, we'll discuss the events in the land."

The queen glanced up. "Hmm." Which Rowan could only assume meant she agreed.

Although he wanted to do both, including taking a long hot bath, Rowan stated, "I'd prefer to stay. I need to know what's happening now."

"Always the warrior." His father patted him on the shoulder, surprising him. "My dear, do you agree?"

The queen 'hmmd' again, agreeing.

The other monarchs returned, gathering around the table. Their retainers were back about their business.

"As we discussed," his mother said, "there have been reports of dark fey finding their way into our land and there has been an illness among our peoples."

The White Queen spoke. "I am able to have more supplies brought for your and the Red Queen's citizens." The White Queen was a beautiful young woman with pale skin and delicate features, which were in direct contrast to her fiery red hair and green eyes. Her voice was soft, yet powerful.

"We appreciate your generosity," Rowan said.

She blushed and inclined her head.

"Indeed," his mother said, more like an afterthought.

"Before we continue…" said the Red Queen. She was the White Queen's opposite in many ways. She wore her dark hair straight down her back. Her angular eyes were as dark and piercing as the strength in her voice. She wore colorful robes that swathed her tall, supple frame. Of course, even she agreed with Rowan's mother. "What news do you bring us, Prince Rowan? What of this armor?"

Rowan didn't want to repeat himself, but he had no choice. He could see his mother's annoyance, but she didn't protest. Perhaps she knew how important this was.

The White Queen's voice trembled when he'd finished. "Harpies. They are fearsome creatures."

"I have no fear of them," his mother said. "With this armor, my son will lead my army into battle."

No one protested, although Rowan wished someone would. It was supposed to be his father who led the army, but Rowan figured the queen had no confidence in the man and, as usual, his father didn't protest. It angered Rowan somewhat that his father was sending him to face their enemies. He accepted the challenge, but already felt the weight of Brigantia's hopes. Then he realized Faith would be there with him. It relieved him to know he had one ally he could trust.

"This all started at the Sea of Tears," the queen revealed. "But we must discover how else they are entering. Taira, have they been coming from the east caves near your borders?"

"Yes, Your Majesty." The Red Queen reached across the map and moved some figures to a certain spot and spread them into a semicircle. "My Chessmen positioned themselves across the hills amid a cave network. Somehow, they still get past them."

"And Millesant, you have seen no trace of dark fey?"

"If they have breached my borders, they are keeping themselves well hidden."

"Your pardon, Queen Millesant," Rowan said. "Perhaps the mountain cold is too intense for them. You may wish to place guards throughout your palace. Seek less-frequented locations. They thrive in the darkness. I would wager any amount that's where they are."

The White Queen drew in a breath and covered her mouth with her hands. She looked at her king and a silent message passed between them. "We will take heed of your advice, Your Highness."

"We don't have enough soldiers to patrol the entire seashore," his mother said. "We need to lure them out."

A sense of dread swelled in Rowan's chest.

"Rowan," his mother said. "You said it's the girl they want?"

Biting back a caustic remark, Rowan said, "Yes, they want *Faith*." Placing emphasis on her name.

"Is it fair to be speaking about her when she's not present?" the White Queen asked.

"I will escort her here tomorrow, Mother. I'm sure she will agree to this plan." Which made Rowan's stomach lurch. Faith would agree, but he hated the idea of using her to draw out the minions of the Rot.

"She won't have a choice." His mother straightened away from the map. "The hour is late, and we will reconvene tomorrow."

Rowan held his tongue. Instead, he bowed to their guests. "Good night, majesties. May your sleep be peaceful." He strode from the room. He needed to be out of his mother's presence.

CHAPTER TWENTY

The commotion outside his room didn't surprise Rowan, given the sudden fierce strikes against his door. "Prince Rowan!"

Rowan pushed himself up and swung his legs off the bed. "Yes, enter."

Several servants piled in. One was a member of his mother's guard. He bowed low at the waist. "Your Highness, the queen has ordered us to prepare you to meet in the war room."

"Yes, of course." Rowan waved them all away. *What's happened now?*

The servants helped him wash and assisted him in putting on his armor. Once done, Rowan headed toward the war room.

The scene inside was like that of the previous night, but the White Queen sat while the King stood beside her, holding her hand for comfort. She was sipping from a goblet and one of her ladies was fanning her.

His mother and the Red Queen were in their places. What drew his attention was the young courier standing before them, his appearance marred by the journey's toll. His clothes were in disarray, stained with blood, and his face was etched with a look of sheer terror and incredulity. He had traversed great distances to deliver news that was likely as grim as his current state. "What has happened?" Rowan asked his mother.

"The White Queen's kingdom is under siege." She nodded at the young man. "Continue your report!"

In a trembling voice, the young man confessed that strange creatures had materialized in the castle within a day of the White Queen and King's departure. While the entities did not physically harm anyone, their mere existence cast a pall of gloom over anyone nearby. Those usually brimming with joy found themselves lost in a fog of sadness or despair, and the calmest of spirits were inexplicably driven to fury. The castle's denizens wandered its halls in a state of dejection, shunning shadowed nooks and shedding tears upon their pillows. A pervasive dread lingered that overwhelming grief might drive some to the brink of self-harm. And the White Queen wept for her people.

"We should go back." The White Queen wiped her tears away with a white-gloved hand.

"You can't," Rowan said. "They will take you."

"I cannot abandon my people." The White Queen's voice grew stronger.

"Your Majesty, with all due respect, I am not saying you should, but if you return, you will fall to this attack." And that's just what it was. Without using blades or magic, the Rot had taken the White Queen's kingdom.

"This is insane!" His mother slammed a fist on the table. "How can…*emotions* bring down an entire kingdom? It seems to me nothing but cowardice!"

"Mother!" Rowan said, ignoring protocol.

The White Queen stood. Through trembling lips she said, "I'll not stay here while my people suffer, Belladonna."

Rowan had never heard any of them call his mother by her first name. The Queen of Hearts' face muscles tightened. "Go back to your kingdom." His mother dropped her gaze and gave a dismissive wave of her hand. "Send word when your people find their courage again." She did not say it in an encouraging tone.

Rowan couldn't stand by and let this continue. "Mother, you don't understand. This evil feeds on fear and sorrow, draining kind-hearted individuals, or it provokes anger and intensifies it. I have felt its influence."

"You are not saying –" his mother's tone held a warning, "– that my son is a coward?"

"My dear," his father began, "if he were a coward—"

"I did not ask for your opinion." His mother kept her gaze on Rowan. "Make yourself useful. Retrieve the girl. Tell her what is expected of her."

Rowan spared a glance at his father. His expression matched his mother's. Yet he bit his tongue and turned to the White Queen. "Majesties, may I escort you out?"

"Of course."

Out of hearing range, Rowan pleaded, "Please. Both of you take care when you return."

The king and queen exchanged a knowing look. "And you take care of Lady Faith." The queen smiled, and Rowan felt his face warm. "Let your mother know we will send word of the situation as soon as possible."

"I will. Safe travels."

Silently, he wished them well. They would need their strength once they returned to where the Rot was holding their kingdom hostage. For now, Rowan had to see Faith. He called a nearby servant and commanded them to go to the stables and have Epione ready for travel.

As he strode through the palace, he contemplated not telling Faith what the queen wanted. Then Rowan shook his head. No, he would not keep things from her anymore. Whatever she decided, he'd support.

★　★　★

The things that had attacked him didn't appear. But the air and surroundings still sent shudders through him. Rowan recalled when all the bright colors, quirky animals, and nonsense annoyed him. He longed for Brigantia to return to its former state. Not the stagnating, murky place he rode through now. Rowan made a silent promise to embrace his homeland.

"Your Highness!"

He'd gotten lost in his thoughts. But his concern was short-lived when he saw who was coming down the path toward him. "Faith!"

"Greetings again." Her smile, even in the dim light, brightened the atmosphere.

"How is your father?"

Her expression dropped a little. "He's doing as well as possible. They infected the food and water with Rot. He said the White Queen brought provisions."

"Not enough to feed both kingdoms." Rowan looked around.

"The farmers and elder citizens are helping each other," Faith continued. "Some have recommended eating salted foods only since they harm fey and negate their magic."

"But it will also cause intense thirst."

"Yes," Faith said. "People have been boiling water, of course." She smiled. "Father must have his tea, so it works well."

"Of course." Rowan managed a slight smile. "We have much to discuss. Were you going to the palace?"

"Yes."

"Then we'd best be off."

Rowan said nothing while they rode. He wanted to be facing her when he told her of his mother's plan. It was dark when they arrived back at the palace. Rowan suddenly felt exhausted. As he dismounted, he saw Faith yawn.

"Sleepy?"

"Yes," Faith said, "how unusual."

"I wasn't until a few moments ago."

"It's the Rot," Faith said.

"Damn it all," Rowan muttered. There would be no convincing his mother now. "Before we go in, there is something we need to talk about." Rowan told her about his mother's plan to have her lure the Rot into a trap. He hid nothing from her and looked her straight in the eyes the whole time he spoke.

When he finished speaking, he noticed Faith was biting her lower lip. Rowan waited for her to respond.

"All right," Faith said. "Then that is what we will do."

Rowan released his breath; his shoulders fell. He'd hoped she would refuse.

"Rowan." She brushed her fingers across his left cheek. "Don't worry."

"Of course I'll worry," Rowan grumbled.

The palace denizens looked at them with renewed awe. This was their first time seeing them together, both in armor.

"I've never been in this part of the palace," Faith commented.

"You have, remember?"

"I have?"

"Do you recall, you snuck in via the pantry window and—"

"Yes, I recall now." Faith smiled. "Yet you still sneaked out of the palace."

"Which wasn't easy." Rowan returned the grin. "We visited the Caterpillar…when she was the Caterpillar."

"I hope she is doing well." Faith's expression fell. "Maybe we should have visited her before—"

"I believe she is," Rowan said. "She is a fey being and resilient."

As they entered the war room, the miasma affected everyone present. "Mother?"

She and his father were sitting in chairs on one side of the table while the Red Queen and her husband sat across from them. His mother straightened in her chair and leaned over the map table. "You brought her."

"Mother, this is the Rot, stealing our vitality."

"We thought as much." The queen turned her gaze to Faith. "Did the prince tell you what we command of you?"

Rowan flinched. *We?*

But Faith just said, "Yes, Your Majesty."

"Mother, the White Queen wanted me to tell you she will send word when she discovers how her kingdom is faring."

"Very well." He'd not seen his mother this lethargic in, well, ever. But she seemed to fight it. His father slumped in his chair dozing. Just as well.

"I beg your pardon, Your Majesty." Faith spoke into the lengthening silence. "How shall I proceed?"

Annoyance flashed in the queen's gaze at the question. "We need to address this lethargy," she said, straightening and stretching. Her gaze went from Rowan back to Faith. "Why aren't both of you ready to faint?"

Rowan exchanged a look with Faith. "It has affected us," Rowan said, "but I believe this armor may provide some protection." He hadn't wanted to draw attention to the armor again.

"Perhaps we should ask Jade?"

"The Caterpillar?" the queen said.

His father regained consciousness and agreed, "Yes, the Caterpillar is a good idea."

"There is nothing more to do until we have more information or receive word from the White Queen," the queen continued. "Take some soldiers with you. How do the commoners say it? Watch your back, at the very least."

"Yes, Your Majesty." Rowan bowed, and Faith followed suit. "By your leave."

"And take care!" It was his father, much to Rowan's shock.

Rowan turned back to him. There was a light in his father's eyes, something he'd not seen before, and Rowan couldn't help but feel proud. "We will, Father."

★   ★   ★

The accompanying soldiers appeared unaffected by the miasma. Still, they rode along in the darkness. It was an unpleasant ride. No wildlife sounds, no murmuring flowers, not even insects were present. The lanterns that the soldiers carried barely illuminated their surroundings, no matter how brightly they burned.

However, as they got closer to the Grotto, the soft green glow spilled from within, and the plants grew as normal, although the flowers were silent. There was also wildlife gathered in this obviously safe space.

"She's fighting it," Faith said.

"Stay here," Rowan ordered the guards, and he followed Faith.

The light filled them with strength. They breathed in the scents of health and life until the fog cleared. Jade sat, arms and legs crossed, her eyes closed, her body bathed in that ethereal light.

The two continued with caution. Both said nothing. And they waited.

Jade's eyes snapped open, but her gaze was far away. She opened her arms wide. Rustling showed approaching animals, but plants sprouted near the mushroom. They were of different types. Some were familiar to Rowan, but most were not. Obviously, Jade had called them forth. Rowan looked at Faith but noticed she had the same faraway look as Jade. Rowan was about to speak but thought better of it when Faith walked forward.

She halted right before the mushroom and laid her hand on it.

The light flowed from Jade and up Faith's arms to fill her entire body. At first Faith stood calm and still. Then she gasped and snatched her hand back. The light drained from her body and returned to Jade, who folded her arms back again and returned to sleep.

"Faith?" Rowan couldn't stay silent any longer.

"I'm all right," she said. "We need to gather these herbs. Jade says they may help with the illnesses."

"What are they? What should we do with them?"

"Jade told me, however," she said with a perplexed expression, "there are certain ways to prepare the herbs. This is not my affinity."

"What do you mean? You're a witch, correct?"

"Yes." Faith shook her head in contrast to her response. "But…" She didn't speak for a few moments as she gathered her thoughts. "The Vine grants the Gift. You have witchcraft, sorcery, necromancy, and alchemy. And perhaps many others we haven't discovered yet."

This was all news to him. Rowan had never heard her speak of such things before. Did this happen because of her connection with Jade?

"But some with the Gift are also given a power that is unique to them," Faith went on. "For example, some witches have an affinity for herb or hearth lore. Often, they take different names like an herbalist or hearth witch. If I had that affinity, I could, in fact, change the food we're eating into something else or remove the poisons."

Rowan was understanding now. He waited for her to continue.

Faith sighed in frustration. "If that fails, you can prepare these herbs to help."

Rowan took her hands and squeezed. "Don't worry, I have the utmost confidence. And of course, I'll be here to help you."

She gave a fleeting smile. "Jade also gave me a vision of where the Rot may strike next, but..."

"What?"

"Jade wasn't certain if the Rot was trying to deceive us, but I sensed its influence," Faith said. "I'm sorry we can't predict where the Rot will encroach next."

"No," Rowan said, "don't apologize. You have given so much already and now you're willing to—"

Rowan halted. There was a sudden tightness in his chest. It was Faith who squeezed his hands then. "Come on now. We have work to do."

CHAPTER TWENTY-ONE

Faith, don't be afraid.

I am not afraid.

As the light traveled over her body, a warmth filled Faith, chasing away her tiredness. It was like when she'd spoken to Jade when she entered the chrysalis at Tidaholm. The Grotto faded into the light, and Faith was standing amid the, well, *green.*

It remained among the most beautiful things Faith had ever seen.

But there was also the sense of Jade fighting against the Rot.

When we spoke last, it had consumed me.

Are you well? What may I do?

I am…keeping it at bay.

Where is it?

Eastward, toward the Red Queen and the Sea of Tears, just a hairbreadth away.

Faith discovered Jade's truth as visions flashed around her. They were brief, and Faith realized Jade didn't want to draw too much attention to herself. Not that the Rot wasn't already aware of her presence.

It cannot be everywhere. It would spread too thin. Listen. Feel.

Faith wasn't certain at first of Jade's meaning. She tried her best to do what Jade had bidden. She went silent, steadied her breathing, and closed her eyes. The veils appeared before her, moving back and forth. They encircled her, their movements resembling a dance that allowed her glimpses into other places. Faith couldn't glean anything from the visions, except that the Rot was indeed present in Brigantia, everywhere, yet distant from everything. Faith couldn't comprehend why she felt that way.

She sensed that the Rot had not finished with her.

Look to the earth for the answer. I will show you.

In the next vision, the world around Faith blurred and shimmered with an ethereal light. Slowly, the ground beneath her feet began to glow, casting an otherworldly aura. The soil seemed to pulse with a life of its own.

As if guided by unseen hands, the earth parted, revealing an underground network of glowing roots and tendrils. The plants glistened with a soft, bioluminescent glow, weaving an intricate tapestry of nature's secrets.

Faith watched in awe as the roots absorbed the mystical energy from the soil, their strength growing with each passing moment. Slowly but surely, the plants began their ascent. They spiraled and twisted, drawn upwards by an invisible force, bursting through the surface in a riot of colors and scents. The air was filled with a delicate fragrance, and the plants seemed to hum with the vibration of life itself.

In that moment, Faith felt connected to the very heart of the Vine. It was a vision of pure wonder, a glimpse into the mysteries that lay hidden beneath the surface.

Faith's gaze fell upon cocklebur, its spiny pods shining brightly. Next, she saw eyebright, its delicate flowers glowing softly. Sandalwood rose with a graceful elegance, and sweetgrass released a gentle, soothing fragrance into the air.

Faith felt a profound connection to the plants and their healing properties. It was as if she could sense their energy and purpose, guided by Jade's wisdom and the magic that flowed through the very earth beneath her.

Jade named a few other plants that were familiar to Faith. She recognized that some were used in making tea. While Faith had a bit of knowledge about medicinal herbs, she hadn't been formally trained in their uses. She pondered this and thought, perhaps there would be more information in the Burrow or the palace library.

Faith continued to focus on the growing herbs, so much so that she didn't notice a dark shape rising inside a veil to her right until it lunged, but the veil stopped it. Faith was shocked enough to be pushed from within the light.

Rowan approached, worried and inquiring. Faith tried to explain about the plants and why she was uncertain what to do with them. But they needed to gather herbs and return to the palace.

"How should we do this? I can cut them with my sword?" Rowan suggested.

"A dagger would be quicker. Maybe one of the soldiers has one?"

Rowan nodded and walked from the Grotto. When he returned, he said, "The guards are very nervous. I suppose I can't blame them. They claim that things have attempted to attack." Rowan had gathered two daggers.

"Let's be quick about this," Faith said.

Movement within the armor was easy, so they had little trouble harvesting the herbs. That wasn't the issue. "I have a thought." Faith continued to work. "Despite my limited experience, there are books that can help us prepare the herbs. There could be some in the palace library or the Burrow."

"We should finish quickly and return to the palace. We shouldn't tarry outside any longer than needed."

"Agreed," Faith said.

They continued their work. Faith couldn't help but glance at Jade every so often, who remained unmoving. After finishing, they carried the bundles to where the soldiers and mounts awaited, then returned to the palace.

★   ★   ★

When they arrived, a frantic servant girl rushed toward them.

"Your Highness, your pardon, but the queen has fallen ill!"

Rowan looked at her briefly and broke into a run.

"Take the herbs to the kitchens." Faith hoped they would listen to her and hastened to follow Rowan. She had to rush to keep up with him as they ran to the royal chambers. Rowan didn't slow until they arrived. The two guards didn't hesitate, and one opened the door. As Faith went to step forward, one of the guards blocked her. "No commoners!"

"Let her in, damn it all!" Rowan commanded.

The guard moved aside. Faith stepped inside and the guard closed the door. She didn't approach the bed, allowing Rowan to see his mother. They hadn't been gone that long. What had happened?

"Mother?" Rowan said. The queen didn't respond.

The queen was lying still. Her once smooth and glowing skin now showed signs of aging, with deep lines around her eyes and mouth. It was as though she'd neglected her daily regimens, and time had caught up with her. The queen's eyes were closed, and Faith thought she was sleeping. Rowan approached the bed. Faith could tell Rowan didn't want to wake her, but she sensed his need for her to know he had returned. "Mother?" He laid his hands over one of hers. She didn't stir.

"Faith." She heard the catch in Rowan's voice. "Would you ask the guard where my father is?"

"Of course." Faith opened the doors, and the guards stood to attention, remaining even after recognizing her.

"Ro— His Highness wants to know where the king is?"

"The war room, milady."

Rowan heard them. With much hesitation, he moved away from his mother's bed. "Follow me," he said.

They ventured farther into the palace, exploring new sections unknown to Faith. She knew about the war room but was unsure what it looked like. When they arrived, Faith's surprise grew as she saw several people slumped over chairs or curled up asleep on the floor. The Red Queen sat with her head leaning over the back of her chair. The Red King was not present. Only the King of Hearts was awake and active.

"Rowan, Lady Faith!" The king grinned and approached Rowan with his arms wide and embraced his son. "I am so glad you've returned. I was beside myself."

"Father," Rowan said, "what happened to Mother?"

Was that a brief look of annoyance?

"I'm sorry, son," he said. "We can't do anything for her. She and the Red Queen—" he nodded once at the Red Queen's slumped form, "—succumbed to the miasma."

"And you?" Rowan asked.

"I'm uncertain," the king said. "I just felt better."

Faith examined the table in the room, which featured a map of Brigantia. Someone had placed tiny figures in different areas, most of which were at the borders of the White Queen's kingdom.

"Where is the Red King?" Rowan asked.

"I don't know," the king said. "Did the Caterpillar have answers?" He directed the question at Faith.

"Yes, Your Majesty." Faith thought it was strange how he didn't know where the Red King was.

"Oh." The king waved her words away. "There's no need for an honorific. Just a simple yes or no will suffice. Although if you don't feel comfortable, you can use sir."

"Well..." Faith was uncomfortable. She felt distant from the king, but she didn't want to upset him. "All right, sir."

"Splendid!" the king said. "What have you to report?"

Rowan positioned himself so the king's attention was on him. Faith tried not to sigh aloud with relief. She didn't know why, but the king made her wary.

"Jade gave us medicinal herbs requiring specific preparation," Rowan explained. "Faith and I will need to use the library to determine how. After completing that, Faith can produce more of what we require."

"Hmm," the king said. "Very well. You two be at it."

"Yes, Father." Rowan turned to Faith, held out his hand, and she took it.

"Oh, Rowan?" the king said.

Rowan turned back toward his father.

"A moment alone with you, please?" the king asked.

Now Faith was suspicious. It didn't seem the Rot had taken hold of him, but why was he no longer victim to the miasma? Rowan glanced at Faith again.

"I'll wait outside," she said.

It was obvious that Rowan was not happy with this secretive meeting. Faith exited the room and proceeded down the hall. Despite her desire to eavesdrop, she prioritized respect.

Rowan came bursting out of the room, his stride angry and his fists tight at his side.

"Rowan?"

He stopped, seeming to notice her for the first time.

"Are you all right?" Had the king accosted him somehow?

"Yes, he just..." Rowan began, "...judged on a certain subject."

"Can you tell me?" It wasn't hard to figure out that it had been about her.

"I..." Rowan sighed.

"Listen, if it's difficult to do so right now, I can wait until you're ready."

His expression was one of profound relief. "Thank you." He brushed his fingers down her cheek.

They studied in the library all night and called servants to carry messages to the kitchens. Faith didn't mention the private conference. She would keep her word to wait for Rowan to find the strength to tell her. For now, they concentrated on their task.

Before too long, a multitude of books was stacked between them on the table. Some were brief, others were extensive and detailed. They found what they needed with the help of spells in books.

"Here." Faith gestured to a drawing. "Put the cocklebur in a sachet to ward off hexes. It is also a deterrent against goblins."

"Can you make enough for our entire army?"

"I can't promise, but I'll try."

"Brewing eyebright in tea would make it easier to distribute," Rowan said. "It makes more sense. It's used to clear the mind and deter memory loss."

"Is there anything else besides that for the miasma?"

Faith pulled another book over. "For protection and healing, burn sandalwood." As she read further, Faith furrowed her brow. "But it must be with certain types of spells." Spells she didn't know. "Finding the spells should allow me to cast them, but no guarantees." She never had to cast spells.

"The sweetgrass is to summon good spirits." Rowan traced a finger down as he read. "I suppose we can use those too."

As they continued with their research, Faith noticed something in one of the books that made her chuckle. Rowan looked up from his book.

"What?"

"I found you." Faith grinned.

"Pardon?"

"The rowan."

"Oh!" Rowan ducked his head down. "Yes."

"It suits you," Faith said with all her admiration. "It's for protection."

Rowan's expression softened as he smiled, then lowered his head back into the book, but not before Faith saw his flush. They continued in companionable silence, except when Rowan was giving instructions to the servants. After finishing and gathering all the information they needed, they both walked down to the palace kitchens.

The cooks had already begun to hang and dry the herbs. Faith and Rowan were relieved to find some already in the kitchen. There was not enough for the entire kingdom, so Faith took a seat at one of four chopping blocks. "Your Highness, would you bring me a stalk of each herb, please?" Faith asked.

She half expected him to say she could dispense with the honorific like the king had, but Faith realized Rowan knew how uncomfortable it made her to address him with familiarity around the servants and soldiers. Faith started working once she had what she needed. It was perhaps not a simple thing, but with one of the herbs in her grasp, she was able to cause multiple plants to grow from the original, even without water or dirt. Like she'd told Rowan before, she couldn't change one *organik* thing to another, but she could make *facsimilia* of them.

It took hours. Somewhere in the palace, a clock struck two in the morning. She was on the verge of dozing off, unrelated to the miasma. She noticed Rowan was setting up a tea service, which Faith figured was for the queen. Faith slid from her seat and asked for a service herself. To her knowledge, the Red Queen and her servants remained in the war room. She informed Rowan of her plans.

He nodded and Faith carried the tea service back upstairs. On entering the room, she noticed the king was gone. The Red Queen sat in her chair as the servants lay scattered around the room. Faith assumed the King of Hearts went to see his queen.

Faith approached the Red Queen with the tea service in hand and set it down on the floor. "Your Majesty, can you hear me?"

To Faith's relief, she stirred. The Red Queen lifted her head and raised her hand to her face. Her eyes opened. "Who?"

"Your Majesty," Faith said, "it is Faith Carter."

She blinked several times and turned her head to look at Faith. Her eyes were unfocused. "The Mad Hatter?"

Faith didn't respond. She wasn't fond of that description. Her father was eccentric, but he wasn't *mad*. Faith poured the tea. "Here, drink this."

The Red Queen reached out with trembling hands. Faith guided the cup to her lips. "Will this make me better?"

"It should," Faith said. "Drink it all down."

It was rough going and some of it spilled down the queen's chin, but she emptied the cup. "Your Majesty, where is your king?"

"I...I don't know."

Not a good omen. "Come, I'll escort you to your room."

The Red Queen seemed to regain her wits. She allowed Faith to help her to her feet. Faith walked her to her guest quarters. The bed remained made. "Where is Percival?"

"I'll find him." Faith put her to bed. Knowing she was breaking all manner of protocols, Faith removed the queen's slippers and pulled back the blankets. She wished to assist the queen with her robe but it was troublesome. Besides, the queen appeared to be asleep again. One last thing Faith did was remove the jewel-encrusted combs that held her hair in silken folds and put them in the drawer of her nightstand. No one would steal them, but the queen would feel more comfortable.

Faith left a lamp burning in case the queen woke up later. She yawned as she left the room. She couldn't recall the last time she'd slept. She went in search of Rowan and found him in his mother's bedroom, trying to coax her to drink tea. Faith rapped on the doorframe with her knuckles.

Rowan looked up at her, defeated. "I can't keep her awake long enough to drink the tea."

"Let's try a different approach," Faith said, disregarding protocol as she climbed onto the bed and crawled toward the queen. Faith sat and as gently as she could drew the queen's head up and tipped it back, causing her lips to part.

Faith saw the queen vulnerable for the first time. Gone was the hot-blooded woman named for a poisonous flower. The one who would cry "Off with their heads!" at the slightest perceived insult.

"Use the spoon," Faith instructed. "You'll be able to put the tea down her throat."

Rowan released his breath and smiled. They spent time, Faith holding the queen's head and Rowan spooning the tea into her mouth. Faith then placed the queen's head on the pillow and moved to the edge of the bed, touching the floor with her feet. Rowan was there, and he caught her in a tight embrace. "Thank you."

When Rowan drew back, he held Faith at arm's length. "You should get some rest. We don't know what tomorrow will bring."

"I believe you mean today," Faith said. "But I can't just yet. The Red King is missing."

Rowan frowned. "When did we see him last? In the war room?"

"When I was helping the Red Queen to bed, she asked, *where is Percival?*"

Rowan released a deep breath and rubbed his eyes with his thumb and index finger. "Perfect timing for him to wander away. Let's get whoever we can to search for him."

Some servants had recovered and joined the search. Faith and Rowan searched together. When they asked about his recent sighting, everyone answered unanimously: the war room.

"I'll ask my father," Rowan said. "If he's still there. It's late and he may have retired to…other chambers."

"I'll return to the kitchen," Faith said.

"Are you sure you're all right using your Gift?" Rowan was obviously worried she would overexert herself.

"To be honest…" Faith could feel a tiny spark of her Gift remaining. She would need food and rest to recover. "I would like to try. I don't believe I'll be able to sleep with everything that's going on."

"All right." He was still wary. "I'll meet you there."

Faith returned to the kitchen. She asked the cook for something to eat and was given a few slices of toasted dark bread and honey-butter and a cup of medicinal tea, although she didn't feel the need, but why not be cautious? It helped. The spark became glowing embers. As she worked, she noticed a few of the maids carrying the completed, tied bundles off somewhere. She was told that they were taking the bundles to hang in the cellars.

Faith never ventured into that section of the palace, where provisions of food and wine were stored. A sense of comfort greeted her as she entered the grand chamber, noticing the staircase adorned with glowing lanterns. The sight was reassuringly ordinary: crates stacked to the brim and dried meats suspended from the wooden beams above. To her left stood a door, and to her right, a corridor bathed in light beckoned. After seizing a lantern from its hook, Faith proceeded down the illuminated path.

Upon entering the next chamber, Faith stifled a scream. At the heart of the room, encircled by barrels and glass vessels, stood a sinister tree, its thorns twisted into a malevolent tangle. Ensnared within this thorny prison was the Red King. His visage was etched with an expression of utter surprise and agony.

CHAPTER TWENTY-TWO

In that peculiar moment, Faith's instincts screamed for her to cry out, to escape the confines of the cellar, yet she was rooted to the spot, paralyzed by the scene before her. Clutching the lantern, her hand quivered uncontrollably as she gazed upon the Red King. Time seemed to stretch into eternity as Faith stood there, transfixed by the ghastly tableau, her voice lost to the silence.

The Red King's left eye moved and focused on Faith. He was still alive.

Faith's silence shattered into a piercing scream. The lantern slipped from her grasp, tumbling to the ground without breaking, its light throwing bizarre shadows across the walls. Despite the eerie scene, Faith stepped forward, closing the distance between herself and the figure ensnared in thorns. With a deep breath, she steeled herself and extended her hand toward the sharp brambles.

"Faith!"

Faith's gasp was sharp, a reflex to the sudden appearance of Rowan, who emerged with a cadre of servants. Their voices rose in a cacophony of shock, some screaming, others hurling exclamations and invoking prayers into the tense air of the cellar.

Rowan shouted, "Get out! All of you out! And say nothing of this!"

The servants wasted no time making themselves scarce.

"Faith, get away!"

"No!" Faith said. "He's still alive."

"Dear gods!" Rowan said.

"I'm going to free him."

"Take care!" Rowan needn't have warned her.

Now they would see how powerful the armor was. As she called upon her Gift, the thorns grew unexpectedly. They would have pierced her hands had it not been for her finger gauntlets.

"No!" Rowan drew his sword.

"Rowan I'm all right." Faith assured him. "Let me concentrate." Faith summoned her power once more. The thorns resisted but couldn't stop her from channeling her Gift from the roots to the very ends. Though the spark of her power waned, she pressed on, her resolve unyielding even as nausea took hold, and her head throbbed with intensity. Her perseverance bore fruit. The thorns withered, their substance turning to ash, and finally, they disintegrated into nothingness.

The Red King's body fell forward and would have knocked Faith to the floor if Rowan hadn't been there and pulled her away.

"Faith?" Faith heard the pain in Rowan's voice. She wanted to tell him she was all right but couldn't. Rowan cradling her head in his lap was the last thing she saw.

★ ★ ★

A scream tore Faith from sleep as dawn's gray light spilled through the window, casting a pallid glow over the bedroom to which she had been whisked away. This was a scream laced with raw anguish. It resonated, relentless and demanding, intertwined with a voice that was unmistakably familiar to Faith – a voice that cried out for truth amid the torment.

The Red King is dead. Long live the Red Queen.

Faith listened to other voices attempting to console the Red Queen, but it was clear that she rejected their efforts. Faith thought of her father, whom she'd not seen since coming to the palace. Certainly, Minerva was with him, but had they gotten the medicinal tea to her household?

Faith had to know. But she wasn't certain she could rise. She noticed she was out of her armor. Now just who had undressed her?

She was relieved to see her armor was hung up on the other side of the room.

Faith blew out a breath. She knew the Red Queen had sons, but as Rowan had said before, they weren't of age yet to do much of anything.

"To lose your husband at such a young age," Faith said aloud.

There was silence in the hallway now. Faith's exhaustion weighed heavily on her, but as she finally drifted into slumber, a tickling sensation invaded her nose, resulting in an uncontrollable sneeze. When she opened her eyes, she saw a familiar cloud of smoke forming over her.

"Cheshire?"

The reconstruction was a slow, almost laborious process. The figure that Faith knew so well took its time to materialize, with limbs and features hesitantly seeking their rightful places. Faith mustered the strength to push herself upright, her gaze fixed on the gradually forming silhouette. "Cheshire?" she said again.

For a fleeting moment, the smoke coalesced into a ghastly form, a jumble of contorted limbs. Faith's scream pierced the air as the abomination collapsed onto her, revealing itself to be Cheshire. The grim realization dawned on Faith when she noticed the dried blood clumping his fur. Lifting him gently onto her lap confirmed her fears; his pained cry betrayed the hidden puncture wounds beneath the matted patches. "Dear Vine!" Faith stroked his furry head. "Somebody help!"

Her door came open and Faith was relieved to see Rowan standing on the threshold. "Faith?" His gaze fell on Cheshire.

"What in the nether hells—?"

Rowan turned away and began yelling out commands to unseen servants. Someone brought in a pitcher of warm water, a bowl, and some soft cloths. Faith didn't recall who they might have been and didn't care. The only person she was glad to see was Rowan. He poured the warm water into the bowl and dipped in the cloth, which he handed to Faith. There, with Cheshire sprawled on her lap, Faith bathed him.

Rowan sat in a nearby chair. Someone else entered the room. Faith ignored them even when Rowan had a whispered conversation with them. At one point, Rowan gave her another cloth and Faith continued. When she finished, Faith wrapped Cheshire in her own blanket.

"Faith?"

Hearing her name, Faith awoke and saw that Cheshire was conscious and gave her a rather frightening, feline smile.

"Are you all right?" Faith saw Rowan out of the corner of her eye. He'd fallen asleep in the chair but awoke, rubbing his eyes and stretching. Faith wondered when was the last time Rowan had slept. He carried the chair over next to the bed and began scratching Cheshire behind the ears.

"How are you feeling?" Faith asked. "You must stop scaring me like that!"

"My apologies."

"Where have you been all this time?"

"I went to spy in the White Queen's kingdom. I figured I should after she returned home."

"You should have said something," Rowan admonished him.

"Then, my dear prince, it wouldn't be spying."

"This is nothing to jest about," Faith scolded. "You must tell us everything. It is important with everything that is going on."

"Yes, of course." Cheshire was repentant.

"What happened to you? You didn't face the Rot again, did you?"

"Not by choice," Cheshire said. "It tried to stop me from coming here."

"I saw something…" Faith began.

Cheshire was silent for a moment, then he said in as serious a voice as she had ever heard him use, "I'm sorry about that. What you saw was my body being pulled back and forth between the veils."

"It must have been horrible." Faith scratched him under his chin.

"It was necessary. I had to get home. There are things you both need to know."

"What did you find out?" Rowan asked.

"The miasma has taken over much of the kingdom," Cheshire said. "It tried with the White Queen and King when they arrived at the border."

"Oh, no," Faith muttered.

"But they were able to fight its influence and deployed their soldiers. They are on their way here."

Faith didn't know whether to be relieved or not.

"You were correct about the Rot finding its way in through cracks and shadows. Its hold is not as powerful as it may believe. It's the people that give it the ability to enter, but with the queen and king returning, they were a symbol of hope."

"I see why the Rot didn't want you to return," Rowan said.

"Cheshire," Faith said. "Where was it last?"

"You can see where it has spread along the borders between the kingdoms," Cheshire said.

"Cutting us off from one another."

"Is it at our border?" Faith asked.

"Yes," Cheshire said.

"Cheshire, I hate to ask this of you, but would you be able to reach the farmers and all our citizens near the border and have them come here?"

"I will do whatever my Lady Faith and His Highness command."

"Then do this," Faith said. "Tell the people we are coming. They can find medicine for illness. Do not leave anyone behind."

"Should I visit your father?"

"No," Faith said. "Minerva won't be able to move him. I will visit him as we march."

"March?" Rowan said.

"We know if I am near, the Rot will know. This is what the Queen of Hearts wanted. The people can flee while we go forward and face it. If fortune is with us, the White Queen's forces will guard our rear."

"I will visit the White Queen if I can and tell her of our needs."

Faith sighed, tired. She would need her strength. Rowan seemed to notice and stood. "Here, go back to sleep. You both need rest. Cheshire, when you are strong enough, make the journey. We will wait for your return."

Now Cheshire yawned. "Yes, Your Highness."

"I'll let my father know of our plan."

"All right," Faith muttered.

Cheshire curled up on her legs and purred. The sound lulled Faith to sleep.

★   ★   ★

For three days and nights, Faith slumbered, her spirit adrift in a realm of half awareness. During this time, a revelation was bestowed upon her, not through spoken word but through a vision. On the dawn of her awakening, as the veil of sleep thinned, she found herself in that tender moment of pre-dawn lucidity.

Amid this tranquility, a cascade of emerald jewels rained down, heralding the arrival of Jade. Faith's eyes fluttered open, a drowsy smile gracing her lips – a smile she felt more than expressed. Jade drew near, her presence as calm as the forest's whisper.

"Faith, hold fast to your name, to the essence of your being," Jade murmured, her voice a gentle breeze. With a tender kiss from Jade upon Faith's brow, the world bloomed around them. Leaves unfurled, vines spiraled, and sprouts reached out, caressing Faith with a touch as light as a butterfly's wing. Laughter bubbled from Faith's lips, a fleeting joy that soon gave way to a profound sorrow, reminiscent of her entrapment by Serval. Yet, from the depths of despair sprang hope, resilience and a profound connection to the Celestial Vine.

As the Vine wove itself into her being, intertwining with her Gift, Faith understood. In her vision, she extended her hand to the vibrant green life, and with a touch as nurturing as nature itself, she encouraged it to flourish.

★   ★   ★

The time came when Cheshire returned.

Faith, fully recovered, expected to be called to the war room and she was not disappointed. A servant came to the door but before they could say anything, Rowan appeared, dismissing them.

"Cheshire is here."

Faith threw off the blankets and swung her feet over the edge of the bed. It took her a moment to orient herself.

"Are you sure you can manage?" Rowan reached out a tentative hand.

"Yes, just let me get washed and dressed."

He nodded and closed the door.

She would need someone to help her with the armor. Faith forewent asking for help and checked the wardrobe in the room, which, not surprisingly, had a variety of clothes – dresses, trousers, and shirts. Faith guessed Rowan had a hand in the selection. She dressed quickly in a shirt and trousers, feeling a bit naked without a top hat, but it couldn't be helped. She ran a brush through her hair, which she realized she hadn't washed since Tidaholm, and made a noise of exasperation.

"Not much to be done now." If someone was so concerned about her hair – well, they needed to rethink their choices.

She left her bedroom and walked to the war room. It shocked her when she entered and found the Red Queen present. Cheshire was in her lap, and she was scratching him behind the ears. There was a slight smile on her face and Cheshire purred in response. It was said a cat's purr could soothe and since Cheshire was a fey creature perhaps his contentment held an even greater power.

"Ah, Lady Faith," the king greeted her. "I take it you are feeling better?"

"Yes, sir." Faith bowed slightly.

"Cheshire, give your report," the king commanded.

The Red Queen stood and gently set Cheshire down. The

cat vanished and reappeared sitting on the map. "The White Queen and King have been working to keep the Rot at bay. With the information supplied to them, they are also preparing the necessary medicines."

"Yes, yes." The king's tone revealed his annoyance. "What about her soldiers?"

Cheshire lowered his lids, his pupils going wide. "She merely needs the day you plan to attack, although she made no guarantees her soldiers are at your disposal."

"Excellent," the king said more to himself. "We attack tomorrow."

"So soon," the Red Queen said matter-of-factly.

"The sooner we destroy these invaders the better," the king said. "Think of your late royal husband."

"Trust me, Leopold, I am."

If the king was upset by her use of his first name, he made no indication. "Then we will march at dawn. Take this day to prepare yourselves."

★   ★   ★

"Did you ever believe you would lead an army?"

Her Gift at full force and in her armor, Faith rode Argestes down the path to the beach. "To answer your question, never."

Cheshire was curled up on the gryphon's shoulders. Faith was glad, but to be honest, she wasn't in the mood for talking.

Faith found it surprising that the Red Queen rode with them. Her Chess Soldiers, numbering one hundred, came through the Looking Glass. The Red Queen possessed unique armor that astonished Faith. She'd cut her long hair to shoulder length and had powdered her face in white with symbols that Faith didn't know painted on both cheeks. She was grim and determined as she rode, handling her mount with precision.

Their forces remained unchanged, four lines of soldiers, led by Rowan, the King of Hearts, and the Red Queen.

Faith tried not to think about her father, whom she'd left at their home. She'd given a supply of herbs to Minerva and instructions on how to prepare them. Then she'd climbed the stairs to her father's bedroom. She told him about what happened to the Queen of Hearts and the Red King. He tried fussing over her, insisting that she not do anything like that again.

"I can't promise that, Father. I must help where I am needed."

"You don't have to do this, my love." The Hatter pressed her hand. "The queen had no right."

"She had every right," Faith said. "And now I know how I may protect all of Brigantia."

He framed her face with his hands. They were pale and thin, like the rest of him.

"I do this for you as well. I am the Hatter's Daughter, and I will not fail you or Brigantia."

Her father wept, which tore her insides apart, but Faith continued, "Father, we are going to ride along the shore of the Sea of Tears until we reach the border of the Red Queen. The White Queen's forces are to steal up behind our foes and, with luck, we can stop them from further movement."

"But how?" the Hatter said. "You have said this Rot has no corporeal form."

"But it takes form," Faith said. "Or if mortals accept it, they turn into— They are no longer human."

"So, the soldiers will fight them if necessary."

"Yes. And I will trap the Rot by transforming it. I will also remove it from wherever it has encroached. The Spinner Queen taught me much during our stay there."

"I still say this is not your duty." But he spoke with a resigned voice. "Very well, my dear, you will come home no matter what. You will tell me all?"

"I promise."

If I come back. Even as she continued to ride, Faith could not stop the thoughts from coming.

The washed-out sun hung behind gray clouds, casting a muted light on the scene. As they approached the Sea of Tears, the gentle sounds of the waves surprised them. The tree line stood before them, untouched by the Rot. At the head of the line, the king raised a hand, signaling for them to halt.

"Lady Faith!" Even to where she stood, the king's voice carried.

"Go, Argestes."

Cheshire floated above them as Faith rode the gryphon between a line of their soldiers. She moved to stand between Rowan and the king.

"Go forward," the king commanded.

"Father—" Rowan began.

"It's all right," Faith said. She assumed the king believed the Rot might attempt to capture her if she got separated from the rest of the group.

"I will protect you, milady," Argestes said.

She believed him. He had changed since Tidaholm. No longer was he the cowardly creature he once was but wore the pride of his people like a shield. Yet, he was in no hurry and treaded forward.

Then he halted.

"They are coming."

Faith's gaze swept ahead, tracing the curve of the beach as it vanished around a bend. At first, nothing met her eyes – only the gray expanse of sand and the distant line of trees. But then, like a shadow creeping forth, the Rot emerged. Its filthy tendrils slithered along the shore. Faith had seen this before; it was the relentless march of decay.

Yet, this time, there was more. Things she'd never encountered in her lifetime. Creatures whispered about in hushed tones, meant to frighten naughty children into obedience. Nightmarish beings.

"Heroine, protect us," Faith murmured, her voice barely audible over the crashing waves. She knew the Rot's hunger, but what followed was beyond her reckoning.

Harpies – feathers black and glistening – descended upon the scene. Their human faces twisted with hatred as they soared forward. The largest among them, claws curved like scythes, took the lead. Faith's heart clenched. Were these the remnants of the Tidaholm battle? Had they triumphed against the Spinner Queen?

The thought churned her stomach. But there was more. Goblins grinning with rotted teeth, mouths oozing poison. Some wore tattered rags, others were naked, their skin mottled and decayed. Ghouls mingled with them, snapping at each other, their hunger insatiable. Both ghouls and harpies feasted on the dead.

And then, the most unsettling of all: minuscule, winged beings – upper bodies of beautiful women, lower bodies serpentine.

Faith's breath hitched. The beach, once serene, now teemed with horrors. The Rot was merely the beginning; what followed was a nightmare woven from forgotten tales and forbidden myths.

"What in the nether hells are those?"

"Nether hells indeed," Argestes said. "They are called lamia. They steal babies to feast on them."

Faith's heart hammered in her chest. She noticed the dark fey had stopped their march. Faith wondered why. Then, of course, she knew. They were waiting for her. Rowan had moved beside her. "Faith?"

"We're outnumbered." Not just outnumbered. Outmatched. They had not suspected this. "I'll go talk to her." Faith assumed the towering harpy was the de facto leader.

"No, you can't—"

"Stay with the army. Your father will need to call a retreat."

"Faith—"

Faith nudged Argestes on his flanks, urging him on. The harpy issued commands. Her voice was lost in the wind. And then, with a grace that belied her monstrous form, she stepped forward. As the gap between them narrowed, Faith pulled Argestes to a halt. The harpy mirrored her wings half spread, talons digging into the sand. Suspicion hung in the air, a taut thread connecting them. Perhaps the harpy sensed a ruse, or maybe, like Faith, she understood that proximity to such creatures was perilous. Either way, they stood there, two wary souls on the precipice of an unknown fate.

"I am Lady Faith Carter," Faith said. "Daughter of Theophilus Carter – the Mad Hatter." Faith figured using that name lent an air of menace. "What do you want here?"

The harpy hissed a laugh. "I am Uryphe. I know not who sired me. And you are aware of what we want, Lady Faith Carter."

"You want me to tear open the veil at the edge of the Sea of Tears so you and your kind may have free rein?"

The harpy's lips curved in a smirk. "Do this and we will spare the people of Brigantia."

"So you may wreak havoc on the world like you did before the Farm Boy felled the Vine," Faith said, not believing the creature's words for a moment.

"We aspire to be in the light again!" Uryphe said. "For thousands of years after being forced to Deep Earth, we have had to struggle every day to stay alive, to not become extinct. We deserve life!"

"At the expense of human lives?"

"Mortals are our prey. And mortals we shall feast upon. If you cannot protect yourselves, that is your affair," Uryphe said. "If you do not wish to suffer the same fate, destroy the veil."

Faith climbed down from Argestes and stepped forward. She gathered her Gift.

"I can see what you are doing." Uryphe grinned with jagged teeth. "So have you agreed?"

Faith crossed her arms and uttered a single word. "No."

Uryphe shrieked and launched herself into the air toward Faith. Argestes flew to meet her, and their struggle began. The Rot pulsed forward in a wave down the expanse of sand and to the tree line. Faith fell to her knees and sank her hands into the sand, pouring all her power in, concentrating on where the Rot slithered along and the dark places it tried to hide. Around her, the armies of the Red Queen and the Queen of Hearts charged around Faith in a wave. She couldn't worry about the dark fey. It was the Rot that had her full attention.

The oily black continued to poison everything nearby, leaving a wake of darkness. Fortunately, the farmers and other citizens had evacuated to the palace, but Faith knew her father remained at their home. Determined to keep the Rot away from him, she braved the cries of battle and the metallic taste of blood on the sand. Closing her eyes, Faith resisted the encroaching darkness, unaware of how she found herself there.

Faith spotted Serval sitting on the stones, a familiar sight. However, when he turned toward her, his face resembled melted wax.

"What are you doing?" Serval asked. "Why are you fighting?"

Faith didn't answer. Instead she directed the flow of power at him.

Serval screamed and leapt from the rock, running back to the line of dark fey. No, he wasn't getting away from that.

Faith stood at the crossroads of two realms – the tangible darkness of her world and the spectral shadows of another. She witnessed the valiant clash of their warriors, a brutal battle where many met their end, torn asunder by the malevolent dark fey. With her attention on them, the Rot used the opportunity to make a savage advance forward, destroying what she had transformed. Faith returned to her task, driving herself into the heart of the darkness.

And Faith understood that this place could ensnare her. As she delved deeper, a realization dawned upon her – the entity at the core, glimpsed just once prior. If only she could attain it—

Something took hold of her, and Faith screamed a protest. "No, no! I was there!"

"Retreat!" she heard the king call. "Fall back!"

"Faith!" It was Rowan. He had her by the shoulder. "We need a barrier!"

She wanted to scream at him for bringing her back, yet as her gaze swept across the beach, now tainted with the rust-hued stains of blood, she understood the imperative – they must hold back the dark fey on this very shore.

Faith channeled her essence into the air that the dark fey breathed, transmuting their flesh into unyielding marble and glittering gold. The surviving goblins, driven by greed, abandoned the fray to seize their petrified allies, now invaluable in death.

Expending her final vestige of strength, Faith conjured a tempest of biting sands, ensnaring the winged terrors in its wrath. With a whispered incantation, she morphed the sand into a flurry of glass daggers, piercing the harpies' wings so that they cried out in agony, grounding them in defeat.

Faith persisted, her magic flowing freely as she sculpted the sand anew. This time, she erected towering spires of glass, stretching them across the beach and deep into the woods, forging a barrier that divided them from their foes. As the crystalline barrier reached the forest, the Vine intertwined with her power, sprouting a barricade of thorns where her influence waned, offering sanctuary to the people and thwarting the dark fey's desperate flight through the forest.

"Argestes!" Rowan called, and the gryphon responded. "Take Faith away from here, now!"

Rowan lifted her up and placed her on the saddle, then he slapped Argestes on his haunches. "Go! Go!"

"I'll take you back to the palace," Argestes said.

"No." Faith leaned forward and closed her eyes, resting her head on the gryphon's neck, her magic depleted. "Take me home."

CHAPTER TWENTY-THREE

Faith didn't speak as Minerva helped her out of her armor.

Useless. Completely useless.

What was all this for? The journey to Tidaholm? The armor, the medicine? Questions filled every part of her mind. From where did those dark fey emerge? How did they enter Brigantia if not through cracks? Then again, perhaps they had. How many times had Serval intruded, using the Rot as his point of entrance?

Why not send thousands if it were true?

Questions lingered in her mind as she ascended the stairs. Minerva drew a bath. Upon reaching the landing, they heard a constant pounding at the back door. Minerva went to answer.

"Is Faith here?"

Rowan barged in without being invited and rushed to Faith, which didn't surprise her. He was still in his armor, which was smeared with mud and dried blood.

"Faith, are you…?"

"I'm fine."

He noticed her tone. "You are not fine. When I discovered your absence from the palace—"

"I asked Argestes to bring me home. He sustained an injury. Minerva saw to him."

"Faith—"

"What happened? How many did we lose?"

Rowan lowered his head and took her by the shoulders. "Are you sure you want to—?"

"Yes."

"Not as many as expected, considering. We have around one

hundred. It would have been less without you."

"Didn't they find a way around the wall?"

"From what we can tell, the wall encompasses the entire woodlands. None of the flying beasts have come over it and the others won't come near it."

"They fear the Vine," Faith realized. "Wait, what about the White Queen's forces?"

"We don't know. They hadn't arrived when Father called the retreat."

"No." If they'd arrived after she'd raised the wall... "I cut them off from safety."

"You did no such thing." Rowan lifted her chin with two fingers, so she looked him in the eyes. "And the fey would have killed everyone if you hadn't."

"What will we do now?"

"Faith?" Her father called from his room. "Is someone there?"

"Yes, Father," Faith called back. "Prince Rowan."

"Bring him to me, please."

Faith led the way as they climbed the stairs. Her father was sitting up again, sipping on the medicinal tea. He looked better, although not altogether himself.

"Evening, Master Carter," Rowan said.

"Faith told me that the battle was lost," her father said, as he set down the teacup on the nightstand.

"Yes, sir," Rowan said. "My father is readying our remaining troops for another assault."

Both Faith and her father gasped.

"Seriously?" The Hatter rolled his eyes. "And they say *I'm* mad!"

"What else can we do?" Rowan asked.

"I need to remove the wall, but I'm unsure how," Faith said.

"I'll let my father know," Rowan said. "Good night, sir."

Faith walked downstairs with him and paused at the door. "The king plans to make another assault?"

"So he has told me. For what it's worth, I agree with your father."

The words tasted bitter on her lips. "Then Brigantia is lost."

"I..." Rowan began, "...perhaps we should return to Tidaholm? Maybe Sylmare can spare some soldiers?"

"Should we ask her for such a favor now? Especially when she has her entire kingdom to protect?"

Rowan sighed. "No."

They stood there in silence for a few moments. Then Rowan said, "I'm sorry, Faith." And he hurried away.

"Miss Faith, come inside." Minerva closed the door. "Take your bath before the water cools."

Was it possible for her to enjoy a bath right now? She should be... doing what? Faith didn't have the wherewithal to refuse Minerva's request, so she allowed the housekeeper to lead her to the bathing room. Of course, as she stripped down and slipped into the steamy water, her mind filled with questions again, about their defeat in battle and how they'd lost so many of their numbers.

Faith submerged in the water, but the muffling of sounds around her only gave a louder voice to her thoughts. She knew two ways to enter Brigantia: the Looking Glass and the Burrow. Obviously, their enemy couldn't have come from the Burrow, otherwise they would have been at their rear.

Faith surfaced, her hands gripping the edges of the tub. Could the Looking Glass be the secret entrance to Brigantia?

That was the Red Queen's domain.

Surely, she couldn't have...?

The smaller dark fey could come through, but the harpies were too large as far as she was aware. Then again, she didn't know how the Looking Glass worked. Only the royal family knew, yet the Red Queen kept some secrets hidden. Faith recalled how stoic the queen looked as they marched. She couldn't accuse the Red Queen of treason without proof.

She was done with her bath. After climbing out of the tub, Faith grabbed a towel from the cabinet and wrapped it around her. She returned to her room. She wasn't quite ready to sleep yet, so she slipped on an old pair of trousers and a threadbare shirt she used when puttering around in the garden. She took out a favorite book and tried to read, but she couldn't concentrate on the words and when they blurred, Faith tossed the book aside. She lay back with her hands behind her head.

Tears escaped from her eyes, but she did not wipe them away. Her beloved home and her failure to halt the Rot consumed her thoughts. Faith turned to her side and drew her knees up to her chest. It was difficult to breathe.

Faith cried until, exhausted, she fell asleep, or at least she thought she had. She could see her room, the lantern's light fading with time. And as her room darkened, Faith noticed something moving by her bedroom door. She realized she was in that place between sleep and full wakefulness.

Whatever it was, it moved like a serpent, but it was translucent gray like fog. It split at its head, with the left side continuing down the hall and the right side entering Faith's room. Sleep paralysis caught Faith as she tried to move. Her vision blurred as the serpent persisted. When a faceless blob peeked over the edge of the bed, Faith struggled to wake herself. Then it was on her, covering her nose, and Faith couldn't help but breathe it in. The smell of it was rotting food. It went down her throat and made her cough violently.

When that happened Faith finally found herself able to move as her muscles spasmed. She whipped her body around and continued to cough as she pushed herself off the bed. Hitting the hardwood floor. She heard coughing somewhere else in the house and she remembered the second fog snake.

"Father!" Faith scrambled to her feet and dashed out of her room and down the hall. Her father's chest rose and fell, lifting his torso off the bed as the smoke filled his mouth and nose.

"Minerva!" Faith screamed as she ran to the bed.

Minerva came running in. Faith was trying to wrest her father's body from the bed. Needing no instructions, Minerva rushed forward and climbed onto the bed, pushing from the opposite side until they got Faith's father on the floor.

Then Minerva screamed as the snake entwined around her body. Faith did not know if it would work, but she leapt onto the bed and plunged her hand into the fog, which sent icy pinpricks across her flesh. She transformed the body into ice by using the cold. Faith could have sworn she heard a shriek as she did so. She saw the other end of the snake leave out of sight.

Faith shattered the ice that held Minerva.

"Help me." Her father was still coughing, but not as violently. They struggled to lay him back in bed.

"I'll fix the tea," Minerva said. "Milady, what was that?"

"The Rot," Faith said.

"But I thought someone had caught it?"

"They did," Faith said. A sudden realization followed. It was her fault. Her feelings of defeat and guilt had attracted the Rot. She had invited it into her home.

"Miss Faith?"

"Please fix the tea," Faith said.

"Of course."

Her father was calm now and seemed to doze. What would happen if she didn't have the strength? No, she wouldn't consider it. These thoughts were the cause. She resisted the anger building within her to avoid attracting the Rot. She needed to remain calm.

"Father, I'm sorry." Faith didn't know if he heard her.

★   ★   ★

Faith had fallen asleep, because the next thing she knew she was being awakened by the sound of someone knocking at her front door. She pulled up a chair next to her father's bed, determined not to leave him alone. The tea set was on the nightstand. Warm, to Faith's surprise. Minerva must have made it fresh, anticipating they would sleep until morning. The limited light made it difficult for her to see.

Her father coughed, and Faith hurried to pour some of the tea. "Father?"

He was already awake. "Try to drink some." He looked frail and sickly again, and Faith hated it. Knowing it was her fault.

"What happened?" he asked.

"The Rot attacked us both last night," Faith said. "It was my fault!"

"Why would you think that?" the Hatter said.

"I was so – I felt so—" Faith began. "Father, we are not going to lose our home. I vowed to save it."

"Hush, dear girl." The Hatter reached for the teacup. Faith took it first, and he allowed her to hold the cup for him to sip the tea. "We are not warriors. Even the soldiers. When have they ever seen battle?"

"But I—"

"Milady, milord?" Minerva was at the threshold. "The White Rabbit has arrived."

Faith was about to tell her to send him away, but her father said, "Ask him in, Minerva."

The White Rabbit entered and bowed. "Forgive, milord and lady." He seemed much better since the last time she'd seen him. Likely having drunk tea. "Lady Faith, the king requests your presence at the palace."

She fought the urge to tell the king to piss against a wall. Instead, she said, "My father has taken ill again. Would you tell the king..." Another idea occurred. Faith changed tactics. "White Rabbit, would you ask Prince Rowan to pay us a visit?"

"Well..."

"Please?"

"Well, all right."

Faith knew she was putting the White Rabbit in a spot. If he didn't come back with Faith as the king commanded, he would likely be reprimanded. "Thank you very much. I appreciate this."

"Of course!" The White Rabbit bowed again.

"Why Rowan?" the Hatter asked.

"I know what the king wants me to do. He wants me to destroy the barrier. I don't want to do that, but I doubt he'll listen to me."

Faith continued to help her father drink the tea. Minerva brought him some porridge, but the moment he tried to eat it he started coughing again. Faith had never felt so helpless. She could see her father was in pain.

The next time they heard a knock, it was, thankfully, Rowan. Faith rose and walked over to give him a hug. "Thank you for coming."

"Father wasn't pleased that you refused his summons."

"I know, and I'm sorry if I caused you any grief." Faith told him about the attack. "Despite the king's wishes, I won't take responsibility for additional deaths by removing the barrier."

"You weren't responsible for those!" Rowan said. "Listen to me, there was nothing any of us could have done." He lowered his head. "Not even I."

"Rowan!"

"It's true," Rowan said. "Training can't prepare us for something like this. We became complacent because of this peace we have experienced. Nonsense, but near perfection, or so we thought."

"What should we do?"

"When I return to the palace…" Rowan drew in a sharp breath, "…I will tell my father we should abandon Brigantia."

"No!" Faith raised her hand to her lips.

"What choice do we have?" Rowan said. "No one can help us."

"Faith…"

They glanced at her father.

"Come here, both of you."

Faith and Rowan moved to her father's bedside.

"We can't leave Brigantia. It is our home, and I refuse."

"But sir," Rowan said, "we have no choice. You can't stay here."

The Hatter swallowed, coughed again. Faith went to reach for the tea, but her father waved it away.

"The two of you will leave Brigantia," her father said. "You must find help."

The Hatter held Faith's hands and spoke. "You must find Alice."

CHAPTER TWENTY-FOUR

Alice.

All Brigantia knew about the Heroine. Rowan had heard countless tales of her feats since childhood but doubted their plausibility. The Hatter, his parents, and the two other queens were present at the times she visited. Some said she was only here twice, while others said she visited many times, making her mark throughout the land. The people and Brigantia were young. Alice's absence had lasted for an unknown period.

The Hatter sounded mad, suggesting finding a legend's whereabouts or existence.

"Master Carter," Rowan said, "how will we find her?"

"I wish I could tell you," the Hatter said. "When you return, you may know where to start."

Rowan and Faith exchanged a look. It was an expression of both fear and hope. "I will need to inform my father." This time Rowan reached out his hand and Faith squeezed it. "Will you wait here for me, please?"

"Yes, of course."

"I'll return as soon as I can," Rowan said.

"I'll be ready," Faith said.

Rowan's mind raced as he left the house and walked to where Epione waited. He'd grown quite fond of the gryphon. In fact, he'd asked her if she would be willing to stay on as his personal steed. He clarified she was not obligated to accept. But she had.

"Home, Your Highness?" Epione asked as he approached.

"Yes," he said.

She took to the air. "If I may ask, what happened?"

Rowan told her about the conversation. He needed to say it out loud to convince himself it had happened.

"This Alice must be a mighty warrior," Epione said.

"So I've been told."

"You have never met this Alice?"

"She hasn't visited Brigantia since before I was born."

"How old was she then?"

"I'm not sure," Rowan said. "Some claim she was a mere nine-year-old child. Some say she was a beautiful young maiden, maybe in her twenties." Rowan wondered what anyone knew about the Heroine.

Upon Rowan's return to the palace, he found his father still in the war room. His initial summons to Faith was to discuss where she would bring down the wall, but the White Rabbit had advised him Faith wanted to see Rowan. It did not surprise Rowan to find his father in a foul mood, which was unlike him. In fact, since the queen became ill, his father had become a different person. Only a few servants were present, while the Red Queen sat near the map.

"Rowan!" The king bellowed when he caught sight of his son. "Where is the girl?"

Rowan gritted his teeth before saying, "The Hatter has fallen ill again. The Rot attacked them both last night."

"What? How is this possible?"

"I don't know, but it somehow got in," Rowan stated. "She begs your pardon and asked to be excused." He'd tell Faith what he'd done later, hoping she would understand.

"Well," the king grumbled, "I suppose that's all right."

"In fact," Rowan continued, "the Hatter suggested we needed help from outside Brigantia."

"The Spinner Queen?" The king leaned over the map.

"No, sir," Rowan said. "Alice."

His father's head came up, and he pierced Rowan with his gaze. "Alice." His voice had a mocking tone.

"It has been so long," the Red Queen commented. "Is she still even alive?"

"Probably not." The king returned to studying the map. He was silent for a few moments. "Then again, I suppose it wouldn't hurt to consult with her, if you can find her."

"I will do my best, Father."

"We must keep this confidential," the king went on. "We can't give the people false hope. Be covert in your handling of this." He looked at the Red Queen. "Don't you agree?"

"Yes, it's best." The Red Queen stood. "However, you mustn't tarry too long in the outside worlds. How long will the wall last?"

"Until Faith brings it down," Rowan said.

"Five days," the king said. "If you do not find the Heroine, the king commands your return."

Rowan thought to protest, but realized it was useless. "Yes, sir. I'll go to prepare."

"Good fortune to you," the Red Queen said.

Rowan bowed to her. Prior to returning to Faith, he had one final task.

There were two maids in his mother's room. They had just changed the sheets, as evidenced by the pile on the floor. They straightened up upon seeing him. The elder of the two said, "Good morning, Your Highness."

Rowan nodded to them, and they both exited after one gathered up the discarded sheets. They left a fresh tea service. Rowan poured a cup. "Mother, can you hear me?" She wasn't getting better like the rest, and Rowan didn't know why. "Please stay with us, Mother."

It was difficult without help, but Rowan lifted her head under one arm and used his free hand to spoon the tea in. "Mother, Faith and I are leaving to find the Heroine. We need help due to the current situation."

Rowan closed his eyes to hold back the tears and clenched his fists on his lap. "I'm sorry. I'll be gone for five days and if— when I return, if we haven't found Alice, we may need to leave Brigantia. Of course, having her here may not mean a thing."

He wondered if they could escape to Alice's world. There must be similarities between the two worlds since Alice had visited several times.

"No matter what happens, I'll take care of you. I promise." Rowan hated seeing her this way. Although she sometimes infuriated him, he was now sorry for the times he'd thought ill of her. Rowan finished feeding her the tea, then he leaned in and kissed her on the forehead. "I will see you soon." He refused to say goodbye.

★   ★   ★

Rowan packed his own supplies. He also took gold with him, recalling the White Rabbit's words that everyone accepts gold. As much as it concerned him, he decided not to take the armor. He wasn't certain if they had such in Alice's world and if they didn't, well… Instead, he requested commoner clothes for which he paid despite the protests from the supplier. Rowan thought discretion was indeed the better part of valor.

Later, Rowan spoke to the White Rabbit, telling him what they were going to do. Rowan asked him how they could travel to Faith's birthplace.

The White Rabbit assured him, "The Burrow knows where to take you. Just like it knew to bring Faith here."

"Thank you." Rowan bowed to him. "May we see each other again soon."

Upon arriving at the stables, Rowan discovered Epione was already saddled and ready. "I am sorry, my loyal mount, but we will have to leave you and Argestes at the Burrow. We don't want to risk you getting hurt. We don't know what Faith's birthplace is like."

"I understand, Your Highness."

He found Faith was waiting for him when he came to her house. Argestes was saddled and carrying a pack of provisions.

"I thought," Faith said, "we shouldn't pack too much."

"And be inconspicuous in our dress?"

She smiled. "Yes."

"I thought we should leave our mounts at the Burrow."

"Agreed," Faith said as she stroked her gryphon's neck, uncertain about what lay ahead.

"Are you ready? Did you tell your father?"

"We've already said our farewells." Her voice caught with her pain. Rowan said no more about the matter.

They rode alongside each other in silence. Everything remained unchanged around them. Still no birds, insects, or beasts. The flowers still had their heads bowed. Their world was ending.

It all depended on them.

When they neared the Burrow, the familiar small tempest of smoke appeared, and Cheshire took his form and settled around Rowan's shoulders.

"Coming with us?" Rowan said.

"Of course," Cheshire responded. "Someone has to look after you."

Rowan chuckled and looked at Faith. She was smiling too. It didn't last long.

Nothing attacked them as they continued to ride, each lost in their own thoughts. Rowan supposed they both should pay attention, but it was impossible. His thoughts revolved around their discoveries. What was this world like? It was not long before they reached their destination. Both dismounted.

"Don't wait for us," Rowan said. "Epione, return to the palace."

Faith was hugging Argestes around his neck and buried her face in his feathers.

"I will go home, Lady Faith, and guard the Hatter."

Faith was crying. "Thank you, Argestes."

"I wish you great fortune."

"Yes," Epione said. "We both do."

They removed their packs from their mounts and fitted them on their backs. Faith still had the Burrow keys, so she unlocked the door. They were relieved to see the Burrow remained unchanged. It was likely due to the Vine's protection. They walked to the middle of the room.

"How may we do this?" Faith said.

"I asked the White Rabbit," Rowan replied. "He said the Burrow will lead us."

Faith stepped closer to him, and they embraced.

"Take us back," Faith said. "Back to the place of my birth."

A soft wind began to circle them, growing in strength but not in ferocity. It carried with it an array of items – books, candles, utensils – swirling around yet never touching them. They stood at the center, untouched, like in the eye of a storm.

The wind continued to whip around them. Rowan felt Faith tighten her grip on him and he could feel her tremble. Of course, she was frightened. He had to admit to himself that he was too.

Rowan sensed Faith's shock when she tightly grasped his shirt collar. They lifted in the air, just inches above ground, as if the Burrow sought confirmation of their desire to venture into the unfamiliar darkness.

Rowan felt Faith against his chest. The storm continued around them, and they floated upward. Then the speed of their movement increased. Rowan held Faith tighter against him, knowing that if he lost his grip, she would fall. But it was the Burrow. The power here, supplied by the Vine, would never allow Faith to be injured. Rowan had to trust.

Their ascent continued, causing the familiar objects nearby to fade into darkness, but not to the point of obscurity. The candles, furniture, paintings, lanterns, and whatnots from their journey now settled into their places.

Rowan hadn't considered the arrival time. It might be pitch-dark. Imagine a place with no daylight. What if this world was dark? He hoped it was just his worry, and the thought was absurd.

The air continued to rush around them, and they flew at a frightening speed, but Rowan continued to trust as the light fell away around them and the sudden scent of loam filled his nostrils. Had they gone beyond the Burrow? The lanterns revealed dirt walls, with roots bulging out. Night air wafted down, and with that scent Rowan was grateful for the lanterns. In perpetual darkness, they would possess these. Rowan craned his neck to look up, and he thought he saw…stars?

With a sudden final push from below, they broke through a layer of dead leaves and branches, and emerged.

CHAPTER TWENTY-FIVE

Night had fallen, but the horizon glowed with a soft blue light as Rowan stood. And the light continued to bloom, rising over the tree line in a blink of an eye. Without warning, Rowan was dizzy, which worsened as the light continued to fill the sky. His stomach lurched, and he feared he would vomit. What in the nether hells was wrong with him?

"Rowan?" Faith reached for him as he fell to his knees. His head pounded and the world spun. The remaining stars moved rapidly across the sky, disappearing into the light, creating streaks in the sky.

Rowan couldn't stand it anymore.

He collapsed onto the grass, overwhelmed as a brilliant light scorched the heavens. Above, a vast orb of fire ascended, its glare unbearable. Rowan clamped his eyes shut, seeking refuge in darkness.

"Cheshire, help me!" Faith called. "Get the waterskin!"

Rowan, unable to move or speak, wanted to tell Faith about the situation. Faith turned him over and lifted his head into her lap. She pressed the spout to his lips. "Drink."

It was about all he could do, and the water helped somewhat. Rowan hoped too much time wasn't passing. What if he didn't get better? He couldn't leave Faith to do this alone, but he hadn't felt this poorly since he was a child and suffering from swine ache.

He must have dozed off because the next thing he knew, Faith was dabbing at his forehead with a wet cloth.

"Is this the Rot?" Faith inquired.

Oh, Heroine, no! Surely it didn't follow us here!

"I don't believe so." Cheshire sounded uncertain, which didn't fill Rowan with hope.

"What could it be? He was fine until we breached the hole."

"Hmm," Cheshire said. "Rowan is not of this world. And I would guess it is not affecting me because of what I am."

"We should have him go back."

No! I will not leave you alone!

"I've traveled with him before," Cheshire said. "I could take him back and then rejoin you."

Gathering what little strength he had, Rowan lifted his hand and grabbed Faith's where she held the cloth. "No."

"Rowan—"

"No."

"Don't be ridiculous," Cheshire said. "It's obvious that you shouldn't be here. Do you plan to lie here in the forest until you waste away?"

He was about to respond – at least try to respond – when Faith pushed the spout of the waterskin into his mouth again. "Men."

Rowan wanted to stay awake but dozed off. The next time he woke up, he was feeling better. He remained in the same position, head on Faith's lap. The light was much better now. He appeared to have slept all day.

"How are you feeling?" Faith asked.

"Better." Rowan smiled at her. "The world has stopped spinning."

"Spinning?"

"It was strange," Rowan said. "It was pitch-dark when we first left the Burrow."

He could see she was confused. "But it wasn't. It was daylight."

"Likely, he saw something different," Cheshire said.

Stars disappeared as the sky filled with light, like a quick morning. Rowan explained about the ball of fire and how it followed the light. "It was so bright it blinded me."

"What do you see now?" Faith asked.

"Still too bright. I mean, it's not as bad as when I first woke up."

"Remarkable," Cheshire said. The fey cat stretched his body out and rolled in the grass. "Time must flow differently here."

Faith drew in a sharp breath. "What if it affects you, Rowan? What if—?"

"We don't know what may happen," Rowan said.

"The first sign that you are affected, you're going home. I don't care if you're my prince. I'll not be responsible."

"I'm sorry." He would not lie to her. "I won't leave you to face this alone, whatever happens, but I promise if I'm feeling sick again, I will tell you."

He could tell she didn't like the idea. Despite that, she said, "All right."

"I believe the larger issue," Rowan said, "is if Cheshire still has his magic."

Cheshire answered by disappearing into the cloud of smoke. Only his mouth was visible. "It would seem my magic is intact so far."

"Still, take care. We are unsure what will happen if you get injured." Rowan sat up despite feeling unwell. "Am I correct in thinking it will be dark soon?" It appeared to him that it was still early afternoon.

"Yes," Faith said, "we must find a place to stay."

Rowan stood a bit unsteadily, but he was able to reach out his hands and help Faith to her feet. He got a good look around. Like in Brigantia, the Burrow's entrance was by a large willow's roots. The trees stood thinly spaced, and a large, grassy pathway stretched in both directions. Rowan was relieved to hear familiar noises of birds and insects. Things were alive here.

"Which way?" Faith asked.

"I'm not sure," Rowan said. "Nothing seems familiar to you at all?"

Faith frowned. Like Rowan, she looked around, her brow furrowed as she fought to bring the memories forward. "Wait..." Faith pinched the bridge of her nose. Then she pointed to their left. "That way."

They started off. Cheshire made himself scarce. Faith continued to look like she was fighting to regain whatever memory she had. And it seemed to work because once the tree line ended, they came upon a wide-open field. Another line of trees stood before them, but like before, they were sparse.

Faith was shaking her head. "It feels familiar, but I can't—"

"It's all right," Rowan said. "Don't fight. Let whatever come naturally."

They entered the open field. Rowan followed Faith's lead.

"Look there!" Faith said.

In the middle of the field was a ramshackle wood building. As they approached, it seemed deserted. One of the two doors was off its hinges.

"Wait here." Rowan slipped through the opening. He couldn't help but smile as the place was lit, allowing him to see every detail. It was empty. There were some burlap sacks piled in the far corner to his left. But what he saw to his right confused him. They were large, tiled squares of what looked like hay.

"Rowan?" Faith had stepped in and joined him. "What are those?"

"It looks like hay, but—"

"How do they make it stay in a rectangle like that?" Faith wondered.

"Perhaps a magic spell?" Rowan approached them. "They're moldy."

"I can fix that." Faith spoke, and the hay became fresh. Next, Rowan approached the sack. The burlap tore. "Apples. Well, at least they were apples."

"Bring some here," Faith said.

They sat, munching on fresh apples, and deciding what to do next.

"I wish I could be more helpful."

"Surely you jest?" Rowan said.

"I mean to say, finding out which way to go."

"You started. We'll continue."

The cozy warmth of the night embraced him, providing solace and comfort. Rowan sat against the stacks and allowed Faith to sleep first. He still wasn't quite healthy, although he figured he was well enough not to worry Faith.

"Rowan?"

"Yes?"

"Come up here with me, won't you?"

Rowan turned to look at her, and saw her stretched out, her back facing him.

"Faith..."

"That can't be too comfortable."

It wasn't, but...

Rowan stood, then climbed onto the stack.

"I'm – I'm just a bit—" Faith said.

"I know, it's all right."

Faith turned to face him. Rowan didn't protest when she moved against him. "Do you believe we'll find Alice?"

"We have to." Rowan circled his arms around her. He decided. "Faith, I'm ready to tell you."

"About what your father said?"

He couldn't help but chuckle. "Yes."

"Is it about me?"

"Yes." Rowan steeled himself. "My father thinks...that we should be married."

He felt her stiffening, and she looked up at him, her eyes wide. "I see." Faith lowered her head. "And you don't want to."

Rowan sighed. "On the contrary, I do."

Her head snapped up, and her expression was one of utter shock. "You do? But you seemed so upset."

"I was," Rowan said. "I wanted to ask you on my own terms. I didn't want him or you to think I did it because it was his wish."

"Oh." He heard the smile in her voice.

"Faith—"

"Don't ask me now," Faith said. "Wait until we have succeeded. When everything is right in Brigantia." She snuggled closer and buried her face in his chest. "Besides, don't you want to ask my father for permission?"

"Oh, yes, of course!" Rowan had forgotten.

"You needn't worry," Faith assured him. "Good night, love."

Delighted, Rowan said, "Good night."

★　　★　　★

Rowan hoped he might adjust as daylight streamed through cracks and the shed's lone window. Faith was still asleep so Rowan, as carefully as he could, moved himself from Faith's embrace, as much as he hated doing so. He needed—

Rowan frowned at a sudden familiar sound. Were those horses? Rowan exited the barn and circled the wall. It was indeed horses. Five in total, being ridden by men in clothes somewhat like his. When Rowan stepped out to meet them, they pulled their mounts to a stop.

One of them spoke. He was a powerful man, with a shaggy beard, bushy eyebrows, a large bulbous nose, and small, mean-looking eyes.

Rowan couldn't understand a word he was saying.

The same man spoke again, seeming to ask a question.

Rowan didn't know what to do. He shook his head.

Another member of the group spoke. He was a thin weasely-looking man, who whistled with every word.

"I am Pri— Rowan, I'm searching for someone."

The two men exchanged blank looks.

Damn it to the nether hells, he was getting nowhere. He only hoped Faith would stay hidden. "I'm looking for someone named Alice."

"Alice?" A third member of the group spoke. He was younger than the rest, with a face still chubby from baby fat.

"Yes!" Rowan nodded. Finally, they understood a word.

Big Nose yelled something to the boy.

The boy began to speak, but Big Nose yelled at him again.

Big Nose reached behind his back and pulled something out that Rowan didn't recognize. It had a long and thin shape, combining polished wood with sections of metal. He leveled it at Rowan and closed one eye. He spoke in a low, menacing tone.

Rowan recognized threats, even in foreign languages. He fell to his knees and held his hands out in a pleading gesture.

Big Nose lifted the stick to point skyward. He muttered something that included the name Alice.

The only word Rowan understood was Alice. He nodded, hoping that was the right reaction.

Rowan turned to the boy and asked, "Alice?"

Big Nose rolled his eyes.

Chubby Boy pointed behind the group in the direction from which they had come. "Alice."

Rowan bowed his head to him. "Thank you."

Big Nose grumbled something.

Rowan had a good idea what the man had said. They must be careful to avoid being seen on their return. Big Nose spurred his horse forward, and the rest followed.

"What an unpleasant cur." Cheshire appeared, sitting beside him.

"Did you understand what they were saying?"

"Not immediately," Cheshire said. "Although the last few words became intelligible. Nothing you want to know about."

Rowan turned to walk back to the barn. "What was that thing he leveled at me?"

"No idea," Cheshire said, "but I felt it was as unpleasant as its owner."

Faith was up and wide awake when he slipped into the barn. "Are you all right?"

"Yes, I'm fine." Rowan said. "Did you hear?"

"Yes," she said. "What horrid men! Threatening you was inappropriate. Even if it is his land."

Rowan's jaw dropped. "What did you say?"

"I was so worried when he threatened to kill you!"

"Wait, you understood them?"

"Yes," Faith said. "You didn't?"

"No."

Faith squeezed him tight. "He warned us about trespassing on his land, so we need to be cautious on our return."

"I was thinking the same thing."

"I heard them mention Alice," Faith said. "One of them knew where she was."

"Just a general direction," Rowan said. "We're going to have to depend on you to translate. Until Cheshire can handle it, at least. Only at the end of the conversation did he grasp their meaning."

"Let's go," Faith suggested, packing up. "I want to be far away when they return."

"So do I." What was that saying? Being a fish out of water? Rowan felt like a fish out of water, but at least they had useful information.

CHAPTER TWENTY-SIX

Faith couldn't help but look back as they walked through the field. She expected the return of those awful men before their possible getaway. She'd heard one call this *his land*. But something made Faith feel that wasn't quite true. Something in that voice that dared to threaten her love.

That thought made her smile. Rowan loved her. Although it had been unspoken, she knew him well enough to recognize the truth. For years, he had felt that way. The thought brought her momentary joy. Notwithstanding her desire to hold on to it, the mission's importance remained her top priority.

They eventually reached the once distant trees, bringing some relief to Faith. It did not last long.

"Faith?" Rowan noticed her unease. "Is anything wrong?"

"I don't know…" Faith checked behind them again. "I feel like…"

Although it was good weather, it was shadowy underneath the trees despite the shafts of light that found their way to the forest floor through the leaves.

"You must follow your instincts," Rowan said. "It's uncertain if magic exists here. Even with Cheshire's being fey, he may not be able to call upon his own magic."

Faith nodded. She wished she didn't feel this way, but perhaps it was for the best. This prevented anyone from sneaking up on them. Still, she felt silly. "Are you sensing anything?"

"I'm afraid not," Rowan said. "That doesn't mean there isn't anything. We've already established we can't trust my senses. Being from this world, perhaps you are more attuned to it."

"We should keep moving," Faith said.

But the feeling persisted. In spite of Faith's attempts to ignore it, she succumbed and quickly turned to look. A small, grayish thing concealed itself behind a tree.

"Rowan!"

"What is it?"

"There is something there."

"Where?"

"It ducked behind that tree." Faith pointed to a nearby maple. "It was small, almost, but its face was—" She could not fully describe it. "It was all in gray."

"Now I wish I had my sword." Rowan looked around. "Hold for a moment."

Rowan walked a few steps away to another tree while Faith kept her eyes on where she'd seen their stalker. She looked at Rowan when she heard the sharp crack of a tree branch. Rowan had broken one off and set it aside to rummage through his pack.

Using a small knife, he removed the bark and leaves. Faith saw the creature two more times during the longer-than-desired process. Once, she glimpsed its furious, clenched face.

Rowan finished and studied his handiwork. "Well, it's not perfect, but it should do."

"Good." Faith wrapped her arms around her middle. "Let's go now, please."

They walked on, and Faith struggled to resist the urge to turn around, but it became unbearable. She was about to scream, but a bell stopped her. They exchanged glances and started running.

The trees broke, and they found themselves on a small hill with a sprawling village below them. Outside the shadowed forest, Faith no longer felt the presence. Faith sat down in the grass. "It's gone."

Rowan knelt beside her. "Are you all right?"

"I'm exhausted," Faith said. "I was so worried about that thing…"

"Now that I think on it, I'm not feeling too well myself." Rowan sat beside her. "Does the air seem thicker here to you?"

"It does." Faith hadn't realized it before.

"Let's rest here a minute. I don't want to stay for too long."

Faith nodded and leaned against him, and Rowan draped his arm around her shoulders. She was just dozing when Rowan nudged her. "We'd better go."

Faith didn't want to. The soft grass, the late afternoon sun…she could have slept there. They continued down the hill. After a while they came to a road into the village made of small square stones placed unevenly. Faith and Rowan stepped aside for carriages and riders, the horses' hooves making a clip-clop noise on the stones. Faith noticed that they were being watched with looks that ran the gamut from disgust to anger.

"Why are they looking at us like that?" Rowan asked.

"I don't know." It made Faith uncomfortable.

Some people stopped to stare at them as they continued. One man on a horse pulled it to a stop, then turned his mount and followed them down the street.

"I don't like this," Faith said. "Why all this attention?"

Rowan looked around. "This way." He took Faith's hand and led her across the street and into a space between two buildings. It was a narrow path the length of several houses and filled with piles of garbage. Faith had to hold her breath against the stench. Rowan continued to lead her down the narrow pathway.

They stopped in a place where they could move through, between two stone walls, one with a single and narrow lighted window.

"I wonder why they build their houses this way. Why are these paths so narrow?"

Rowan shook his head. "I must say, I'm glad they're here. It doesn't seem like many people traverse these paths."

"We're too conspicuous this way." Faith sighed. She didn't want to do this. "Did you notice back aways, the laundry hanging?"

Rowan's shoulders fell. "Wait here. I'll be right back."

It was starting to get dark, but light came from one window. Rowan returned carrying a thin cloak and a shawl. "We'll try these."

Faith took the shawl and wrapped it around her head, pulling it forward, while Rowan donned the cloak and raised the hood. "Let's hope this works."

They returned to the street, keeping close to the buildings again. They still received looks, but many of them now were disinterested. Still, they kept their heads down and hurried along.

The village was a hive of activity. The streets were lined with a variety of shops they thankfully recognized, like the blacksmith clanging away at his forge, the baker with his fresh loaves of bread, and the butcher displaying cuts of meat. The air was filled with the sounds of horse-drawn carriages and the calls of street vendors selling their wares.

"Where should we go first?" Faith asked.

"Some kind of gathering place must exist," Rowan speculated. "We'll have to just ask."

They avoided the people moving along. Faith noticed a solitary old woman at the front of one of the narrow paths. She was tending a stall. It was just a wheeled cart on which sat an odd machine, stacks of clay cups, tiny loaves of bread and blocks of butter. There were a few other sealed canisters marked *milk*, *sugar*, and *honey*.

"Good evening, mistress," Faith said.

"Good eve to ya, what can I get for ya?"

"Well..." She was hungry and figured Rowan was too. "May we have two loaves of bread with butter and honey?" Faith pointed to the machine. "What is that?"

The woman misinterpreted her question. "Coffee o'course."

"Two cups, please."

"That'll be two bob, please."

Faith glanced at Rowan, who shrugged and retrieved a silver coin from his pack. He handed it to the lady.

"What in the world?" She squinted at the coin. "Eh, now, what's this?"

"Silver," Faith said.

"I know this looks like it. You tryin' ta cheat me?"

"Of course not!" Faith exclaimed.

The woman bit the coin. "Well, I'll be damned. I can't change this. Where you from, anyway?"

"Across the sea," Faith said. It was as good an answer as any. "Perhaps we may purchase some information instead?"

The woman raised an eyebrow. "What kind of information?"

"We are looking for someone. A woman named Alice."

"Alice what?"

"Your pardon?"

"What's her last name?"

"I'm afraid we don't know," Faith said. "She was just Alice."

"I need more than that."

"Well," Faith said, "she used to live outside of town. The land was purchased by someone else, according to a young man we ran into recently."

The woman tapped a dirty fingernail on the stubble of her chin. "Matter of fact −" she went to work fixing their meal, "− did her family have a big house that burned down?"

That explained why she remembered fire. Faith tried not to sound too eager. "Yes, I believe so."

"Yeah, the man moved his family to town here. Promptly keeled over and died." She smiled with green crooked teeth. "Heard he had a thing goin' with some slut servant. She bore a child with him too."

Faith fought to keep her voice calm. "What happened to the woman?"

"Died in the fire as far as I know." She took two cups and filled them with dark liquid. "You just throw them in the wash bucket when you're through."

Faith gazed at the cup, then at the bucket of murky water nearby. When she took a sip, the searing bitter liquid had her coughing.

"Good stuff, eh?"

Rowan had a look of pure disgust on his face but drank it down. The woman handed them bread wrapped in paper.

"Can you share anything else with us? Where might we find more information?"

"A gathering place," Rowan said.

"A gathering place?" Faith asked.

"Well, you can try the Wooden Raven Tavern," she responded. "Get ya a pint there real cheap. Straight down the lane." She pointed.

"Thank you, mistress," Faith said. "We appreciate the information."

The woman waved Faith's words away with a cackle. "Call me Missus Abagail. I ain't nobody's mistress. It's my pleasure."

They finished their coffee and moved away from the cart as others were gathering. They stepped onto another nearby walkway. Faith leaned against the wall and opened the now-greasy paper. She translated what she needed to, keeping Abagail's crude words about her mother to herself.

"Are you all right?" Rowan asked. He touched her on the shoulder.

"Yes," Faith said. "I am sad that I'll never meet my mother, but I don't remember anything about her." Faith took a bite of the bread. It wasn't too bad. "As for my father, well, I'm uncertain, but he didn't protect my mother, so I have no concern for him."

"I'm sorry," Rowan said.

"Don't be." Faith smiled. "Brigantia is my home, and Master Carter is my family and soon you'll be family too."

Rowan smiled back before starting on his bread too. Once they finished, they didn't have a place to wipe their hands, so they wiped them on their trousers.

"Ick," Faith said. "Perhaps it will give the impression that we're ordinary people searching for jobs during difficult times."

"Good idea," Rowan said.

Nightfall accompanied their return to the street. The tavern wasn't hard to find. It buzzed with rowdy activity. People gathered on steps and spilled from the doorway, some already drunk. Rowan hesitated.

"I don't like this," Rowan said. "Perhaps you should stay outside?"

"With them?" Faith nodded at the group outside. "Absolutely not."

"You're right," Rowan said. "Let's just keep our heads down."

People filled the place, making it overcrowded and dark. Acrid smoke from tobacco and oil lamps filled the air. It mingled with the scents of greasy, rotting food and unwashed bodies. The single open window didn't make things any better. There were people crowding around it and conversing loudly with those outside.

"What a vile place," Rowan muttered.

No tables were available, causing a momentary dilemma. After several minutes, a woman approached them, grinning. She carried a tray in one hand. "Can I get ya anything?"

Faith struggled to find the right words. "To be honest, we're looking for someone named Alice."

The woman snickered. "I doubt she's here. Women don't—" She stopped, leaning to the right, eyeing something behind them. "What the fuck—?"

Faith and Rowan looked to see what caught her attention. Two figures stood on the threshold. They wore long blue cloaks, and voluminous hoods hid their faces. It remained unclear if they were males or females. When someone noticed them, the noise level decreased. Although she couldn't see their faces, Faith got the impression their attention shifted to her and Rowan. A shiver rushed along Faith's skin.

"Friends o' yours?"

Before Faith could answer, one of the drunk revelers pushed in between them. "Outta my way!"

A dark-skinned, emaciated hand reached out from the sleeve of the robe and grabbed the man by the collar. His body seized up in one giant spasm. His eyes went wide, and his mouth opened. Time paused, then he was released and turned to them. His eyes filled with darkness and spilled from his mouth, and he collapsed.

Chaos erupted as the patrons rushed to escape in their panic. Avoiding the two, they moved toward the tavern's back. Meanwhile, onlookers entered, overpowering and forcing both robed individuals down.

"Faith!" Rowan screamed over the din. "The window!"

Patrons left through the window, making room for others to reach it. Rowan took Faith's hand, and he bullied their way to escape. Rowan lifted Faith up and out the window and followed.

Unsure of the direction, Rowan guided them to the closest narrow walkway. They stood, pressing themselves against the wall as they watched patrons escaping from within.

"What were they?" Rowan asked.

"Servants of the Rot." Faith was certain. "What I saw in the forest must have informed on us."

"We can't stay here. We should go," Rowan said.

Faith was the first to turn and cry out at the sight of the two cloaked figures blocking their path. How, by the Vine, had they escaped that panic so quickly? Faith feared for any innocent that had gotten in their way.

An eerie light emanated from their bodies, enough for Faith to see by. They both reached up and lowered their hoods. They were both women. Their faces, resembling the hand she had witnessed, appeared starved of nourishment and light. Faith knew their identities.

"Dokkalfar," Faith whispered.

"We won't let you take us!" Rowan said.

"We haven't come to take," the one to their left said. "We are here to ask you to return to Brigantia. You are not safe here."

A third figure appeared behind them, much taller than the women. He was also wearing a long cloak that hid his features. "Faith."

That voice! It sent a lance of fear through her. He moved to stand between the women and removed his hood.

"Serval," Faith said.

"Please," Serval said. "You must go home. If you stay here, you will die."

CHAPTER TWENTY-SEVEN

"What treachery is this?" Rowan demanded.

"No treachery," the woman said, "just truth."

"I don't—" Rowan began.

"Wait." Faith stepped in front of Rowan and reached back, placing her hand on his chest. "I believe them." Faith took a few steps forward but made certain she didn't get within reach. "You're Dokkalfar."

"Yes."

"What are your names?"

The woman didn't respond.

"So, I suppose your truth doesn't include who you are."

"Call me Echo," the woman said, nodding to her companion. "She is Nightshade."

"Very well, Echo," Faith said. "Now speak your truth."

"You have noticed the way your vigor has drained away," Echo said. "And how heavy the air seems? It will only worsen."

"We have," Faith said warily. "So, exactly what do you want us to do?"

"Return to Brigantia. We will make certain no one follows you or causes you harm."

"Really." Faith crossed her arms. "For what price?"

"We know you are wise," Echo said.

"So, you still want me to allow you to breach the veil," Faith said. "It seems you've already found your way in. You don't need me."

"We do!" Serval spoke up. "If you and the prince join with us, we promise you—"

"What, power? Glory?" Faith mocked. "An old story and we both know a lie."

Echo took two steps forward, but Faith held her ground and gathered her Gift at the same time. Echo must have realized or seen and stopped. "You will let us in!"

"Keep your distance!" Rowan said.

"I figured," Faith continued, "there are only two ways your people could have gotten in. The Burrow or the Looking Glass. If you'd used the Burrow, you would have trapped us. Also, I doubt the Vine would have allowed it. That leaves the Looking Glass."

"Faith?" Rowan said.

"I'm sorry, I meant to ask you about this, but it makes sense, doesn't it?"

"But the Looking Glass is in the Red Queen's—" Rowan halted. "The Red Queen?"

"She let you in, didn't she? Why did she kill the Red King? Did he discover your trespass?"

Their response wasn't immediate. Both women looked at Serval.

"That is not for you to know," Serval said.

"Hmph," Faith said. "We are going to find Alice and ask her for help. We won't let you stop us."

"You believe that?" Echo said.

"Yes," Faith said. "Because you are not in any condition yourselves. How long have you been here? Were you looking for Alice too?"

A shrill whistle pierced the silence, making them all flinch.

"What in the nether hells..." Rowan moved to the narrow entrance. Faith continued to stare at the three cloaked figures.

"Faith, let's go," Rowan said. "There are many uniformed people coming this way."

"We can't let you—" Serval began.

Faith unleashed her power, just as she had with the wall in Brigantia. The stones to her left and right expanded, rising from underneath. Before the three could react, they found themselves ensnared.

Rowan took her hand, peeked from behind the wall again. "All right."

They ran, but only got as far as the end of the street when a voice shouted behind them, "Halt in the name of the law!"

They recognized that order. With no discernible direction they continued straight on.

"I said halt, or I'll shoot!"

"What does he mean?" Faith said.

Before Rowan could answer, he ducked into another narrow passage just as something whizzed past Faith's ear and struck the corner of the wall, blasting shards of it away. Faith screamed as some of them sliced into her face.

"Faith?" Rowan stopped and took her by the shoulder. Faith felt the blood trickling down her cheek. In disbelief, she reached up her hand and it came away bloody. "I'm bleeding!"

"Cheshire!" Rowan called.

"I am here, oh prince." Cheshire appeared, floating above them just as the light of a lamp illuminated the path. As Rowan had said, there was a man in a blue uniform. He held something in his hand, but neither could see what it was.

"Mary, Mother of Jesus!" he cried. "Witches!"

"Who is he calling a witch?" Cheshire grumbled.

"Cheshire, take Faith away!"

"No, wait!" Before Faith could protest further, Cheshire became smoke and wrapped himself around her body.

"No, no, Rowan!"

Then she was somewhere else.

"Damn it to the nether hells!" Faith turned on Cheshire. "How could you?"

"You need to be treated," Cheshire said. "I'll go after Rowan."

"But—"

"Alice! I found Alice!" His face and mouth separated from his body and appeared at the walkway of a cottage, then they both vanished.

Faith looked at her surroundings for the first time. No longer were they within the town proper but Faith guessed somewhere on the outskirts where there were cottages, like the ones back home. The only sounds Faith heard were of crickets and somewhere, faint music. Faith waited, while wringing her hands, for Cheshire and Rowan. She refused to move until they returned.

It seemed forever, yet only a few moments before Cheshire appeared. The spiral of smoke clearing revealed Rowan. Something was very wrong. Rowan lay at her feet. There was a dark red stain on his right shoulder. Rowan moaned in pain.

"Rowan? What happened?" Faith knelt beside him. When Faith touched the spot, like with her face, her hand came back bloody. "Cheshire!"

"I don't know," Cheshire said. "There was a flash of fire and Rowan cried out in pain as I tried to bring him."

"You said you found Alice?"

"There." Cheshire dipped his head toward the house.

"I can't carry him over there by myself."

Cheshire retreated, transforming back into a cloud. It swirled and expanded, reshaping until it matched Faith's shoulder height. The smoke congealed, and to Faith's astonishment, he loomed gigantic. Even more remarkable, he stood on his hind legs like a man. Cheshire then slid his arms gently under Rowan's shoulders and began to drag him across the lane. Faith drew in a breath when Rowan cried out. She'd never felt so helpless.

Faith had no idea how far away they were from those men who were chasing them, but they seemed very far away indeed. When they passed the arch at the front gate, Faith noticed a small, engraved sign made of polished wood on which was carved, *Hargreaves.*

Faith ran ahead and pounded on the door. *Please let this be her.*

Cheshire vanished as the door was opened by an old woman wearing a frock and apron, her hair under a kerchief. "Yes, may I—?" She looked down and saw Rowan. "What's all this now?"

"Dinah, who is it?" a voice called from within.

"Please," Faith said. "I desperately need to speak with Alice."

"What's going on with him?" The woman knelt. "Bloody hell, he's been shot!"

"What?" Another woman appeared. She was tall and slim. Although there were signs of aging in the lines at her eyes, she was still quite lovely with a heart-shaped face and smooth skin.

"Are you Alice?" Faith said.

"Dinah, let's get him into the house," the woman said. "Take his legs."

Faith didn't think it was possible, but the two women managed to half carry, half drag Rowan into the house. With each movement Rowan grunted in pain.

"Dinah, get me the tweezers, some bandages and disinfectant."

"Yes'um."

"Help me get this shirt off," the woman said.

Faith stood there, unable to move or comprehend. She continued to stare at Rowan, who was still bleeding from the wound.

"I'm Alice!" the woman said, exasperated. "Now, help me."

Faith knelt by Rowan across from Alice. *Alice, it's really her, it's the Heroine!*

"You're hurt too," Alice said as they struggled to remove Rowan's shirt.

"I'm fine," Faith said.

"Well, you're not fine, but we'll take care of you next."

Dinah returned with everything Alice asked for. Alice opened the bottle of disinfectant. "You may want to hold him down."

It was a good call because when she poured it over the wound, Rowan cried out, his eyes opening wide before he fell unconscious again.

"Who shot him?" Alice said as she picked up the tweezers.

"Who did what?" Faith asked, confused.

Alice shook her head and positioned the tweezers over the wound.

"Wait, what are you—?"

Rowan began to struggle again, and Faith continued to hold him as Alice dug into the wound and finally drew out something that resembled a metal ball. "Hopefully he won't get infected."

"What was that thing?" Faith asked.

Alice and Dinah exchanged glances. "You've never seen a lead shot before?"

"No," Faith said. "And you don't need to worry about infection." Knowing it would likely get them sent away, Faith laid her hands over the wound and repaired it. When she leaned back both Alice and Dinah were staring at her with shocked expressions.

"Mother Mary, preserve us." Dinah made a motion with her hand, touching first her forehead, the center of her chest, her left shoulder then right. "She's a witch!"

"Dinah," Alice scolded gently. "Please get us a clean blanket. He'll be much better near the fire."

Dinah curtsied quickly and hurried off. She returned soon with a silk blanket. Faith and Alice turned Rowan onto the blanket and then dragged him into the next room, which Faith surmised was a parlor. There was a fire burning in the hearth and once they situated Rowan near, they turned him back on his chest and pulled the blanket over him.

"Dinah, would you make us some tea, please?"

"Yes, Missus Alice."

Alice sat in a chair across the room, arranging her robe, and steepled her fingers, leveling a cool even gaze at Faith. "Now, tell me who you are and why you have brought such chaos to my house."

Faith took a deep breath and drew herself up and, as she had done with Uryphe, said, "I am Lady Faith Carter. Daughter of Theophilus Carter. You know him as the Mad Hatter, although I'm not fond of that name."

Alice's mouth opened in shock. "You—you're the Hatter's daughter?"

"Yes."

"The Hatter took a wife?"

"No," Faith said. "I'm an orphan from this world – your world."

"And who is that?" Alice nodded at Rowan.

"He is Prince Rowan, son to the Queen and King of Hearts."

"My word." Alice fanned herself with one hand. "I have been gone a long time." Then her attention went back to Faith. "Wait, you said you were from here? How did you get to Wonderland?"

"If you mean Brigantia," Faith said, "the same way you did, through the Burrow."

"Yes," Alice said. "In my young mind, I saw all the wonders of the place and named it as such. I believe someone tried to correct me, but I wanted things my way." She smiled at some unknown memory. "How old were you when you went down the Rabbit Hole?"

"An infant."

"But how could you have—?"

"Lady Alice," Faith said, "please forgive me for interrupting but Brigantia is in dire need of your help."

"Me? But why?"

"You are the Heroine of Legend," Faith said. "We have tried to fight our enemies, expel them from our home but have not been successful. My father sent me to find you."

"Heroine of Legend? I may have resolved some issues whenever I visited, but a legend? I'm just an ordinary woman."

"But…" Faith couldn't say anymore. Had they come all this way for nothing?

"And I'm finding this all a bit hard to believe."

Dinah returned with the tea service and poured a cup for Alice, but Faith refused any. "Finding what hard to believe? Who else would know what Rowan and I know?"

"You've told me very little," Alice said. "For example, you say you went down the Rabbit Hole, how? How could an infant do such?" There was an almost accusatory tone to her voice.

"All I know by the word of my father is that I was found in the Rabbit Hole, after he'd been given the message by the Caterpillar."

Alice took a sip of her tea. "All right."

"I recall being in a fire but no more. Then I was floating—"

"Wait!" Alice held up her free hand. "You said there was a fire?"

"I believe so. I remember flames and smoke."

"We were visiting friends at their summer home," Alice said. "The lord of the manor, Grayson Kennedy, and his wife, Molly, invited us often, along with my whole family. They loved throwing lavish parties.

One night their manor burned down. Well, I didn't understand the gossip and rumors at that time. Kennedy was rumored to have got—" She halted, her expression was astonished. "It's you!"

"Beg pardon?" Faith asked.

"Why didn't I see it? You look just like her!" Alice said.

"Like whom?"

"There was a maid named Charity, who was pregnant," Alice said. "They said Kennedy was the father and Molly Kennedy burned the place down to kill the baby. They never found the body."

Alice set her tea aside and stood, walked over to Faith, and took her hand. "Someone must have stolen you away and…" Alice hugged her. "I'm so glad you're alive. I loved Charity and told her about my adventures in Wonderland all the time. She was the only one who ever believed me!"

So that was her mother's name. Charity.

Alice stepped away and sat down again. "Please, tell me of this trouble."

Suddenly tired, Faith sat in the chair next to Alice and began to speak.

★　★　★

Faith wasn't certain when she finished. She was so sleepy that she wasn't even certain she was talking. Maybe she was dreaming she was talking? Faith yawned heavily.

"I'm curious, how did you and the prince get to my house?" Alice asked after Faith finished her tale.

"Cheshire brought us," Faith said.

"Cheshire is here too?" Alice almost squealed in childlike glee.

"He comes and goes," Faith said. "I'm assuming he didn't want to shock anyone in the house."

"He's welcome here," Alice said. "I didn't know magic truly existed in this world."

"I suppose it does," Faith said. "Or, perhaps it was given to me by the Vine."

"The Vine?"

"The Celestial Vine. It is the source of all magic in our world."

"Fascinating," Alice said. "You are obviously exhausted. We can talk more tomorrow. I'll have Dinah fix up the guest room. My husband and children are away on a journey."

So, she'd started a family. Life seems to be going well for her. Meanwhile, they were struggling to save her Wonderland.

"I'll stay here. I want to be near Rowan when he wakes."

"Very well."

The last thing Faith knew was Alice draping a blanket around her and she gave herself to sleep.

CHAPTER TWENTY-EIGHT

Faith was away. That was all that mattered.

Now facing the shouting man in the uniform, and still not understanding a word he was saying, Rowan hesitated. He didn't know if he should run or wait and hope Cheshire came back in time. "Please, I mean you no harm," Rowan said.

This seemed to fuel the flames of the shouting man's anger. He continued to wave the device menacingly. Rowan knew it was the thing that had shattered the wall and sent the shards of stone to slice Faith's cheeks. That made Rowan angry.

More figures appeared at the head of the walkway, and they were making their way steadily forward.

"Damn it all." Rowan turned to run and found Cheshire floating there, which sent Rowan's pursuers into a panicked frenzy. Then there was smoke moving in the vortex around him. And at the same time, there was that telltale flash of light and a sharp crack and then—

There was no true description of it. The pain tore through his very being. Rowan screamed in agony. It was the fires of the nether hells concentrating into a tiny sphere rending his flesh. The pain was unbearable and stayed with him as the world went dark around him.

Everything after that was just flashes of memory and reality, or so he thought. It was impossible to tell because the pain came and went. He thought there was another woman – no, two women, both strangers to him. They were all speaking but again, Rowan didn't understand. He welcomed unconsciousness.

The next time he awoke he found himself lying on a hearth before a low fire. There was light coming from somewhere. Rowan turned his head to his left and saw Faith sound asleep, sitting in a chair. Someone had draped a blanket over her. The light he found was coming from a lamp affixed to the wall. Rowan's gaze went back to Faith. Her face was peaceful in slumber, the light lending a soft sheen to her skin. If Rowan hadn't already been in love with her, he would have fallen madly now.

He noticed his shoulder, although stiff, no longer hurt as much. Faith, of course. He knew it immediately. He watched her for a little longer, before going back to sleep.

★   ★   ★

Someone moving about nearby woke Rowan. He turned to look at Faith and found she was still sleeping. However, it was the sound of conversation coming from the next room that had Rowan pushing himself up to sit. Rowan guessed it was early morning. He drew the blanket aside and although it took some doing, climbed to his feet. As he did, Faith woke up.

"Rowan." She was up and launched herself at him. She started kissing him all over his face.

"Gently now," Rowan said.

"How are you feeling?" Faith asked.

"A bit sore, but much better, thanks to you."

Faith heard the voices and they went to investigate the next room. Upon entering, they found themselves in an arboretum. The woman Rowan had glimpsed was sitting on a plush couch with her legs curled up, leaving room for Cheshire, who was sitting at the opposite end. A light repast of muffins and – thank the Vine – coffee had been set up on a rolling cart.

"Good morning," Cheshire said brightly when he saw them.

"Good morning, indeed." The woman turned her gaze to them.

Rowan sighed with relief. He understood her. "Thank the Vine."

"What?" Faith asked.

"I don't know why, but I can understand her." Rowan approached and held out his hand and she laid hers in it. Rowan kissed it. "I am Rowan, the Prince of Hearts. Milady, might you be Alice?"

"How polite!" she said. "Yes, I am Alice."

"Thank the Vine!" Rowan said. "I'm assuming Faith told you of our quest?"

"Rowan…" Faith said.

"What is it?"

"She did," Alice said, "but…"

"She can't help us." The defeat in Faith's voice tore at him.

"I don't understand." Rowan frowned.

Alice swung her legs around and lowered her feet to the floor. She stood to face him. "I'm sorry, but as I told Faith, I'm no heroine. I'm sorry you came all this way for naught."

"No." Rowan couldn't believe what he was hearing. *Brigantia is doomed.*

"However," she said. "I do have some gifts for you to help. I wanted to wait until you awoke, Prince Rowan." Alice motioned to the rolling cart. "Please, help yourselves. I'll return shortly."

When the three were alone Rowan said, "I suppose we should eat something. We have a long journey back."

"I'm sorry," Cheshire said. It was the soberest they'd ever seen him. "I don't know what's happening." He began to walk back and forth on the couch in a cat version of pacing. "There is something… not quite right."

"What do you mean?" Rowan poured coffee for Faith.

"I don't know," Cheshire said. "We were talking for hours and there were just…"

Cheshire shook his head as though he was getting rid of something tickling his ears. "That…she…she isn't Alice."

"What?" Rowan and Faith said together.

"I mean to say," Cheshire continued, "she *is* Alice and yet she isn't."

"Cheshire, dear, you're not making any sense," Faith said.

"I know!" It was a wail. "It's a feeling I have. I can't explain it. It's like we stepped into another place and time but not where we expected."

"It doesn't matter either way," Rowan said. "She's already said she can't help us."

They quieted when they heard footsteps. Alice returned with an engraved wood box under one arm and a long item wrapped in burlap. "I've kept this hidden for some time. I knew my husband wouldn't understand." She handed the wrapped item to Rowan. The box went to Faith.

Rowan carefully unwrapped the burlap. "By the Vine!"

As the remaining coverings slid away, Rowan discovered a short sword in a scabbard. Drawing it, he observed that the blade bore intricate runes, while the pommel took the form of the Jabberwock's head. "Is this...?"

"The Vorpal Blade," Alice said, as though it were an everyday thing.

"You've had it all this time?" Rowan said incredulously. It certainly explained why the book said it was lost. "How did you come by it?"

For the first time, Alice seemed nervous and hesitant. "It was a gift from your father."

Rowan was certain he hadn't heard right. "My father?"

"I didn't understand why at the time," Alice said. "I felt it was inappropriate, but I was so young, I didn't want to make him mad."

"Inappropriate," Rowan said to himself. He didn't know what to make of it. It was a simple gift, wasn't it? What did she mean by inappropriate? Rowan decided not to ponder it. "Thank you for returning this." He wrapped it again in the burlap.

Faith had opened the box and now stood staring at the contents in confusion. "What are these?"

"Pistols," Alice said.

"Pistols?" Faith inquired.

"It is a modern weapon," Alice said. "One of these was the cause of Rowan's injury."

"What?" Faith said in disgust. "Why are you giving these to me?"

"They may help so you may protect yourself."

Faith looked at Rowan, distressed.

"We need any advantage we may get," Rowan said.

Faith still looked uncertain but at least he'd taken the responsibility away from her, somewhat.

"Let me show you how to use them."

They spent the rest of the morning under Alice's tutelage. She showed them what *ammunition* was – apparently small steely balls like the one they'd picked out of Rowan's shoulder. How to load them and how to keep them clean. Rowan understood but couldn't even guess how the whole thing worked. When they felt they could not absorb any more information, another older woman, who Rowan later found out was the maid, Dinah, called them for lunch. It was around this time that Cheshire said he would do some skulking on his own.

After lunch, Alice gave Faith a belt that had two strangely shaped outer pockets attached, which Alice called holsters, where the pistols would fit. Alice told Faith about something called the *fast draw* but couldn't really explain how to do it. Alice told Faith to just pull the guns from their holsters, aim, and pull the triggers. Faith did not appear to be the least bit comfortable with this.

"We'll leave at dusk," Rowan announced. Perhaps by then they could figure out a way out of this predicament.

★   ★   ★

Alice asked more questions as they sat down to dinner. Neither had much of an appetite but they knew it was essential to keep up their strength. Besides, Rowan had a few questions of his own. "Lady Alice, who were the men that pursued us and shot me?"

"Local constabulary," she said. "Law enforcement officers."

"Shouldn't they be protecting people instead of trying to kill them?"

Alice sighed. "Yes, they should, but I needn't tell you what the smallest taste of power can do to a man."

"They have no superiors?" Rowan asked.

"They do," Alice said. "But sometimes they are even worse. And how far are you supposed to go?" Alice set down her coffee cup with a clink, annoyed. "This is not the perfect paradise you come from. This is not Wonder—"

"Brigantia." Rowan realized that Cheshire was right. This wasn't their Alice.

"That was impolite," Alice said.

"Your pardon."

"We appreciate your assistance," Faith said. "Perhaps you'll return and visit us someday."

"I'm afraid that isn't likely."

"Of course."

The ensuing and awkward silence was broken by a soft knocking at the door.

Alice let out an exasperated breath and threw down her napkin. "Now who is that at the dinner hour?"

Who indeed, Rowan thought. "Please excuse us, but we should go, milady."

Rowan slid out of his seat and stood, waiting for Faith. As they both exited the dining room, Rowan heard Alice say, "Hold a few moments, Dinah."

Rowan had left the Vorpal Blade wrapped up and lying on the couch, next to the holstered pistols. Rowan took the sword up now. Faith quickly belted the holsters around her waist. "I don't like this." He knew she was speaking of the pistols.

"I know," Rowan said.

Alice entered the room with two coats thrown over her arm. "Take these," she said. "Women may carry firearms, but it is probably best you keep them hidden. Now, with the sword, I recommend the same, although the laws may be complicated."

"Thank you again," Rowan kissed her hand one more time.

"Faith," Alice said, "please give the Hatter my regards."

"Of course," Faith said. "Take care, milady."

They stole out into the yard through the arboretum. Rowan looked back and saw Alice standing in the doorway. Her expression was impassive as though it could have been anyone visiting her and not a part of her past life. Not people who had come to her for help to save the world where she was renowned. Rowan turned away.

"We need Cheshire," Faith said. "We have no idea where we are."

Rowan realized belatedly that she was right. As they crossed the lane, Rowan chanced to look back to see two figures at the door. They weren't wearing robes, but were bundled up in coats, hats, and boots as if it were the middle of winter.

"Rowan!"

Cheshire had appeared. Well, at least his eyes and grinning mouth had.

"We are running out of time," Faith said.

"What is it?" Rowan asked.

"I am afraid... my magic seems to be fading," Cheshire said. "I didn't believe it possible."

"We've got to get out of here," Rowan said. "Cheshire, do you have enough magic to get Faith back to the Burrow?"

"Stop it!" Faith hissed. "Stop treating me like some fragile maiden who needs to be rescued."

"I—" Rowan began.

"Faith," Cheshire chided, "you know he only acts that way because he cares."

Faith calmed. "I know." She stepped forward and framed Rowan's face with her hands. "We have to do this together."

"I know," Rowan said. "It's just that—"

Faith placed a finger against his lips. "I know."

"I'll try and lead you away," Cheshire said.

They followed the bobbing grin and eyes as the sun dipped below the horizon. There actually were lights along the streets, lined up in neat rows so they did have light to see by. While they were in the wealthy part of the town there weren't many people around, but as they came to a bridge crossing a river, the surroundings became more urban and soon they were back in the town proper.

Rowan knew he should be relieved that they made it this far without drawing much attention. Whenever someone drew near, Cheshire would vanish entirely and come back with only the smile and eyes, which seemed to take longer each time. Rowan and Faith were not immune. They often had to take breaks to catch their breath.

When the area in which they walked started looking familiar, they stuck to the alleys – that's what they were called apparently – but even so it was more difficult to move around. A bell tolled five and the streets bustled with activity, and they figured the workday must be ending because they saw the tavern and dining halls were quickly filling.

"We'll need to cross that wide street," Cheshire said.

"Yes, I recall this area. We're not far from that lady with the cart," Rowan said.

"Cheshire," Faith advised. "Save your strength. We can find our way from here."

"All right, but I'll be close by."

Cheshire vanished completely.

"We'll continue on this side until we pass the old lady just to be safe." They walked, trying to keep an even pace and seemed to be making progress when Faith suddenly gasped in horror.

"What is it?" Rowan asked.

"Don't turn. Look out of the corner of your eye to your left."

He saw what she had in one of the shop windows. Two hand-drawn *Wanted* posters with their faces.

"What in the nether hells?" Rowan said. "Keep walking. Eyes down."

Again, they tried not to rush although it was nearly impossible and the urge to look at people by sheer force of habit made navigation difficult. They caught sight of the old woman and her cart across the street. Rowan was relieved they were going the right way, but on the other hand—

Rowan didn't know what it was, fate or mere coincidence, but as they passed by the old woman, he forgot himself and looked right at her in the same instant that she glanced up, and with the streetlights she'd likely gotten a good look. Rowan cast his eyes downward again and realized in a moment he was too late.

Her shrill cry went above the crowds and filled the air. "Witches! There are the witches!"

Rowan only heard the word *witches*. He didn't need to hear any more.

"Rowan?" Faith said in a desperate whisper.

"Keep moving." They picked up their stride. Rowan hoped the crowd would hide them.

"The witches! There they go, the witches! Across the street!"

The crowd was becoming agitated. People were looking around, shoving and tussling as arguments and accusations broke out. The old woman was still screaming until suddenly she was cut off and her screams became ragged, gasping cries.

Both Rowan and Faith couldn't help but turn to look. It was the Dokkalfar, that was the only explanation, as a gray shriveled hand reached out from the voluminous sleeve of the hooded cloak and grasped the woman by the throat.

"No!" Faith cried and she dashed across the street.

"Faith!" Rowan was right behind her. A coach nearly ran her over, but the driver pulled on the reins just in time.

"Damn it to the nether hells!" Rowan said as he grasped the rearing horses by their bridles.

The driver cried out what Rowan assumed were curses. He ignored them and ran for Faith, who was facing the Dokkalfar who turned out to be Nightshade.

"Leave her be!" Faith screamed and went to grasp her arm, and Echo appeared from the shadow of an alley and came up behind Faith, wrapping her arms around Faith's torso. She said something and Faith stopped moving.

"Get away from her!" Rowan cried. Echo did what he demanded, much to his shock, and he took Faith by the shoulders to draw her away just as the sound of a shrill whistle came from down the way. It was the law enforcers. The last thing they needed.

"Let's go!" Rowan took her elbow, and they ran.

"They killed her! They killed the old woman!"

"Murderers!"

"Witches!"

Several large bodies blocked their path, their intentions clear. The enforcers were calling for them to halt but then the men suddenly began to shout various oaths, and when Rowan and Faith turned, they saw Echo, holding a sword. How she'd managed to hide it, they didn't know. She took the head off one of the officers.

Faith screamed. Echo turned to another, who dropped his pistol and raised his hands. They knew he was surrendering but Echo held the sword straight out to plunge it into the officer's heart.

It never happened.

While watching Echo take lives, Rowan hadn't noticed Faith drawing one of the pistols. It was the sharp crack and the flash of fire that told him what she had done. When the ball hit its mark, Echo screamed and exploded in a blast of fire and black smoke.

Nightshade wailed and threw herself forward, reaching out her hands to embrace what was left, but there was nothing but ash.

Chaos erupted. Within it all, Faith stood motionless, the gun still in her hand. Her expression was one of horrified shock. Neither of them had expected this. Rowan snatched the pistol from her hand and jammed it through his belt. He grabbed her hand and ran, following the flow of people fleeing the grisly scene.

CHAPTER TWENTY-NINE

You're going to kill them, aren't you?

We must protect you no matter what the cost.

Faith shuddered as Echo embraced her from behind. When the Dokkalfar attacked the cart woman, Faith didn't consider her own safety. Even though Missus Abagail had betrayed them, Faith would not allow her to die. Before Faith could act, the alley shadows came alive and trapped her underfoot. Then Echo moved behind her into some twisted circle of protection.

"Leave this place," Echo whispered close to her ear. "Return to Brigantia before you lose your life. Then how will you save your home?"

"Get away from her!"

Rowan. Faith was unsure if it was Rowan's command or the advancing enforcers that caused Echo to let her go.

"Let's go!" Rowan's touch liberated Faith from her paralysis.

The people behind them screamed curses and oaths, saying the word *witches* with hate or disgust. *What is wrong with these people? Why are witches treated with such disdain?* Before they could escape, four brutish men blocked their path. Behind them, the officers yelled for them to halt. Faith's heart sank. They would never make it back home.

Faith spotted Echo holding a sword. Before Faith could ask where Echo had hidden it, the Dokkalfar decapitated the closest officer with it.

Faith screamed in anguish and guilt for the innocent life lost. Echo turned to the next officer, a man not far into adulthood. He dropped his pistol and raised his hands high, terrified. He surrendered, giving Echo no reason to harm him.

Although Faith couldn't see Echo's face, her body language and the way she held her sword drawn back with the blade pointed at the cowering young man left no doubt in Faith's mind. Even if any of these people harmed her, Faith wouldn't allow them to be murdered.

Faith drew one pistol and with a quick prayer to the Vine that her aim was true, pulled the trigger as Alice had taught her. The force of the explosion knocked her back a few steps. The sound made her ears ring, and she smelled the acrid scent of metallic smoke. Alice had not told her about that!

Nor had their *Heroine* told her what would happen in the aftermath.

Perhaps Alice hadn't known. After all, these were fey creatures. But the cry of intense pain resounded, then was silenced as Echo's body exploded and burned, the flames consuming her flesh like a candle devouring paper until only ash remained.

The world around her was silent.

Faith stared at the pistol, a foreign and wicked object. Regret overwhelmed her, tearing at her insides as if she too would dissolve into ash for ending a life. She had intended to wound, but the creators of this terrible machinery desired more. Survival hinged on luck or circumstances.

Chaos engulfed Faith, like a crashing wave on the Sea of Tears. Rowan snatched the pistol from her hand and shoved it into his belt. Then he pulled Faith after him. She did not look back.

*   ★   ★

The full moon was the only light they had once they'd fled the town limits. Faith wondered if they witnessed the identical moon in Brigantia. Such an absurd thought, given the circumstances.

Rowan stopped when they reached the tree line. "We'll stop here and rest."

Faith plopped down right where she stood. The dampness made her uncomfortable, but she didn't care. She kept seeing Echo consumed by flames and hearing her scream, followed by Nightshade wailing.

"Faith." She hadn't noticed Rowan kneeling next to her. She could see his face. "It wasn't your fault. You didn't know."

Of course, he'd know what she was feeling. "Then whose was it? I not only killed her, I— it's not what I wanted to do." Faith wanted to cry, but no tears came.

"I know." Rowan took her hands. "She would have killed that young officer, even though he was terrified and unarmed."

Faith took a slow breath. "Yes, I know."

She curled her legs up against her body and wrapped her arms around them. "I want to go home."

"So do I," Rowan said. "I've had enough of this violent, filthy place."

A faint light appeared moments later, and Cheshire floated above them. His body was translucent.

"Cheshire!" Faith reached for him, but he vanished just as quickly as he'd come, leaving a false light in his wake, floating like a wil-o-wisp in the air. "Dear Vine, I hope he's all right."

Seeing him and knowing what he risked by appearing before them and leaving this bit of himself to guide them back to the Burrow, filled Faith with new resolve. She stood. "Let's not tarry here any longer."

Faith assumed the lead as they journeyed toward the forest. She had no plan to save Brigantia, just longing to return home to loved ones. The walk back was filled with silence.

When they crested the top of the hill, Faith chanced to look back at the town below them. She couldn't see what was happening, but smoke was billowing from several places and half the lights had gone out, and if she listened hard enough, she could still hear screams and shouts in the distance.

"Do you believe they'll destroy themselves?" Rowan was looking back too.

"Yes," Faith said. "But it's not our concern anymore."

Alice was not the woman they had hoped for. Even Cheshire had sensed it. Faith wanted a good life for Alice, and hoped she wouldn't get caught in the chaos.

★   ★   ★

As they walked, they sensed pursuers – men and dogs – trailing them. The Burrow loomed ahead, and they hastened their steps, guided by the ethereal glow. Questions swirled in their minds: How had they been discovered? And why did it matter? Meanwhile, their town burned, flames licking at its heart. At that moment, their emotions were a mix of anxiety, curiosity, and a sense of impending danger.

"It's likely they won't follow us into the Burrow," Rowan commented.

"I'm going to make sure they don't," Faith said. She would never let this evil enter their world, even if they had to leave Brigantia.

As they reached the Burrow, bathed in a faint, welcoming glow, several figures materialized. Their pursuers had spotted them and released the dogs.

"Go!" Faith said. She waited, making certain they saw what she was about to do. If they feared witches, then she would become one. Her true self. Faith called on her power and beseeched the Vine at the same time. It didn't take long to heed her call.

Twisting vines, with needlelike thorns and sticky burs, erupted from the earth, forming a barrier between her and the relentless dogs. Despite her reluctance to harm the helpless creatures, those who persisted in their pursuit became ensnared. Faith stepped back, allowing herself to descend into the safety of the Burrow. Once inside, she coaxed the nettles to curve protectively over the entrance, while the tree roots multiplied, weaving a formidable net of branches and prickly stickers.

Faith sensed her vigor returning in an instant. Her very being restored itself as she breathed in the earthy scent of the Burrow. She looked down and saw Rowan sitting in one of the floating chairs. "Are you all right?" he asked.

Faith settled in his lap. "Yes, I'm fine." She snuggled against him. "Let's rest before we go on."

Faith couldn't help but yawn. "You're right."

It didn't take long for Faith to fall asleep. Yet she remained aware of her surroundings. Did the Vine give her this vision? She saw Alice's home in the world above. The men gathered where she'd closed the entrance to the Burrow. There were five of them and they stood muttering to themselves, while the poor dogs were limping around and whining in pain.

Faith felt bad for the animals. The men were paying them little attention. Faith focused on their voices.

"What should we do?"

"Burn the witches!"

"Chop down that damnable tree!"

"Are you mad? Do you wish to bring curses upon us?"

"You can't believe—?"

"You saw! You saw everything!"

"I'll not do it!" The one who had spoken turned away. "I have ta get back to my family!"

"Yeah, I ain't stayin' neither. You do what you want." He whistled. One dog was his and the poor thing limped after him.

All but one walked away. He stood before the nettle and branch covering and raised his lamp. The last dog lay down at his feet with his head resting on his paws and whining.

"Shut up, you mangy beast!"

He was struggling to operate the lamp when a brilliant light illuminated the space, banishing the darkness. The dog, despite his injuries, yelped and dashed off.

Cheshire appeared before the man, the size of Argestes. His simple *meow* was a roar to the man. He shrieked in terror, turned, and followed his companions into the night. Faith smiled as Cheshire returned to his normal size, then became smoke as he passed through the barrier. The famous grin and eyes appeared. Cheshire then shrank to the size of a house cat and curled up on Faith's lap. They were safe.

★　★　★

"I fear what lies beyond that door," Faith admitted.

"It's fine," Cheshire said. "We are fortunate not much has changed."

"Is that fortunate?" Rowan said.

Cheshire sat on his haunches, and used his legs to shrug, although Faith was certain his legs should *not* be going that way. When they stepped back into Brigantia, they saw Cheshire was correct. The passage of time seemed to halt, leaving everything as they had left it. Faith couldn't decide whether she should feel relieved or disheartened.

"All right," Rowan said. "I'll go back to the palace and inform my father about what happened and our suspicions of the Red Queen. Cheshire, would you come with me? Please bring Faith with you when things are prepared. Is that ideal for both of you?"

"Of course," Cheshire said.

"Yes." Faith smiled, reassured. "First, I would like to check on Jade's well-being. Don't worry, I'll be fine."

Despite his hesitant expression, Rowan agreed.

They parted ways at the Grotto, and Faith stood outside and waved until Rowan and Cheshire were out of sight. Faith entered the Grotto, then gaped when she saw Jade sprawled across the mushroom cap.

"Jade?" Faith rushed over to her and climbed atop the mushroom. She was unconscious. Faith noticed the Grotto remained alive, untouched by the encroaching Rot. Careful of her wings, Faith turned Jade over on her back. "Jade?"

Her eyes came open, much to Faith's surprise. "Faith?"

"Jade!" Faith kissed her on the forehead.

"You are home."

"Yes," Faith said. "I wanted to see how you are faring."

"I am better," she said. "The Rot has receded."

"It has?"

"Yes," she said. "It leaves me very suspicious. They may plan another assault."

"Jade," Faith said. "We found Alice, but—"

"Did she not wish to assist?"

"She…" How could Faith explain it without wasting time they didn't have?

"You needn't tell me," Jade said. "There are things of greater import."

"Jade, if you are able, please send a message to the Spinner Queen. Inform her of the harpies' attack."

"She is already aware," Jade said.

"Good," Faith said. "Will you be safe here if I return home?"

"Yes."

"Good," Faith said. "Then I have one more message for Sylmare."

★   ★   ★

Faith's sudden fury toward Alice seemed irrational.

She sat at her father's bedside and told him of their…*adventure* in Alice's world. Her father sat up in bed and listened while drinking tea. His own emotions went from worry to fury to disappointment. That was the source of Faith's greatest anger.

"Perhaps —" the Hatter set his teacup on the nightstand, "— we expected too much of Alice. Or made too much of her."

"Father." Faith laid her hands over his. "She was the Heroine, but Alice was not a symbol of strength and courage. We must find our own."

"I'm not sure if any are remaining." Her father's voice filled with despair.

"Please don't give up," Faith said.

Her father tightened his grip on her hands. "It must be you, my dear."

"Me?" Faith said.

"You must be our symbol, our Heroine now. I know you can do this."

Faith didn't feel a symbol was necessary. What good were they? As for her being the Heroine… "Father—"

Cheshire appeared but did not materialize, just his head and tail.

"Cheshire!" the Hatter said.

"Faith!" Cheshire's distant voice called out. "I have an urgent message from the prince!"

"He needs me at the palace," Faith said.

"No, no!" Cheshire protested. "You must stay away from the palace!"

"I don't understand," Faith said.

"The prince is imprisoned," Cheshire said. "He was betrayed."

CHAPTER THIRTY

"Prince Rowan!"

Once again, the guards failed to recognize him, but upon closer inspection a group of servants, though fewer than usual, surrounded him. He learned his father had sent some soldiers to keep watch over the wall. His mother remained bedridden, while the Red Queen joined the soldiers at the front. The citizens were surviving, and the king had spent his time examining the map with almost fanatical attention.

He had no valid reason to do so. The wall prevented the enemy from advancing, leaving them with limited mobility options.

The absence of the Red Queen from the palace was a stroke of luck for them. The challenge was to breach the wall, reach the Looking Glass, and destroy it without the Red Queen's knowledge or interference. He was still pondering this as he climbed the stairs to the royal chambers.

Guards remained by his mother's door. As Rowan approached, a maid emerged from the room carrying a tea tray. The maid bobbed a curtsy.

"She is still being fed the medicinal tea?" Rowan asked her.

The maid looked stricken. "No, Your Highness. The king said not to."

"What?" Rowan said.

The girl cowered. "I'm sorry, Your Highness, it was the king's orders."

Rowan fought to calm himself. "Didn't anyone realize how pointless that was? Get her the medicine now!"

"Yes, Your Highness." The maid scurried away.

Despite his desire to visit his mother, Rowan walked to the war room. Rowan found his father there, as expected, observing the untouched figurines on the table.

"Father!"

The king straightened, startled. "Rowan! You've returned. Thank the Heroine! Did you find her?"

"I did," Rowan said. "And there is no reason to be thanking her. Father, why did you command the servants to stop giving Mother the medicine?"

An expression of puzzlement crossed his father's features. "She seemed to get sicker the more we fed her, so I thought perhaps it isn't as safe as we thought."

"I ordered the maids to give it to her again, but if there is a problem, I'll rescind my command."

"There will be plenty of time for that," the king said. "So, tell me all of your journey."

"Before I do," Rowan said, "I must tell you about our suspicions concerning the Red Queen."

"She is at the wall with her soldiers and ours."

"I know," Rowan said. "But Faith and I—"

"How is Faith?"

The interruption annoyed Rowan, but he kept his peace. "She is fine. She went to see her father. About the Red Queen?"

"Let's not worry over her," his father said. "We need Faith to breach the wall before we can do anything."

"I had the same thought," Rowan said. "Father, we believe the Red Queen is using the Looking Glass to allow the enemy inside. We must figure out a way to destroy it without the Red Queen's knowledge."

"That will be a difficult feat," his father said. "Did the Heroine refuse to help?"

"She is no Heroine, father. At least not the one we believed she was."

"I don't understand."

"It's hard to explain." Rowan shared Cheshire's words with him.

"Such a disappointment." The king stroked his beard. Then his attitude brightened. "Well, at least Alice gave you the Vorpal Blade, so I'm sure the Red Queen will be easy to take care of."

Rowan stiffened. "Yes, Father."

"Tomorrow we shall gather the rest of our troops and travel to the wall. You'll have Faith bring it down. We'll deal with the Red Queen then."

"Of course, Father," Rowan said, as his heart fell into his stomach. "I'll visit with Mother now. I will fetch Faith in the morning."

"Good." The king bent back over the map to stare at the immobile figures. Rowan kept his pace even as he walked out, his stride leading him to his mother's room. He reminded the guards, "No one, except the servant girl and I, have permission to enter Her Majesty's room, understood?"

"Yes, Your Highness." They looked confused. They likely wondered why the king was not included in this order. The serving girl who had arranged the tea tray before was the same one. "If questioned, inform them it's my direct command. Continue to bring the medicinal tea."

"Yes, Your Highness."

"Close the door."

Rowan moved a chair to his mother's bedside. "Mother, please come back. We need you." He realized he missed her whooping and hollering and her commands of "Off with their heads!" Now she seemed ancient, her face pale and wrinkled around her eyes and mouth, and with streaks of gray in her hair. "I don't want to leave you again, but I must. A terrible decision lies before me."

He wanted — *needed* to see Faith. He had an important matter to attend to. "Be strong, Mother."

When Rowan stepped out of his mother's room, the sound of rushing footsteps made him turn to his right. His father, followed by three guards, was coming for him. "Damn it," Rowan muttered. He thought he'd have more time. He had wanted to retrieve his armor, but now it was too late.

"Rowan, halt!" his father shouted.

Momentarily disoriented, the two guards hesitated, granting Rowan an opportunity to flee.

"Seize him!" his father roared. However, it took a few moments more before the guards pursued.

"Summon more guards! Rowan is not leaving this palace!"

Rowan couldn't believe the danger that now chased him in his own home. Heart pounding, he bolted down the nearest staircase and sprinted through dimly lit halls. The side door beckoned – his escape route. But echoing footsteps closed in from both directions, threatening to trap him within the very walls that should have been his sanctuary.

"Rowan!" a hushed voice said. Rowan was barely aware of where he was. The nursery wing. Seven beckoned to him from a cracked-open door. Despite not wanting to, he hid in the children's room. Seven closed and locked the door behind her.

He realized he'd not seen his sister in almost a month. Rowan knelt and embraced her.

"What's going on?" Seven asked. "Everyone is so angry, and we're all scared."

All the other children were asleep snug in their beds.

"Why are you up so late?" Rowan asked.

"I heard them yelling. Why are they mad at you?"

"I..." How could he explain it? How could he reveal to her that their father was the real enemy?

"Seven, sweetheart, I need to ask you a favor. Stay in the nursery."

"I have been. We all have. Father commanded we stay here for our safety."

At least his father had some honor left in him. "Then that is what you must do. Promise?"

She nodded.

"I'm putting you in charge." Rowan removed his signet ring and gave it to her. "Find some chain and wear my ring around your neck."

"I will." She threw her arms around him. "Be careful."

"I promise."

Rowan straightened. "Lock the door behind me."

Glancing, he entered the hallway, turned left, and approached the exit. Silence enveloped the area, making it impossible for him to detect anyone's location. As he reached the hall junction, he heard footsteps and whispering voices. *Damn it to the nether hells!* Going the other way would lead him straight to the throne room. It was evident that he had only one option. Rowan took a deep breath and stepped out into the open.

Both guards halted, shocked, then they tried to take on menacing expressions as they drew their weapons.

"Stay where you are, Prince Rowan," a tall grizzled older guard said. "We have orders to place you under arrest."

Rowan remained calm. "On what grounds?"

"Treason and attempted patricide."

Patricide? Would the king go that far? "I am innocent. Do you honestly believe those charges?"

The younger guard looked at his elder for guidance. The grizzled guard scrutinized Rowan.

"I need to go to Faith. Only she can put an end to this."

The older guard lowered his sword, then tossed it at Rowan's feet. The younger guard followed his action.

"Thank—"

The blade of a sword thrust through the center of the elder guard's chest. Shock and pain crossed his face, his head lowered, and he crumpled to the floor, dead.

The king turned on the young guard.

"No!" Rowan dashed forward and put himself between the king and the guard.

"Traitors must die!" the king said. Rowan was disgusted to see the Rot swimming in the king's eyes and filling his mouth, giving him a tone Rowan had never heard from him before.

"Go now." Rowan motioned with his head and the young guard dashed down the hall. Rowan thought the king was too focused on him to care. When he heard the guard's agonized scream, Rowan resisted the urge to look back. His father – no, the Rot – had struck the guard down with no remorse or reason. He kept his eyes fixed on the king. More guards were approaching, although they kept their distance. *An excellent move*, Rowan thought. They were unaware of the challenge ahead.

But Rowan was.

"You gave yourself to the Rot."

The former King of Hearts grinned, revealing black teeth. "Yes."

"Why?"

"Surely you can figure this out for yourself. You're a bright young man."

"Was this the only way?"

"The man I was? Useless and pathetic!" the king said. "Letting some slut cuckold him!"

"You son of a bitch!" Rowan went for him, but the king leveled his sword.

"Take the prince to the lower cells and lock him up."

The guards didn't move. They exchanged nervous or confused glances.

"Didn't you hear me?" the king demanded. "The prince is a traitor! Take him away!"

Two guards stepped forward and moved toward Rowan.

"I will execute anyone who disobeys me!"

The guards who had remained in the background screamed as black thorns pierced their flesh. It was the same thing that had happened to the Red King. The Rot had full command.

"No!" Rowan held his hands out. "Please, no more killing! I'll go with them!"

The king grinned. It disgusted Rowan. "That is more like it. Now then, hand over the Vorpal Blade."

Rowan had no desire to do it. The king was looking at his scabbard and scowled. "Where is it?" the king demanded.

Rowan raised his hand and looked down at the now-empty scabbard. "What in the nether hells—?"

"Where have you hidden it?"

"But I didn't—" Rowan stared at the scabbard in confusion.

"Ah," the king said. "I see you don't know. I have a suspicion who may have it."

He lowered his sword. "Take him away."

"Wait, what of them?"

The guards whom the king had cursed were on their hands and knees. They begged for mercy in their expression. Blood was pooling at their feet. The king sneered down at them. Inclining his head once, they died in a matter of moments, torn apart by the thorns.

Rowan glared at the smirking thing. "Bastard." The two guards approached and flanked him. Rowan went without protest.

When they were out of earshot, one of them muttered, "We're sorry, Your Highness."

"Just do as he says," Rowan said. "If you find the chance, leave. Take your families and look for the Red Queen at the wall."

"Yes, Your Highness."

They took him down, passing the spot where they found the Red King. Not far away, there were cells that were rarely used, if at all. Usually, they held some miscreant for a minor infraction that didn't warrant a long stretch. Or someone whom the queen had sentenced to have their head taken, but soon forgot about once the guilty vanished from view.

Rowan never imagined being here. The guards opted for the first cell and retrieved the nearby keyring hanging on the wall. A guard opened the cell door and Rowan stepped in. The guard locked it after.

"Remember what I said. Tell everyone, commoner, servant, or soldier. Escape the palace if you can."

"Yes, Your Highness."

They left him alone.

Rowan paced until the sound of metal hitting stones drew his attention. He turned to find the Vorpal Blade lying right outside the cell door. And Cheshire sitting there with one paw placed on the blade.

"Cheshire." Rowan grinned at him. "You sly old feline! Get me out of here."

"Um…" Cheshire said.

"Oh, yes, iron bars."

"And the keys." Cheshire nudged the sword closer but turned away. "If Faith could—"

"Gods be damned!" Rowan said. "Faith!" Rowan approached the doors and grasped the bars. "You must warn Faith! Inform her about my father and advise against visiting the palace." He hoped his warning didn't come too late. "Instruct her to find the Red Queen and destroy the Looking Glass!"

"Worry not, Your Highness!" Cheshire said. "I will get the warning to her."

"Take care. The king knows of your involvement!"

Rowan reached through the bars and maneuvered the sword through. It shone with an ethereal light. Rowan raised the mystic weapon and brought it down on the lock. It cleaved it in two. "I'll be damned." Rowan grinned.

Rowan ran from the cellars, taking the stairs two at a time. People were escaping, with only the clothes on their backs, as they followed his command. One of the guards who'd escorted him down stopped and said, "Your Highness, aren't you coming?"

"I'm going for the queen," Rowan replied.

"Good fortune to you. Take care."

As Rowan pushed against the frantic tide of terrified people, an almost animalistic roar reverberated through the air. Onlookers halted in their tracks, their eyes drawn to the figure standing atop the grand staircase. The man they had known as their king was now unrecognizable – a primal force, his humanity eclipsed by something ancient and fierce. "Traitors! Deceivers! All of you!"

"Father!" Rowan had ceased to call him that, but now, with all these people, he needed to keep the king's attention on him. "Will you face me? I am your son!"

The apparition crept down the stairs, his eyes on Rowan.

"Go!" Rowan commanded, and the wave of people went out again, apart from the guards who still obeyed the king. But the king waved them away. "Father, I know some part of you remains. Surely, you did not give up your soul to the Rot?"

"We are power," the king said. "Don't you understand, Rowan? Let them come here. They gave me the strength to rule my kingdom."

"Our kingdom," Rowan said. "What you have is not strength, it's a lie. That's what it is. That is true betrayal of self, your family and the kingdom."

The beast faltered, revealing his father. His voice trembled as he said, "I don't... I'm sorry, Rowan." His eyes held a mixture of anguish and resignation. But as quickly as the human façade appeared, it dissolved, and the primal creature reasserted itself. Rowan's heart sank; he sensed in his soul that his father was irrevocably lost.

"Now," the beast said, "take the girl to break the barrier, or I will kill as many of those who are loyal—"

"You will not."

The voice, although hoarse, rang across the open space of the throne room. Every gaze shifted as the Queen of Hearts descended the stairs, assisted by the servant girl. Once the queen set foot on the landing, she told the girl, "You may go now." She scurried away.

Her pale appearance improved as color returned to her cheeks and she held on to the railing with a trembling hand for balance.

"Mother."

"Leopold," she said. "What have you done?"

A momentary shock swept over it before the beast uttered, "Belladonna?"

"You gave yourself to this thing? This Rot?"

"What do you care?" the beast shot back. "You always treated me like I was nothing. Now, we are strong. Did you feel no love for me?"

His mother didn't respond.

"See!" The beast scanned the remaining people, anticipating their empathy. "You are a vile woman, and it will bring us joy to see you dead."

The queen inclined her head. "Do what you must."

An unearthly cry echoed through the chamber as the shadow stretched across the floor, thorns bursting forth and crumbling the marble tiles. Just as they closed in on her, the queen issued the chilling command, "Off with his head!"

The king, consumed by rage, fixed his gaze solely on the queen, leaving Rowan unnoticed. In that moment, Rowan darted forward, silent and resolute.

The vorpal blade went snicker-snack!
He left it dead, and with its head
He went galumphing back.

Everything was silent. The soldiers dropped their arms and fell to their knees. His mother slumped onto the bottom step.

"Mother!" Rowan ran to her side and knelt before her.

She gave him a wan smile. "The king is dead. Long live the king."

CHAPTER THIRTY-ONE

The wall stood and stretched farther than Faith had expected. Clad in her armor, she instructed Argestes to fly at a low altitude and closely inspect it for any hidden breaches. Despite Cheshire's warning, her immediate desire was to liberate Rowan and reach the palace, yet Cheshire remained adamant. They would need the Red Queen's help and her Chessmen. Faith still didn't like it. She also didn't like the idea of leaving her father and Minerva alone. However, like Cheshire, they insisted.

"It all depends on you now, my daughter. Seek the Red Queen and save Rowan. Both of you must work together," the Hatter told her.

Faith was shocked to find soldiers and common folk gathered at the beach. Still, it wasn't difficult to locate the Red Queen. Among the moving bodies, tents, and crude shelters, she stood outside of the largest tent, in her full armor.

She looked up and stepped forward to meet Faith as the surrounding soldiers moved aside to make room. Faith dismounted before Argestes had landed completely, strode up to the queen and bowed low. "Your Majesty."

"It is good to see you, Lady Faith. Welcome home."

"Thank you, but I must apologize to you." Faith held her gaze.

To Faith's surprise, she said, "You suspected I was the betrayer?"

"Yes," Faith said, despite the excessive grumbling from the queen's people. "I ask your forgiveness."

"No need," the Red Queen said. "How aware are you of our situation?"

Faith shared her knowledge about Rowan's imprisonment by the king. And Rowan's request to have the Looking Glass destroyed.

The Red Queen sighed. "I figured that's how Leopold was allowing them in, but it has its limits. I'm not sure how the harpies got through."

"What do you mean, limits?" Faith asked.

"It's difficult to explain," the Red Queen said. "The Looking Glass won't allow just anyone in at any time. The magic of it makes it somewhat..." She bit her lip and furrowed her brow, trying to gather her thoughts.

"Your Majesty?"

She looked up. "Call me Taira, please."

"When did you surmise it was the king who had betrayed us?"

"I started suspecting after the murder of my dear husband. I understood the situation and realized that this Rot only affects weak-willed individuals. We both know that isn't Belladonna." She smiled and Faith couldn't help but smile too.

"And what of your journey to find the Heroine?"

That took a while, so they moved their conversation into the tent. An elderly woman brought bread, cheese, and wine. Refugees from the palace arrived at the beach, carrying as much food as possible.

The tent had one chair, clearly for the queen, and several cushions arranged on a large wool rug. In the center was a rickety wood table with, Faith discovered, a roughly drawn map of the wall. "I can have someone find another chair," the Red Queen said.

"No need," Faith said and sat on a large cushion.

"Isn't that uncomfortable?" Taira was incredulous.

"No," Faith said. "The armor is very light and malleable. I just need someone to help me out of it, but it's like it molds to my skin."

"The Spinner Queen must have tremendous talent."

"She does," Faith said.

"And the weapons Alice gave you?"

When Faith belted the holster, it transformed into part of her armor, in color and design. This included the pistol's handle but, of course, not the barrel. "It's called a pistol."

"Pis-tull?" Taira furrowed her brow again. "What a disgusting name."

"It's an awful weapon. I don't know why I still have it," Faith said. "Rowan has the other one. I don't trust them to anyone else."

A sudden commotion erupted outside. Taira stood. "What now?" She reached out a hand to help Faith to her feet, and they exited the tent. People gathered at the camp's center. Cheers went up. Argestes bounded over and that was when the crowd parted, and Faith saw – "Rowan!"

Faith ran to him as he dismounted from Epione and met her halfway. Pulling her into his arms, he kissed her deeply. Faith encircled him with her arms and allowed him to lead. The people began cheering again. Faith pulled back, breathless. She embraced him again. "I'm so relieved you're safe."

"And I, you." Rowan glanced over her shoulder as Taira approached.

"Your Majesty." Rowan bowed. "I owe you an apology—"

"No," Taira said. "Faith and I already have spoken of this. And no longer Your Majesty. I am Taira."

"As you wish." Rowan grinned.

"What of your royal parents?"

Rowan dropped his gaze. "I am now King of Uthelan."

"Rowan." Faith drew him against her. Even through his armor, she could feel him shaking.

"Long live—" Taira began.

"Don't, please."

Taira nodded. "Very well. What of Belladonna?"

"She is recovering," Rowan said. "She knew the king was the betrayer."

"I'm glad to hear she will survive."

"Faith told you of the Looking Glass?"

"Yes," Taira said.

Faith turned to look at her handiwork. "We must be ready. We are unaware of what lies beyond. If fortune is with us, it will be the White Queen's army."

"Let us discuss our plan of action."

They gathered in the big tent with the leaders of their army. The initial decision was for those unable to fight to either seek safety in the royal palace or return to their homes. Many remained determined to fight for their home, resulting in numerous tearful wishes for good luck. No one said goodbye.

"Rowan and I should fly to the other side and explore," Faith said.

"What about the harpies?"

"Any remaining uninjured would have attacked already. If they do, I'll stop them again," Faith said. "Rowan, is this agreeable?"

"Yes," Rowan said. "We need to see what we're dealing with."

"We'll concentrate our forces along the beach," Taira said. "My Chessmen guarded the forest but saw no enemy break through."

"Did they feel any sensation of being watched or followed?"

"Yes, they did," Taira said, "many times. I thought it was their imagination, but you claim it's true?"

"Yes," Faith acknowledged. "They are being spied on. Regrettably, stopping it is impossible. Urge them to be courageous and support each other. Light fires and stay close but tell them to be very careful."

"Done," Taira said. She nodded to a nearby soldier, who rushed to carry out her order.

"When you report," Taira said, "we'll arrange troops and proceed accordingly."

Taira escorted them out to their mounts. "Argestes," Faith said, "we will fly over the wall on a scouting mission and report back. We will need your keen eyes."

"I – we – are at your service." Argestes inclined his head at Epione, who repeated the motion. Faith and Rowan mounted, and they were off. The wind whistled past them as the gryphons climbed skyward. Faith had to admit she was impressed with herself and couldn't help but smile a bit. Only when they reached the top of the wall did her smile disappear.

At first glance, the beach seemed strewn with heaps of black seaweed. A multitude of these dark forms lay scattered haphazardly near the rocks.

"What in the nether hells are those? Surely, they can't be dead bodies?" Faith said aloud. "Argestes. Do you sense anything?"

"This may sound unbelievable, but those things are living beings. I can see an aura and yet...?"

Rowan signaled to her, and together they returned to the queen's side.

"How many are there?" Taira asked.

"There are no bodies," Faith said. Argestes let out a small cry. "I intend to say, there were heaps of...we couldn't identify their nature. Argestes said he sensed life within them."

"I don't understand any of this," Taira said. "There was no sign of the White Queen or her forces?"

"No," Faith said. "Let me open a passage. Thoughts on dividing our forces?"

"I am loath to do so," Taira said.

"It may be the best choice," Rowan advised. "We're unsure about those things or the Rot's plans. The king was their connection. We don't know how his death will impact their plans."

"Then we will move forward," Taira said. While she was commanding her soldiers and having them stand in formation in front of the wall, Faith went to work.

Faith pressed her hands against the surface of the wall. The glass felt familiar, its coolness akin to her own voice. As she worked, the glass yielded, shifting and coming apart. Her task was to distribute it evenly along the shore. As the glass slid beneath the odd living piles, they rose slightly, then settled back into place.

"Avoid those things," Taira warned her soldiers. "Take extreme care where you step."

She needn't have told Faith and Rowan. They led the gryphons with their bridles, but the beasts could watch their own footing. Now that they were closer to the things, their putrid scent made it difficult to breathe. The air was filled with sounds of gagging and retching. Faith was fighting to keep the contents of her own stomach down.

Faith sought Rowan's support with a glance. He managed to smile, although she could see he was struggling to continue.

Epione abruptly halted. "Rowan!"

One pile had extended a stringy substance that wrapped around her leg after she stepped into it. "It burns!"

Rowan drew the blade just as Faith rushed over to her. Rowan sliced the strings, which left burning red marks on her fur.

"It's all right." Faith knelt next to Epione and held her hands over her wounds, "I can—"

Bands of black constricted around Faith's torso, pinning her arms to her sides. A sudden jerk yanked her backward. A fleeting thought, her armor was protecting her from being burned but still she was immobile. Rowan sprinted toward her, screaming, only to be swallowed by oblivion. Desperate, Faith fought against the inexorable pull, but the darkness was all-encompassing. Faith realized this was a trap – one that had ensnared them all. The Rot had deceived them.

I will not let you win!

No victory, no defeat.

A voice emerged from the darkness. But she knew it.

Serval.

You owe us this! You murdered our sister!

To the nether hells with you!

Vulgar language, not like you.

You do not know what I'm capable of, you son of a bitch!

The surrounding restraints tightened.

The last person who displeased me found themselves in a similar position. I got what I wanted.

Then kill me now.

We only need you for one thing.

The restraints released Faith, and she fought to move in the floating nothingness. Yet, just as she believed she had gained freedom, something – whether restraints or some other force – seized her hands. When she tried to scream, the darkness filled her mouth, stifling any sound.

Then, a light appeared – a fragile bloom within the oppressive darkness. Faith momentarily ceased struggling as it drew her toward it.

The truth lay hidden behind a veil. No, it was the barrier. They had dragged her beyond the Sea of Tears.

No!

This is all we wanted from you! There would be no death if you had surrendered yourself completely.

Like the King of Hearts?

He was a useful tool.

I will not be yours!

As she floated before the barrier, the sensation of an unseen force took hold of her hands. Faith cried a protest but, in the darkness, her voice became warped and guttural. Her Gift called against her will and filled the space with light as it rippled along the surface of the barrier.

You will not use me!

A rip appeared, which quickly lengthened, opened wide as if a sword had slashed down the middle. She had to act immediately.

She screamed for the Vine to give her strength, to draw from her life force if it needed the power to stop this. Take away her power if it must, or even kill her.

And the Vine heeded her call. But it did not kill her or take her power. It filled her with sudden strength and purity, ripping the darkness from within her. Her Gift replaced the darkness, burning it away, and her aura was made manifest.

The light allowed her to perceive the world around her, including the barrier and shimmering curtain of silver particles, rent open by Faith. And as Cheshire had said, she found herself floating above a great waterfall, which plunged into oblivion.

Creatures, some the likes of which Faith had never seen, pushed themselves through the tear and began moving their twisted limbs, as they swam through.

Faith, with stark realization, knew where they had taken her – deep underneath the Sea of Tears. How was she alive? She was breathing as easily as she breathed the air. She could see Serval floating nearby. He was laughing in triumph. He appeared to have forgotten about Faith's presence. Now in command of her power, Faith realized she could feel the water. She hadn't noticed there was no sensation at first. It was now a tangible presence around her. She was always a strong swimmer and now was glad for it. Faith cut through the water toward Serval. So intent was he on his success that he didn't realize Faith was close to him until she touched him.

Faith could heal, but she never thought of using her Gift to destroy.

He turned to look at her, startled. Then his expression fell to one of disinterest. Until he realized what Faith was doing.

Serval panicked. He tried to pull away from her but, like he had done to her, the Vine that rested in her body lengthened her fingers to wrap around his arms. Despite the growing tendrils and leaves, Faith refused to let him escape and disregarded her worry.

Stop! Stop, you wretched bitch!

But Faith held on.

She could feel Serval losing his senses, his limbs hardening, his heartbeat and breathing slowing. Faith was surprised he still had those parts of humanity.

"Brothers and sisters, to my aid!" He called to the escaping dark fey, but they ignored him. They had what they wanted, and now Serval was a discarded tool. Serval's last movement was to turn his head to Faith, his eyes pleading before they too glazed over and went white. She released him and watched as his body sank.

Now to seal the barrier.

It would take every last vestige of her Gift to seal the rift, which lengthened as dark fey continued their escape. Her Gift alone prevented her from drowning. Concentrating, knowing she had little time left, Faith gathered everything she was into one blast of her power. The fey were trapped between the barrier and the water. As Faith continued, as the rift closed, some thought they could squeeze through, but were sliced in half. When some dared to come near her, Faith transformed them as well. With its imminent closure, the dark fey relentlessly assaulted the barrier, tearing at it, yet once again, it held them back.

At last the hole was knit. The barrier was sealed. Faith used the last of her Gift to fortify it and as she did, it became difficult to breathe.

When water went into her nose and mouth, Faith held her breath and swam upward, going for the dappled light, her lungs craving – *demanding* – air. She knew she would not make it. Just as well. She had done what she needed to do. She was losing consciousness. Yet, she could still see the dappled light of the ocean creating a floating haze. And there she saw—

The two women appeared once more. The witch and the diviner. They stood on the other side of a veil where shadows moved in the void between. The unknown two.

Not yet, Faith. We still have a task before us.

Faith came awake, coughing and sputtering. She sat up, unsure of her location. It felt odd, with the wind rushing, whipping her hair into a frenzy, and the sun warming her face.

"Faith! Thank the Vine!"

"Rowan."

"Is she all right?" Argestes inquired. Faith realized they were sitting on the back of the airborne gryphon.

"I think so, are you?" Rowan asked.

"Yes." Faith held tightly on to his collar. "I did it, Rowan! They forced me to open the breach, but I sealed it."

"As long as you're safe, dearest."

"How did you know?"

"Jade," Rowan said. "She joined us on the battlefield."

"Battlefield. Oh, no, how many got free?"

"Hundreds," he said, and Faith's heart fell. "But do not worry, love, we have help."

As Argestes flew over the beach, Faith saw, with joy in her heart, not only the Red Queen's forces but the White Queen's and—

"You didn't tell me you sent a message through Jade to ask Sylmare for aid."

"I wasn't certain she could spare her soldiers."

"She's there."

"Let's get down there!"

"No, Taira gave us another task."

"The Looking Glass."

"We are going to destroy it."

"The dark fey can still get in that way," Taira had told Rowan. "It won't be enough to just smash the mirror. You need Faith to transform it as she did with the sand."

"Stone." Faith looked down. And their forces were prevailing. Cheers erupted as they flew over the scene, Argestes pumping his wings vigorously to gain more speed.

"Keep aware," Faith said. "I don't know if any harpies escaped into our world."

It seemed they arrived at Taira's castle in no time. Commoners and servants came to greet them, but they had no time to waste. Faith and Rowan sprinted into the palace. No one attempted to stop them as only servants were present. They received odd looks but that was all.

They knew the room where the Looking Glass was housed but upon entering, they discovered another being there. She looked a sight, with her feathers torn out and deep gashes across her skin and her wings shredded.

"Uryphe," Faith said.

"You!" The harpy screeched and leapt rather ungainly toward them.

Rowan drew the Vorpal Blade and Uryphe, thinking better of attacking, dodged to her right and came for Faith, but if she thought Rowan was just going to stand there...

The harpy's wings sliced through the air, abruptly altering her trajectory again. Now she veered toward the Looking Glass, her talons outstretched. In that split second, Faith's instincts kicked in. She drew her pistol and fired. The gunshot echoed in the chamber.

The Looking Glass, that enigmatic portal between worlds, stood half in and half out of existence. As the bullet struck, the glass shattered, its fractured shards raining down like malevolent stars. Uryphe screamed – a sound that seemed to tear at the very fabric of reality.

Faith and Rowan stood amid the shards. The fragments of the glass bore parts of Uryphe within them – twisted reflections of her essence.

One eye, half obscured by jagged edges, peered out. Its wide pupil shifted back and forth, as if independently seeking comprehension.

"Dear Vine," Rowan said.

Faith holstered the pistol, untied the belt, and handed it to Rowan. "Please dispose of this for me, love."

"I will."

Faith knelt, careful to avoid the shards. Did she have any of her Gift left? Faith closed her eyes, searching within her for some remaining embers. Yes, they were there, very weak but enough to transform the shards down to the smallest piece into stone. The Looking Glass was destroyed.

★   ★   ★

The battle's tumultuous echoes faded as the dark fey retreated into the forest, their malevolence yielding to the relentless pursuit by the humans, who had endured great losses. The air hung heavily with both victory and sorrow.

As Argestes alighted gracefully on the sand, Rowan slid off the majestic creature's back, his arms extended, a silent invitation for Faith, who leapt into his embrace. Around them, friends and allies formed a protective circle, their eyes reflecting relief and admiration. The soldiers, weary yet resolute, erupted in cheers, their voices carrying through the clearing.

And there, amid the aftermath of battle, Rowan's gaze held Faith's. His voice, raw and vulnerable, cut through the chaos: "Will you marry me?"

Faith's smile was radiant, her answer swift and certain: "Yes." Their kiss, a promise forged in the crucible of war, sealed their fate – a union that transcended realms and defied the darkness that had threatened to consume them.

CHAPTER THIRTY-TWO

"My dear, you don't want to be late!"

"We won't, Father," Faith grinned. "You just be certain you are ready."

"I am always ready." Her father adjusted his signature hat.

"Then go down and get the coach ready." Minerva waved him away.

Their faithful servant guided Faith to turn around, and she smiled with pride. "Such a beautiful gown the Spinner Queen made for you."

"I know." Faith twirled around again.

"And don't forget this." Minerva picked up the white-laced top hat.

Faith put it on, tilting it at a jaunty angle.

After what felt like an eternity, the sun emerged, bringing joy to Faith. Brigantia was returning to itself. A paradise, Alice had called it. Although not a perfect paradise, it was still home. And it was her wedding day.

Before this, important matters needed addressing.

The Queen of Hearts had recovered, and Rowan ceded the ruling Uthelan to her until he was ready for the throne. Rowan expected a long wait, allowing him to focus on other matters.

Belladonna – *you can call me Belladonna, dear, since we'll be family* – seemed to have, for the most part, calmed that fiery edge, but when something worked her nerves it returned, and "Off with their heads!" could echo throughout the palace. Obviously, Faith was never the target of that. Still, Faith didn't feel quite comfortable with using the queen's name and had taken to calling her Queen Mum, which Belladonna approved of.

And although Faith was not a witness to it, Rowan advised her they had burned his father's body on a pyre and scattered the ashes into the Sea of Tears. Faith thought it was fitting. Initially, Leopold was not evil, but his weakness made him vulnerable to the Rot. Perhaps he would find peace.

Faith descended the stairs, and the pictures of her relatives, now restored to themselves, called out their good wishes. Faith stepped outside to see the large and ornate carriage, courtesy of Queen Mum, and a coachman to transport them to the palace. The Hatter smiled and tears welled when he saw her.

"You are so lovely, my dear. Rowan is a good man. But I needn't tell you that."

"No, Father."

The Hatter helped her into the coach, then Minerva. The Hatter used the cane to tap on the roof and they were off. Smiling, Faith watched the familiar scenes go by, witnessing the world's restored beauty.

"I wonder why Alice left this world, her Wonderland. She could have stayed."

"Perhaps she'll realize her error."

"No way to return now, not from that world," Faith whispered. Now that the Looking Glass was destroyed and the Rabbit Burrow was blocked, Alice's life in that world would continue.

"I would not wish for her to have regrets, so I hope she is content with her choice."

The Hatter looked at her with pride. "You are a decent and kindhearted woman."

Faith felt her face warm as she returned his look. "I am your daughter."

When the carriage came to a stop in front of the palace, the citizens gathered, cheered, and threw flower petals. Some cried out, "Hail to Princess Faith!" as Faith exited the carriage. She tried not to flinch at that. Yes, she would become Rowan's wife, but she was and always would be the Hatter's Daughter.

They entered the palace, and a group of giggling servant girls ushered Faith off to a room where she would wait until the ceremony began. Sitting in a chair, surrounded by running and fussing girls, Faith took out two letters received through the White Rabbit. She needed to ask him how he traveled so much.

She read the first, from Isbet of Rhyvirand. She was one of the women Faith had seen in her visions. Harper, from Innrone, was the diviner. They both planned to discuss combating the Rot with her. Faith had already sensed the situation wasn't over.

Both expressed regret for not attending the wedding as they searched for each other. She wondered how they knew about her impending nuptials but speculated the Vine played a role.

She dictated letters to them, gave them to the White Rabbit, and advised the Queen Mum's loyal servant to assist the two women in finding the others in any way he could. The White Rabbit's heart danced with joy as he complied and elegantly bowed. "With your permission, Your Highness." Again, Faith tried not to flinch or laugh as he hopped off.

The giggling maids did their final preparations and Faith was ready. She walked from the room to where her father waited. The bridesmaids and groomsmen had already started their steady march.

"Did I say how proud I was of you?"

"Yes," Faith said. "But say it again."

The Hatter laughed and as he walked her down the aisle, Faith looked at those who had become her friends. Her family. They had helped her save Brigantia.

Rowan was waiting for her, his eyes filled with love and admiration. The Queen of Hearts tried to look staid but upon seeing Faith, a tear escaped from the corner of her eye.

"Faith," Rowan said. "I will always be beside you."

"I know," Faith said. It satisfied her.

The ceremony began with the customary exchange of vows. It ended joyously, with the Queen of Hearts crowning Faith with a ruby-jeweled crown over her top hat. Despite her love for the Queen Mum, Faith couldn't wait to remove the blasted crown.

Rowan grinned as they ran down the aisle. As always, he knew what she was thinking.

ABOUT THE AUTHOR

W.A. Simpson has been writing since the age of five after a family friend gave her an old typewriter, when she saw that she enjoyed creating works of mystery and suspense that only a five-year-old could. She completed her first novel and started shopping it at fourteen. In later years, she figured out mystery wasn't her thing. It was a story by Ray Bradbury that she enjoyed that turned her towards fantasy.

On a more personal note, she likes to think she is the world's biggest bibliophile. When she's not reading or writing she indulges in her favorite pastimes, which include working in her garden, video gaming and streaming. Come see her on Twitch as Runic Nightshade.

Her previous books with Flame Tree in the *Tales from the Riven Isles* series are *Tinderbox* and *Tarotmancer*.